SHADOW OF A MAN

Books by May Sarton

POETRY

Encounter in April
Inner Landscape
The Lion and the Rose
The Land of Silence
In Time Like Air
Cloud, Stone, Sun, Vine
A Private Mythology
As Does New Hampshire
A Grain of Mustard Seed
A Durable Fire
Collected Poems, 1930–1973
Selected Poems of May Sarton
(edited by Serena Sue Hilsinger and Lois Brynes)
Halfway to Silence

NOVELS

The Single Hound
The Bridge of Years
Shadow of a Man
A Shower of Summer Days
Faithful Are the Wounds
The Birth of a Grandfather
The Fur Person
The Small Room
Joanna and Ulysses
Mrs. Stevens Hears the Mermaids Singing
Miss Pickthorn and Mr. Hare
The Poet and the Donkey
Kinds of Love
As We Are Now
Crucial Conversations
A Reckoning

NONFICTION

I Knew a Phoenix
Plant Dreaming Deep
Journal of a Solitude
A World of Light
The House by the Sea
Recovering: A Journal

SHADOW OF A MAN

MAY SARTON

W · W · NORTON & COMPANY

New York · London

Published simultaneously in Canada by George J. McLeod Limited, Toronto.

Printed in the United States of America

First published as a Norton paperback 1982

Grateful acknowledgment is made to Harper & Brothers, Publishers, for permission to reprint four lines from *Bolts of Melody* by Emily Dickinson, copyright, 1945, by Millicent Todd Bingham.

Library of Congress Cataloging in Publication Data

Sarton, May, 1912–
Shadow of a man.

Reprint. Originally published: New York: Rinehart, 1950.
I. Title.
PS3537.A832S5 1982 813'.52 82-3510
AACR2

W. W. Norton & Company, Inc. 500 Fifth Avenue, New York, N.Y. 10110
W. W. Norton & Company Ltd., 37 Great Russell Street, London WC1B 3NU

2 3 4 5 6 7 8 9 0

ISBN 0-393-30030-7

For

JEAN DOMINIQUE

PART ONE

"Notre vie intérieure n'est pas une mathématique, mais une histoire. Nous ne vivons pas dans l'espace, mais dans le monde des âmes."

HENRI BERGSON

CHAPTER ONE

PERSIS BRADFORD died a few days before Christmas in the house on Mt. Vernon Street in Boston where her mother had died before her, at almost exactly the same age, in her early sixties. The heart attack was over in a few minutes. At four she had been alive, waiting impatiently for the tea to come up to the library, and at four fifteen she was dead. Apparently she had been aware of the condition of her heart but had preferred to pay no attention to it and to tell no one.

In one instant the house, which had been animated by this extraordinary woman, was emptied of all warmth, all grace. Those who remained felt like ghosts. It was she who lived on with frightening power and they who haunted her presence wherever they went. They were two, her son by her first husband, Francis Adams Chabrier, twenty-six years old and a graduate student at Harvard, and her second husband, Alan Bradford. For the first time these two faced each other without her mediating presence. But luckily death brings its own particular busyness with it and for the first few hours Alan and Francis took refuge in the innumerable decisions there were to be made. They had not either of them come face to face yet with grief. Only they avoided the rooms she had used and as a result talked in Alan's study on the fourth floor. It had once been a nursery.

"I think, perhaps, Francis, we had better keep the wreaths up," Alan said after dinner. He was acutely aware that people would resent having to grieve at this season. A funeral just at Christmas seemed almost an imposition. And as Francis, smoking his pipe, said nothing, Alan went on hesitatingly, "But perhaps we should remove the red bows. What do you think, Francis?"

"By all means remove the bows, Alan," Francis, dark and glowering, his eyes very bright and the shadow of a smile on his lips, managed to sound insolent without perhaps meaning to.

"On the other hand, I wonder if it doesn't look a little strange to have the wreaths out at all . . ."

"Oh hell, what does it matter?" Francis got up and paced up and down. "I'm going out for a walk," he announced.

"But your aunts are coming back, Francis. We have things to decide."

Francis was already out of the door and halfway down the stairs. "I'm sure you'll do just as well without me," he called back. "Give them my love."

Alan was suddenly too tired and too defeated to argue or to move. Since four o'clock he had hardly been alone. His mother had arrived at once from Chestnut Hill and stayed to supper. Persis' sisters had come and gone. He was glad to have these few moments where he did not have to think of others and could think of himself. It was extraordinary this instinct for flight one observed in oneself. If he could decently have taken a boat for Europe that night, he would have done it, cleared out, never looked back. He understood very well what drove Francis out to the streets; they at least were impersonal and there one did not have to wear a mask. Death laid a mask on all the faces. One must be brave. One must realize what other people were going through. It would be indecent to break down. Life must go on more or less as if nothing had happened. Only old Mary, the cook, had broken down completely. And, Alan thought wearily, she's the only human being among us. He took out a pad and pencil and began to jot down things that still had to be done. There was the question of the music for the funeral, certainly Mozart's *Ode Funèbre* which Persis had played many times in the last month. Would it be possible to get the music by tomorrow and have the organist practice it? Her records of this were French. Perhaps Sukey would know. White orchids from his mother's greenhouse for the coffin—he must call the gardener in the morning. He felt that everything must be perfect, and he was abysmally nervous of the responsibility. Francis was no help. Alan knew very well that Francis would have preferred to have no public funeral at all, but Persis liked form—Persis—

Even her name seemed remote, the name of someone long dead whom he hardly knew any more. Now she was dead, she had become mysterious and distant. He couldn't yet remember the little things which would stab his heart awake and perhaps bring on the tears. Now he felt simply empty. And he was glad when her two sisters, Alison Adams and Susan Thorndike, came at last to take up the list where he had left off.

They had obviously both been crying and he envied them. They seemed amazingly young, though Alison was sixty-five, a year older than Persis, and Susan must be sixty-three. He looked in vain for a remembrance of Persis in their faces. It seemed hardly possible that they were of the same family. Alison wore her invariable brown Harris tweed, brown felt hat pulled down over mousy brown hair held back with a round comb. Her large gray eyes behind glasses looked out at the world with fire and candor; she had spent her life fighting in every major political battle, a member of every liberal organization from the NAACP to the Civil Liberties. Alan, conservative and unsure of himself, had often found Alison embarrassing. Now he felt her goodness and was grateful.

Sukey, all in black, immaculately dressed, her gray hair done in small curls over her head, was less reassuring. Persis had called her the bird of paradise in a family of mice, but that was to underrate herself. Sukey was fashionable always, but she just failed in distinction, at least so Alan thought.

"Let's have a drink, Alan. This is too grim, really." They had climbed up the four flights to his study and were still slightly out of breath.

"Where's Francis?" Alison asked, refusing the highball he poured.

"He went out for a walk, said to give you his love."

"He was frightfully rude this afternoon," Sukey said drily.

"He can't help it." Alison flushed. "It's hardest for him. We must make allowances."

"All his life people have made allowances for Francis. I never understood why. He's a normal human being, isn't he? Why can't he behave like one?"

This was so much what Alan himself secretly thought that he felt quite guilty. "Dear Sukey," he said gently, "we are not gathered here to discuss Francis. There are certain practical matters," he cleared his throat.

§ 6 §

They all felt relieved to be faced with a list, with words written down, with simple decisions like what should be read at the service. This business occupied them for an hour or more. Then the inevitable silence fell. It was as if they and the house itself were listening for a voice, for a step which would never be heard again.

Persis Adams Chabrier Bradford, to give her all the names she had borne in her life, was one of those people who, without particularly wishing it, or using it as a man would have used it in some career or other, was nevertheless a power, a person whose influence is far greater than any outward manifestation of her life might suggest. Now she was dead, her power would for a time increase rather than diminish. At this moment she entered deeply into many lives. Many people questioned her, asked their secret selves what she had been really like, who she was.

She had been, first of all, an Adams, brought up in that frugal intellectual atmosphere peculiar to Boston where studying Greek for a child of seven did not seem an extravagant idea, but a fur coat would have seemed so. She had not gone to college, but at twenty she spoke French and German fluently and could read Italian with pleasure. She was an accomplished pianist, so accomplished that she had gone over just after the '14–18 war to study with Cortot. She had had no intention of becoming a concert artist, but she wanted to go as far as her talent would take her, for her own pleasure and that of her friends. This attitude puzzled many people—it was a time when women were talking a lot about "careers." But it stemmed from Persis' essential character which was to be an observer rather than a participant. She wanted above all to keep her freedom. A concert artist is always a slave. So it surprised everyone except herself when in 1922 she married Pierre Chabrier and settled down at 43 Rue de Vaugirard to fourteen years of intensely happy married life in the course of which her son Francis was born. Her husband, the son of a lawyer in Tours, was the type of the philosopher-artist-man-of-action which has had its apotheosis in our time in T. E. Lawrence, Malraux and St. Exupéry. He had been an aviator, much decorated in the war; he was a not-uncritical follower of Bergson and James, and when he died at forty-seven he was considered one of the most brilliant philosophers of his day. Unfortunately the work which would have established his reputation had never been written. The boxes of notes and a few published lectures were all that remained.

After his death, which literally cut Persis' life in two, she took the boy, then twelve, and came back to Boston, to the house on Mt. Vernon Street closed since her mother's death, and started to remake her life alone. During the next five years she went back seriously to playing the piano, opened her house to all musicians, painters, school friends of her son's, queer characters, visiting French scholars and anyone whom she found interesting. In a quiet way, she became famous as a hostess. The library with its Picasso etchings, its shelves of paper-backed books, its flowers and the slightly formal atmosphere she created for conversation, suggested to many people a salon in Paris—and this was no doubt quite conscious on her part. She no longer lived in Paris, but she was a different person from the Persis Adams who had gone to Paris to study twenty years before. Amongst other things she had learned to have a confidence in herself which Boston women of her background often lack. She had learned to laugh and she had learned how to make other people talk and to feel brilliant. And she did all this with a rather shy and self-deprecatory air which was still endearingly Boston.

When Alan Bradford, back from years in China as a consul, walked into this room, what he saw was a woman in her early fifties, unspectacular looking, but the narrow face illuminated by penetrating dark eyes, a woman who had obviously, to put it crudely, "lived," and the only woman he had ever seen whom he immediately wanted to marry; within three years he had accomplished that wish. It was an eminently suitable marriage. And Boston congratulated itself that two such intelligent, charming, and rich people had decided to unite their lives. No one thought for an instant that it was an affair of passion, and in this they were partly right. When she accepted his offer Persis made it quite clear that what she felt for Alan was the tenderest friendship, no more. He had married with his eyes open, but he had not reckoned quite with himself. And in some ways the last eight years had been, to put it as he would have put it to himself —he was always afraid of big words—difficult. He had been terrified of his dependence on her, coming as it did late in a life accustomed to solitude. But solitude à deux was different. He had suffered. She had been kind. And her kindness had humiliated him almost beyond bearing. But, unwilling to dramatize himself, Alan believed that many marriages which seem outwardly serene, are the scene of such subterranean struggle, and that perhaps in all marriages someone pays an outrageous price. He was far too generous to count the price, and too sensitive not to blame himself. The portrait of Pierre Chabrier in a heavy silver frame stood between the twin beds on the night table.

During those eight years Alan had buried part of himself in work and was now halfway through his monumental history of China. Persis had proved an invaluable research assistant and their happiest hours together had been here in his study, the hours when she had willingly become part of his world, instead of the hours when he had tried, and, it seemed, always failed, to become part of hers.

During those years, her son Francis had grown up. Alan had been puzzled at first by her relation to Francis, it seemed curiously unmaternal. She left him absurdly free, made no comment on his frequent follies, and treated him rather as an honored friend to whom she felt faintly antagonistic, than as a wayward son who needed disciplining. Their arguments, always in French, went on for hours, and were about everything under the sun from existentialism to Mozart, from Boston politics to Dante's politics. The house was full of Francis and his friends on the weekends.

Francis had accepted Alan by ignoring him. They did not exactly avoid each other, but there seemed to be a tacit understanding that intimacy was out of the question. Until the night of his mother's death Francis had almost never sat down in Alan's study, and this, Alan thought in the silence where he sat with Persis' sisters, may have been one of the reasons why Francis left. What had not happened yet, was not going to happen. Francis had rooms at Eliot House across the river and they would presumably not see much of each other.

For the three people who sat in the book-lined room and let silence take over, the silence held very different things. Alan, holding his loss at bay, was thinking about Francis rather than think about Persis who lay now at the undertakers, and since she was not yet buried, seemed neither dead nor alive, a creature of limbo, neither his nor death's.

Alison was thinking of her mother who had died in this house more than twenty years before and at almost the same age as her daughter, but Persis was in Paris then and had not come to the funeral. This was awful, she thought, but that had been worse, though they had been better prepared by the long months of illness. Prudence Adams had died of cancer and her death had seemed a blessed release to them all. And yet, prepared as they thought they were, at least for Alison who had never married, it had been an immeasurable parting, and in a way the end of her own life. Gentle and violent their mother had been, implacably true to herself. Was it only a matter of generation? Did everyone feel this about his mother, that she had been pure and deep in a way that made all their lives by comparison seem a little superficial, a little shrill? Her mother had not really liked Alison's passionate defense of causes, little and great, but she had always poured oil into the wounds, always been there, listening and quietly judging. And on the night of Sacco and Vanzetti's execution, she had cried bitterly with Alison. They had sat together that night by the fire and shared the agony. Alison felt the tears rising again, but they were tears for her mother and not for Persis. And this seemed strange and a little cruel.

Sukey alone of the three was thinking about her sister. She was bitterly regretting an argument she had had a few days previously with Persis. It was about nothing really, the arrangements about the summer (they shared a house on Mt. Desert) but now it seemed hideous because there would never be a chance to make it up. She remembered how when they were children, Persis had always taken care of her and scolded her and how she had thought she hated Persis, but really loved her and how lost she had felt when Persis went to Paris and never came back all those years and years. Persis found Sukey's husband dull and Sukey resented it. They had never really opened their hearts to each other, and now it was too late. Inside the perfectly coiffed, mondaine woman, sat an angry, warmhearted child with a tear-blotched face, calling, "Persis, Persis, where are you? How could you just die like that? Without giving us a chance? Without letting us know?" Then she turned to Alan and saw for the first time the exhaustion in his face.

"Alan, we must go and let you get some sleep. Have you something to take?" she asked fishing in her purse for the little silver box with pills in it. Sukey was a great believer in medicines of all kinds, perhaps in violent reaction to their homeopathic upbringing which had taught them that aspirin is the equivalent in wickedness of heroin.

"Thank you, Sukey, I think Persis has phenobarbital by the bed." He had said it in the present and blushed, but did not correct himself. Perhaps they had not noticed.

CHAPTER TWO

THE YOUNG MAN in his late twenties, who emerged from the house on Mt. Vernon Street into Louisburg Square at a little past nine that evening, looked at first glance like a hundred other Harvard men. He was tall, dark, wore a sheepskin-lined trench-coat and no hat, so that his crew cut marked him at once as a college man. On the doorstep he lit a cigarette and inhaled deeply. The light caught his narrow cheeks, the sunken wide-apart eyes and brought into sharp focus the curiously intelligent, intense, and yet lost expression. He looked as if he were old for his age on the one hand, or on the other hand perhaps too young for his face. The forehead and eyes showed maturity and intellect, the mouth and chin seemed unfinished, as if the draftsman had hesitated in designing them, as if something there were left to chance or life to complete. Inside this given mask, there was at the moment nothing but chaos. Francis was well aware that he had taken refuge in rudeness and anger since four o'clock that afternoon because he could not yet admit to himself what had happened, because he would not yet allow grief to take him over. He stood on the hill looking down the steep drop to the black lacquer of the river and the lights on the Cambridge side, and for a moment breathed in deeply the quiet of the city at this hour, and its familiar beauty. He was here, on the step of his mother's house, Francis Adams Chabrier, and yet he asked himself, "Do I exist?" For for the last few hours it had seemed as if his very existence were suspended. There was no simple answer to this philosophical question, and even as he asked it, he proved his existence at least as a physical being, by walking quickly down the hill, listening to his own footsteps as if they were somehow reassuring. He was now thoroughly ashamed of his behavior earlier in the evening. It had been inexcusable to be rude to Aunt Sukey, and especially in front of old Mrs. Bradford who was such a stickler for form. He knew very well that he had succeeded only in having another black mark put down against him in the family books. It was all over the question of the funeral, of course.

"We have always been buried from King's Chapel," Aunt Sukey had said.

And he had answered furiously, "Pierre Chabrier would have agreed with me that a formal funeral at Christmas is an insult to peoples' good will." How far he had set himself apart from them by bringing in his father and France he well knew. They had all gathered, the whole damn clan of them, with their ineffable "we do this" "we do that," serenely unconscious that there might be other values, other points of view, even somewhere in the world another "we." Francis had felt the loneliness grow around him like a physical chill. And of course they had won. They were alive.

Even now, though he had begun by feeling remorseful, the

anger seized him again. His stepfather had sided with them, though Francis was sure that in his heart he agreed. He would not have been so concerned about the silly wreaths unless he had felt the whole enormity of a formal funeral at this season.

Francis stopped at the brightly lit window of the coffee joint on the corner of Charles Street. It was empty. The man at the counter stood looking out at the street like a fish in an aquarium and, on an impulse, Francis went in. He had hardly touched his dinner and realized that he was hungry.

"Hamburger and a cup of coffee," he said, sliding comfortably onto the stool where he had sat so often before, comforted already by the usual air everything had here, as if nothing had happened.

"With or without?"

"With." The smell of onions rose in a delicious cloud.

"How are things?" the man asked. Francis didn't know his name, but they had often talked, about the rotten politics in Boston, about the election. Francis knew the man had voted for Truman and had a wife and two children, and lived in Everett. The man knew next to nothing about him. He was standing with his back to Francis now, patting the hamburger down on the hot plate.

"Terrible," Francis answered, wanting to tell this man, this perfect stranger, and so, this perfect friend, wanting so much to tell him that he ran his tongue along his lips as if he were tasting the words he somehow couldn't say.

"It's never as bad as you think," the man said half mechanically. He had a store of such aphorisms which he brought out in just the way he handed out a cup of coffee, with a pleasant and fundamentally impersonal smile. It didn't do in his job to get involved. Half the people who came in here, came in because they wanted to talk.

"I dunno. Maybe not." Francis took a big bite of hamburger. It seemed strange to be eating now, eating to satisfy a real hunger. And he thought, hunger at least is real, the only real thing in the unreal world in which I am. It would be impossible to tell the man. He didn't believe it himself. He drank a big gulp of the oversweet coffee.

"What's eating you?" the man asked, leaning on the counter now and lighting a cigarette, a thing he never did unless the place was empty.

"I want to tell you," Francis said seriously, "only I can't."

"Did you just rob a bank?" the man asked with a grin. "What's all the mystery?"

"It's this," Francis said, pushing the hamburger away half finished. He felt sick to his stomach. "My mother died this afternoon."

"Jeez, that's bad." The man was embarrassed now to have chaffed Francis. "Tough going, son. I'm sorry."

The words fell like balm on Francis' closed heart. Everything he had held all clenched up inside him loosened a fraction. He took another swallow of coffee because he was afraid now of the tears, the thousands of them, that he felt inside him. One doesn't cry. One doesn't, even if one is half French, cry in the brightly lit window of the coffee joint on Charles Street. And to keep from crying he talked fast as if he were telling someone else's story. "She was just sitting there in the library, waiting for tea, and she had a heart attack. She wasn't old. Nobody knew—none of us knew—but she must have known."

"A brave woman," the man nodded sympathetically. "Like these birds that go around dying of cancer and never let on."

"My mother was wonderful," Francis said simply.

To the man at the counter, it was evident. Everybody's mother is wonderful. It's a well-known fact. He nodded sympathetically.

"Well, we all have to die—" the sentence floated off like the smoke. Francis hardly heard it. He was thinking, wonderful yes, but strange, wonderful in her own way, and this nothing to do with what the man at the counter thought. She had been no "mom" to answer cries like "where are my snow-boots?," to have hot meals ready for the returning hero, no maker of pies, dispenser of comforts, dependable in crisis. At moments of crisis she had left her son alone, demanded his best at all times, taken him seriously always, which meant fighting him every inch of the way, testing his mind against her own, forcing him to grow to meet her. Surely it must have troubled her deeply that he still had no idea what he would do with his life, she who always knew exactly what she wanted. And he realized with a thrust of real pain, she'll never know what I become, and added bitterly, perhaps it's just as well. So far she had only been here to watch the fumbles, the inherited brilliance wasting itself because without focus. He had studied history first, then when he finally got out of the army, the most insignificant of soldiers who had never even gone overseas, he switched to French literature.

"You must do what you most mean, Francis, that's all," she had said when he made this decision. Clearly it involved giving up the idea of diplomatic service with which he had toyed before the war.

"But what do you think is right?" he had insisted, longing for her to take the decision out of his hands.

"Don't be a baby, Francis. Nothing is right or wrong in that absolute sense. I can't tell you. It's your problem," and when he answered miserably, "I don't know what I mean yet," just for an instant her tone had changed, all the irony gone and she had said very gently—he groaned aloud when he thought of it and the man behind the counter shook his head sympathetically—she had said, "Your father, you know, took a long time, too."

Oh never to see her again, never to run up the stairs with a book open in his hands, a record under his arm and to say, "Mother, listen to this!" More often than not they disagreed violently, but she had been his standard. Against her judgment he put everything and watched to see how it stood up. Now there was no standard. Whom did he trust? Aunt Alison in a way, because he knew she loved him but how little she knew really, except in that special field of hers. Aunt Sukey? With her emphasis always on manners, clothes, how one behaved. No. Alan? The weight of his own inadequacy flooded over Francis. He had behaved abominably to Alan.

"I must go back now," he said to the man behind the counter, handing him a dollar bill.

"Take it easy, son. You'd better get some sleep. I guess you'll have a day tomorrow, what with people calling up and all—"

"Oh my God, yes," Francis said, realizing for the first time what it was going to be like from now on, until he could escape back to college. There would be Ann first, whom the family was obviously maneuvering hopefully to get him to marry, Ann with her eager puzzled face, so anxious to say the right thing, so afraid she wouldn't. There would be all the old friends. There would be the awful pity to face, and above all his own intolerable anger which he knew would rise against them again and again like a poison, and no one now to laugh him out of it. He climbed the hill slowly as if he were carrying a burden, and perhaps indeed he was carrying the full burden of himself for the first time, and it was heavy. There was a light in Alan's study, a light in the hall, otherwise the house was dark. He stood outside and looked up at it, the dark blind windows and then the lighted one. He shivered then, a long shiver and ran up the steps, leaning his full weight against the door as he put in the key as if he were taking the house by assault.

His aunts' coats lay on the hall sofa, Aunt Sukey's little mink cape and Aunt Alison's brown overcoat, beside them two books from the Athenaeum, Fénélon and an early novel of Elizabeth Bowen's—his mother must have put them there to be returned. He sat down and began to read the Fénélon as if somewhere there between those pages so lately scanned by his mother's eyes, he would find her, looking out at him. There he was discovered by the aunts as they came downstairs followed by Alan.

"Why, Francis, what are you doing in the hall?" Aunt Alison said anxiously.

"I was reading," he said, terribly embarrassed, as if this were some new crime.

Aunt Sukey raised her eyebrows a fraction and said a little acidly, "Something interesting, I hope?"

"I don't know yet," he said stiffly, "these are the books Mother had out of the Athenaeum." Just then a loud sob was wrenched out of Francis before he could do anything about it. He stumbled up the stairs and away from them, up the four flights to his room and slammed the door. Then he flung himself down on his bed with his face in the pillow to stifle the awful noise of his grief.

Alan, unable to face sleeping in the bedroom, stretched out in the armchair in his study and stared open-eyed into the dark. He had wanted very much to go in to Francis, but he had been held back by reticence, the fear of seeming to intrude now upon a relationship from which he had been so carefully excluded always. In the morning when he woke up, stiff from sleeping half upright, Alan felt like a very old man who has failed in all things.

CHAPTER THREE

It was that old man who came down to breakfast the next morning. They sat in their usual places, the head of the table empty. Alan rather awkwardly poured himself a cup of coffee; Francis, absorbed in the obituaries, hardly looked up. He had finished his breakfast. When he did look up finally and lit a cigarette, he was shocked to see his stepfather's diminished, almost wizened air. For the first time Francis recognized that this man had loved his mother; he had until now simply refused to consider the matter at all. He had simply decided in his own mind, "a stranger has come to live with my mother." But now he was, in spite of himself, filled with pity. With an awkward gesture, he put out the cigarette he had just lit. He looked across at Alan again.

"Alan, I'm sorry I behaved so badly yesterday, truly sorry. I'm afraid I was very selfish." It was, for Francis, an immense gift of the self which he usually kept concealed. And Alan was far too sensitive not to know this.

"It's all right, Francis. I think we understand each other. We just have to live this through, somehow—" he said with a vague gesture, a helpless gesture, "as best we can."

"I'm afraid people will start coming and phoning—that's what's so awful, this panoply of grief," Francis said nervously, relighting the black tip of his cigarette. Why did this have to happen now, he thought irritably, just now during vacation when I can't escape?

"After the funeral we might get away," Alan said quietly.

"Where?" Francis was already poised for flight, like a deer who hears a footstep in the forest. You won't catch me, his face said.

"I don't know—the South—" but he knew it was hopeless. How could they go away together when they hardly knew each other and perhaps did not really like each other?

"I should really work," Francis said.

"Yes, yes—of course—"

At that moment the phone began its imperative demands for their attention. It was Alan's mother to ask him out to Chestnut Hill to lunch. It was Aunt Alison asking Francis to lunch with her. Both invitations were accepted with alacrity—anything to get away from each other's grief and from the house. They each felt better after these calls.

"The obituaries," Francis said with an ironic smile, handing *The Herald* and *The Globe* over to Alan. "How is it that my mother's sister-in-law, Madame de Lestanville, is not mentioned among the bereaved? Mother was a member of The Nucleus Club whatever that is, but of course Madame de Lestanville is not considered to be important. She never lived in Boston."

"Oh well, does it matter?" Alan asked wearily.

"I don't suppose it does. But I want something at the funeral which will mean France." He had been thinking about this half the night. "I suppose that I am the only person here to whom it will mean anything, but if there must be a funeral, then perhaps I should be included."

"I think that's a very good idea," Alan said refusing to adopt a hostile tone. "What do you suggest?"

"There must be something of Chausson's," Francis said thoughtfully. "May I try to find it this morning?"

"By all means. As you know, Francis, we wanted you to help in all this. Your aunts will be very pleased."

For a moment the barriers had been down between them but it was as if some devil always came in and took over; Francis felt like a porcupine with all its quills trembling with anger. What he would have liked to shout at his stepfather was "She's my mother, what was she to you, compared to that? What to her sisters? You all have each other. I have no one, nothing. Can't you understand?" But he knew too that they wished to understand and that he himself held them off, would have none of their sympathy, did not really want to be included in their "we," was proud of being an outsider. It is all I have, he thought bitterly, that I am not one of them. He had poured himself another cup of coffee and now drank it down in a gulp.

Alan was looking out of the window. He could hear Persis' voice as if she were speaking now, light and a little harsh, saying, "People Francis' age have to revolt against something, revolted as they are really against themselves. Let Francis have his Boston and hate it. He'll learn." She had refused to be worried. She had been quietly amused. Francis was still her son, not his, and so Alan controlled the impulse to have this thing out once and for all, and instead picked up the papers, and stared for a long time at the old photograph they had dug up of his wife.

When the telephone rang a third time Francis had left the room.

"Oh Alan," the extremely cultured voice at the other end of the phone said and it was charged with drama. Alan braced himself. "This is Fanny."

"Yes, I recognized your voice."

"Sukey told me last night. I haven't slept a wink. My dear, what a blow. And what a heroic creature Persis was to face this alone and not tell anyone."

"Yes," said Alan without expression.

"I had to call you just to say two things. One is the last verse of a poem of Emily Dickinson's—Oh dear Alan, listen to this splendid voice." (Eloquent indeed was the voice to which Alan was forced to listen.)

> "Love is like life, merely longer;
> Love is like death, daring the grave;
> Love is the fellow of the resurrection
> Scooping up the dust and chanting 'Live!'

I just wanted you to have that this morning and—Oh Alan—this one line of Santayana's, 'A perfect love is founded on despair.' I'm thinking of you, dear Alan, every moment. Good-bye." And, mercifully, Fanny Shaw hung up before Alan had to make the proper response. For the first time since four o'clock the afternoon before, Alan smiled, remembering what Persis had suffered from Fanny's eruptions into poetry and wisdom on the telephone. Perhaps not in the way she intended,

Fanny, elderly, eager Fanny with her filing boxes full of scraps of paper culled from years of reading, had helped him over a bad moment. But he foresaw that there was to be no escape from the overflowing souls of his Boston acquaintance. Only too happy were they to leap into the breach, waving a copy of *The Paradiso*. Death was one of their favorite exercises; all the concealed love of drama could now have free play. If only Persis were here, how they could have laughed together, laughed without malice—for Alan did not hate Boston, he appreciated it—but laughed just the same. The Chinese have their ceremonies he thought and Boston has its Famous Quotations. And what would we do without them?

Alan went down to the kitchen to have a talk with Mary. She and Louise, the waitress, were sitting in the big dark kitchen eating their breakfast and Alan drew up a chair and sat down to have a cigarette. There was something very comforting about the kitchen, about Mary's tear-blotched kind red face and Louise's dignified silence.

"We'll be two for dinner, Mary. Can you plan something? I'd be grateful if you would take over for a few days."

"Yes, sir."

"Do you mind if I sit here for a minute, Mary? The rest of the house feels rather strange."

"I know, sir. It's awful upstairs, so lonesome, Louise and I were just saying. And you didn't sleep at all, sir. You must get your rest."

"Oh, I slept, Mary. I just stretched out in my study."

"The papers are full of Mrs. Bradford, sir. Have you seen them? It's going to be a great funeral. Mrs. Bradford had so many friends and relatives. And will they be coming back here afterwards, sir? That is what I was asking myself this morning. Whether we should have coffee ready—or anything—"

"My mother and my sisters-in-law will come to lunch that day. I think no one else," Alan said thoughtfully. He would have to ask his mother at lunch about what should be done. But it was a great relief to be able to talk things over with a person who took it all simply and yet who cared as much as Mary did.

"You're a great comfort to me, Mary." He gave her shoulder a gentle pat as he got up to go.

"Is Mr. Francis all right?" she asked with a trace of anxiety. "It's a terrible thing for him, left alone like this—an orphan like—of course he has you, sir."

"Yes, Mary," Alan said, the chill wrapping him round again, the sense of failure. And very slowly he climbed the three flights of stairs. Apparently Francis had gone out. Alan stood for a moment in the door of the library and looked in. It was horribly the same as ever. The books, the records, the yellow armchair where Persis had sat in the evening. Nothing had changed and nothing would ever be the same again. It might just as well all be burned to ash.

But, he reminded himself, unwilling to dramatize, I expect people get used to these things. I expect eventually I shall be able to go in and sit down.

Meanwhile he had much to do this morning and that too was a good thing. He must telegraph three old friends in New York who might wish to come to the funeral. He went to King's Chapel to talk over the arrangements. He stopped in at Sukey's on his way out to Chestnut Hill to tell her what progress had been made and what still remained to be done. He suggested that they should consider having printed notices in the French way naming all the bereaved and edged in black to be sent to France. He supposed that Persis' address book would be of help. He had not yet opened her desk, where presumably the will would be found. He had not yet had the courage for that.

Francis spent the morning chasing down a piece of Chausson organ music which seemed to be all right. It was not quite what he wanted, but what was lacking would be supplied by the Mozart they had all agreed on. When he stopped in at the house to wash he found a note on the hall table to say that Ann had called. There were three letters for his mother, one with a French postmark from Madame Bernard, a friend he dimly remembered knowing as a child, who had seemed to him then the epitome of elegance, and who had given him the Jules Verne books to read one by one. Without really being aware of what he was doing, he put this letter in his pocket, and left the others, and Ann's message where they lay.

Then he went out again into the bright cold morning to walk over to his aunt's apartment on Myrtle Street. The Adams sisters all had a pleasantly safe amount of money, each in her own right. But Alison, who had not been able to get at any of her capital as it was part of a Trust Fund, compromised by living on about a tenth of her income and giving all the rest to the NAACP, the Civil Liberties Union, The Quaker Relief Fund, the Joint Anti-Fascist Relief Organization, The International Social Service, the Judge Baker Foundation, various clinics and hospitals and innumerable smaller and more temporary organisms. Her mail was a formidable array of requests for money, very few of which she turned down. Her life was composed of lunches and committee meetings, accelerating in pace when the legislature met, and she was a well-known figure treated with tolerance and something like affection by the Irish politicians on the Hill. Francis felt at home in her small shabby flat with its old velvet sofa covered with clippings and liberal journals, its rows of books on economics and history, the photographs of Tom Mooney, Sacco and Vanzetti, Jaurès, and her friends Richard Cabot, Miriam Van Waters, Frances Sweeny and Justice Frankfurter (taken at the time of the Sacco-Vanzetti case). The one incongruous thing was the prevalence also of Botticelli reproductions which Aunt Alison had brought back from a year in Florence when she was just out of college.

"Oh Francis, I'm glad to see you," she said beaming at him in the doorway, and kissing him on both cheeks in the French way, a salute she made with great tact and which had become like a secret sign between them. "Come in, you must be frozen. You should have on an overcoat, child. It's ridiculous to go out like that. There, sit down and pour me a glass of sherry while I heat up the soup." Brisk and matter of fact, as always, her presence seemed infinitely consoling. Even the worn places on the elbows of her old brown sweater were consoling. Francis sank onto the sofa, pushing aside three or four books and a copy of *The New Republic,* and gave a great sigh.

"Gee, Aunt Alison—" he said aloud.

She quite understood what he meant and took the proffered glass without a word.

"Let's talk about your mother," she said after a moment. "That's all one really wants to do, isn't it? I suppose because it's all we can do."

Francis lit a cigarette and puffed at it in silence. At the moment he could think of nothing to say. He felt like a drowning man who touches the shore; he just wanted to lie there and feel safe at last. Alison Adams watched him and said nothing. She was thinking that young men, like perhaps the Furies, are not quite human and that's what makes them so interesting. She was very fond of Francis but she didn't feel she understood anything about him really, his love of argument, his queer rages and defiance, his air of expecting to be put in the wrong, his sudden rather harsh laughter—all this she suspected meant nothing, was not the real person at all. And she wondered what the real person was, how sensitive beneath his apparent insensitivity, how vulnerable under his aggressiveness. Because she was fond of him and because Alison was fundamentally simple she went on as she had begun, whether he responded or not, though she really couldn't read his silence at all.

"Of course she had two distinct lives, that is what we always forgot about Persis. But you never forgot it, did you, Francis?—and I suppose that's why you were closer to her than any of us could ever be."

"We weren't exactly close," he said thoughtfully. "But we respected each other."

"Yes," Alison said with a shy smile, "that's just how she would have put it." Francis was pleased.

"Do you think she was in love with Alan?" he asked sitting up and leaning forward on his knees, frowning. All morning he had been carrying around with him the image of Alan's face as he had seen it at breakfast, like a mask emptied of all interior life. He had not wanted really to see this, but now he had seen it, it forced him to take Alan into account, for the first time in his life to feel with Alan. It was rather bewildering.

"I don't know," Alison said honestly. She was a little frightened of Francis' question. They all knew of course that Francis and Alan did not exactly get on. She did not want to do any damage.

"He was terribly in love with her." Francis went on, "I wonder if he was happy with her. I think now he wasn't and that is why this is worst of all for him."

"That's generous of you." Alison flushed because she was moved and because she was already affected by the sherry.

"No," Francis still had that intense frown, "but I want to understand. You know, I've behaved awfully badly. But maybe I had to. It was a question of loyalty, maybe. Or—no, that's too moral—perhaps more of identity. I exist because of my father. It wasn't easy."

"We all knew, Francis, don't imagine we didn't."

"My mother was such a powerful person, Aunt Alison." He said it almost as if he were accusing his mother, but she thought she understood.

"It's strange because she never did anything, I mean, she never really used any of her gifts as they could have been used."

"She wanted to be a person," he said definitely. "I think as a person she was tremendous. There was nothing she couldn't do. She made herself over for Alan, made herself into a good research assistant in these last years, learned Chinese—did you know that?"

"No, I didn't."

"She took being a wife very seriously, and yet I don't know why she married again. I wish I did."

"Maybe if what you want is to be a person, you find out you can't be it alone."

"Do you believe that, Aunt Alison?" he looked up, startled, into her eyes, and for an instant met her gaze straight on. "I thought you didn't believe that. After all, you're a person, aren't you?" He grinned.

"Yes—and no, not in the sense your mother was, that completeness— I'm just an old fuddy-duddy with bees in her bonnet. I suppose I never grew up. Most people forget what they believed passionately when they were young. I never stopped believing it. To most people, that seems rather quaint." One of Aunt Alison's charms was her humility. She had no illusions.

"Most people compromise. Is that growing up?"

"Well, in a way perhaps it is."

"And you think Mother compromised?" he pressed her.

"I don't know what I'm talking about, Francis," she said with a little embarrassed laugh. "Oh my goodness, the soup's boiled over!" She made a dash for the kitchen.

"I think she did, and I think she knew it," Francis said. "In a way we were close, Aunt Alison, but it was a battle all the time. She was so afraid of being possessive—and I—well, I think I wanted to be possessed. I guess I must be a little drunk to tell you that—drunk on one glass of sherry." His eyes were very bright now and he seemed elated. "I just wish she had once told me what she really thought of me—what she hoped—now I'll never know, never."

"Well, it seems to me," Aunt Alison said matter-of-factly,

"that what's important is what you hope yourself, what you yourself want."

"That's what I don't know," he burst out almost angrily. "That's what's wrong with me, Aunt Alison. I'm twenty-six. Don't you think I should know? I bet you knew at twenty-six!" he challenged her.

"Yes, I did—and look at me now!" She stood with the saucepan in her hands, grotesque and endearing and as pure, Francis thought, as sunlight.

"You were too good to be ambitious for yourself. I'm not. I'm a selfish arrogant young man."

"Yes," she said, smiling at him, "that's just what you are."

Meanwhile at Mrs. Bradford's discreetly elegant house on Chestnut Hill, they were discussing Francis. Sukey was also there. Old Mrs. Bradford approved of Susan, as she always called her, having an aversion to nicknames. Alison was nothing but a communist of course. But Susan with her impeccable manners and her charming clothes was perfectly acceptable.

"Naturally," Old Mrs. Bradford said, "Persis spoiled Francis, her only child. But it has been hard on him, I think." Mrs. Bradford was devastating in her gentleness. Her criticism masked (even from herself) in extreme tolerance was always oblique. She had expected Alan to live with her when he got back from China. His marriage, so late in life, had been a bitter blow, and as Mrs. Bradford was far too good ever to face evil squarely, even in herself, she had never admitted for a second that she was anything but "delighted for poor Alan. Such a *brilliant* marriage," and the inflection on the brilliant suggested that though brilliant it would not, of course, be happy.

"I think Persis knew what she was doing," Alan said gently. He had seen through his mother long ago, but he loved her dearly, more since he had admitted to himself that she was not a saint after all.

"Persis *always* knew what she was doing," Sukey added, leaving Mrs. Bradford out on a limb.

"Of course she did, dear brave Persis—only—now she's not here and so we have got to face things for ourselves. It's rather strange, for instance, it seems to me, that Francis still has no idea what to do with his life. Don't you think soon he had better make up his mind?" She turned to Alan.

Mrs. Bradford was not heartless. She had seen how utterly devastated Alan was and she minded. She wanted to get him to thinking about something beside his own loss, and she relied on his generosity of heart to carry her impulse on. Much later, the time would come when she might suggest that he come home to her and sell the house on Mt. Vernon Street. It was very unlikely that Francis would want to keep it up.

"He's done very well in his studies," Alan said. He felt horribly tired and did not want to be forced to "face" anything. "I expect he'll come through all right. He's intelligent and sensitive."

"The trouble is he's got such a chip on his shoulder," Sukey broke in. She was still smarting under Francis' rudeness of the day before. "He's so critical and savage."

"He's half French we mustn't forget," Mrs. Bradford went on. "It's a difficult inheritance," she conceded.

"Really, Mother, I don't see why." Suddenly Alan was terribly irritated with them, his eighty-year-old mother looking absurdly well and cheerful, and Francis to be coped with. It was just too much suddenly.

"The French are unstable, volatile people—they have plenty of spirit and plenty of intellect but I have always felt that they lack heart, you know what I mean?" She turned to Sukey who was looking out of the window at the sad snowless lawn and the thin trees, and who shivered suddenly.

"Francis has no imagination about other people," Sukey said. "The whole world revolves around himself."

"That's just being young."

"He's not as young as all that, Alan."

But Alan changed the subject. "Persis had planned to go over to Paris with Francis this summer. It was her graduation present to him. I don't know whether she had told him or not. But I think she even had the passages booked for June."

"She always wanted him to be French not American," Sukey said quietly. "I don't think she minded the way he felt about all of us. I think she rather approved of it."

"Persis was a very complicated person," Mrs. Bradford said, a shade too eagerly.

Alan got up and walked over to the window to look out at the desolate day, unseasonably warm. Everything looked damp and sad. Why couldn't they leave Persis alone? He waited what seemed to him minutes before he felt enough in control of himself to speak.

"I would rather not discuss my wife," he said. Only the back of his neck which had turned bright red showed his emotion. Mrs. Bradford, remembering her husband's lack of anger and how much worse his self-control had been than any outburst, held her peace.

"Eventually you'll have to have a talk with Francis," Susan said, to change the subject.

"I suppose so."

"He's having lunch with Alison, isn't he? Those two get on like a house afire." Susan went on, "I wonder why. They couldn't be more different. Francis certainly isn't interested in politics."

"I suspect that he finds Alison human," Alan said out of his anger. That was as far as he could allow himself to go. But he left the house a half hour later, still in a rage. He had not been able to bring himself to kiss his mother good-bye and now he felt remorse. But he couldn't help it. Persis had never once criticized his mother; her standards of behavior would never have permitted that. But of course he knew how little real sympathy there had been between the two women. While Persis was alive, he had succeeded in keeping his two selves separated, his married self and his son-self. Now they seemed to be tangled up together and Alan suffered from the tangle. He drove around aimlessly for half an hour, trying to cool off. And then suddenly made for home, for the house, which seemed now a shelter and the one place where he could find Persis, get her away from all the words and the insinuations, feel again her essence which was part of him now forever and ever. It was anger that drove him forward. He walked straight into the library and sat down deliberately in her chair, his head in his hands.

"He's sitting in the library now, Mary," the waitress reported.

"Is he now? Well and that's a good sign surely. And you'd best take him a cup of tea in there, the poor man."

§ 35 §

Neither alive nor buried, Mary said to herself, the tears falling again into her own cup of tea, these are the hard days. Lonely the corpse, lonely the living, she said to herself. And surely it's a bitter thing to die so young. She was enjoying herself thoroughly, but she did not know that.

CHAPTER FOUR

Persis herself would have been startled by the violence of feeling that rose up around her presence, now she was no longer there. She had not been a woman given to intimate friendships or heart-to-heart talks and yet, it seemed, her mind, her way of looking at things, her standards had printed themselves deeply on peoples' consciousness. And now that she was dead, her death had become a question. It was as if they had all become obsessed suddenly by the intricate problem of a personality, as if each were challenged to solve it once and for all, as if perhaps Persis herself would have no rest until she had been judged by the living, blamed, praised, analysed, re-created in their memories until the reality could take on the sculptured contours of a legend. Then, when she was safely laid away, they could go on living.

In his studio back of Huntington Avenue a young violinist with whom Persis had played once a week during the last year set himself to practice for four straight hours. He had seen her just a week ago, had flushed under her taunt, "Tony dear, how long did you practice this? It's pretty ragged." They had "practiced" together then for two good hours, and he had been worried afterwards to see how tired she looked at the end, had wanted to say something, had been put off, his tender regard brushed away with hardly a word. She cared about music, not about me, he said to himself severely. But was that quite true? She had fed him, scolded him, worked with him. Was that "not caring"? Or was her way of caring her own way, impersonal, built always on something other than personal feelings at least? Tony did not try to answer the question, but he set himself to work harder than he had ever done before.

"Of course," Mrs. de Forest said to her husband after breakfast, watering the plants in the bay window carefully with a small watering can, while her husband sat with the paper open in his hands, shocked by the news of Persis' death, "Persis was a cold fish, out for herself. She never invited any kind old bores to the house."

"She rarely invited us, if that's what you mean," Mr. de Forest said slily. A retired portrait painter, he was the kindest of men and he had always admired Persis. He was twenty years older than his wife, an old man now, sitting in the sun, and he had been shocked as if this visitation so close to them were a private warning. Slowly he gathered his thoughts together and sorted them out. There was quite a silence before he said, "She was interested in ideas, not in people, I think, a strange woman, Boston with a French inflection. I always wished I could have seen that first husband of hers."

"Everybody said they were terribly in love. But he was a failure of course, and she couldn't bear that."

"Come, come, Edna, aren't you being unjust? The man died in his forties."

"You men always defended Persis—I've never understood it. Surely she can't have been very attractive with that long face and those strange dark eyes. Personally I thought she was ugly."

"My dear, personally you just didn't like her," Mr. de Forest said gently.

"She rubbed me the wrong way," Edna admitted with a faint blush. She couldn't understand herself why she should be so mean. After all, Persis was a perfectly good woman—but—there was the day after the poor Miller boy hanged himself. Edna had met Persis at the Codmans' and had been terribly shocked to hear her say, "The Millers have been criminally innocent." It was rumored that the boy was a homosexual and his father had found out and been so upset, poor old man, that he had asked Peter to leave the house. Everybody's sympathy, except, it seemed, Persis', had gone to the parents. Edna could still remember the short silence that followed this verdict of Persis' and then the voices all finding something to say quickly to fill the gap. No, she didn't like her. There was something unpleasant about that unfeeling clarity. It put one off.

"All the Adamses are arrogant, secretive, strange people—look at the son. He's pure Adams in spite of his French father," Sukey's son John, the lawyer, said irascibly to his father.

"Well, you've got some Adams blood in your veins yourself, Johnny." Florid, pompous, very sure of himself, Samuel Thorndike didn't really care one way or the other. He was annoyed, as a matter of fact that his sister-in-law should have chosen to die just at this season. It had upset Sukey, set everyone at sixes and sevens. He wished the funeral were over and all this talk were over too. After all Persis was dead, let her rest in peace. He had never liked her, but that seemed irrelevant now. Samuel Thorndike was not given to reflection. He liked to think of himself as a man who could make up his mind fast and accurately and who never regretted a decision. His son John bothered him with his tendency to worry every issue like a dog with a bone.

John got on well with his father and laughed, "Oh I know. And I admit I'm going to miss the arguments I had with Aunt Persis. She was a formidable antagonist."

"She knew too much for a woman's good, that's my opinion. I don't hold with these blue stockings. Any redblooded man caught in the Athenaeum and meeting one of those faces behind the bookshelves would run a mile," and Samuel Thorndike laughed his hearty laugh. "But there was one thing Persis knew that I'm grateful for—she knew about wine and food. I'll grant you that."

John puffed at his cigar thoughtfully. The Adamses may be arrogant, but they are honest. "I have an idea," he said quietly, "that Aunt Persis knew how to live and somehow or other we all resent it. I wonder why." And then as his father looked completely blank, John went on talking to himself, "I suppose she made us feel accused, in the wrong—but accused of what? That's the question."

Miss Forbes, the principal of Boston's most famous private school for girls, sat at her desk with a snapshot of Persis at seventeen in her hands. Someone was late for an interview and she was grateful for this five minutes' grace. She had hardly had time to realize what had happened, must write to Alan at once she reminded herself. But for the moment she looked at the earnest intense young face in the photograph and thought, I'll never have another such friend, never. And yet she did not see Persis very often. Two or three times a year they went off for a drive in the country and a long talk. But in some way these talks were each important, in some way steadying, as if Persis had been an anchor. Mostly they had laughed about the school problems. Persis, Ellen Forbes thought, had a divine sense of proportion. I wonder how she achieved that? She looked back again at the snapshot. The young girl she had known then had been criticized rather often as "over intense." Her wit frightened people. She had not known how to be gentle, only how to be passionate and because she was so passionate and convinced, seemed hard, self-centered, difficult. But, Ellen thought, she grew up. I wonder if any of the rest of us did. Persis just never stopped growing—always I felt I was running to catch up, catch up with her phenomenal powers of reading and assimilating, of understanding music, politics, philosophy—what was there that Persis didn't pursue for a while as if it were the only thing in the world? And everyone of these interests was matched to a person.

Only last year she had started playing again seriously in order to work with a boy at the conservatory whom she wanted to help, believing he had talent but needed help in practicing. She had learned Chinese when she married Alan to help him in his history. And without his being aware of it, Persis took a good deal of trouble to keep up with Francis' courses. Yes, she put an immense amount of time and thought into her personal relations, there was no doubt of that. But what was interesting to Ellen Forbes was that Persis did all this and yet did not seem to get entangled. "Incandescence" was the word that leapt into her mind, as she carefully put the snapshot back in the small leather frame on her desk. Words meant a great deal to Ellen. She used them circumspectly, but this one she knew to be exact, and so she was pleased, light but not heat, it suggested. But—she hesitated a second longer before pushing the bell to the office to say she was ready for the interview—perhaps after all one must have experienced passion once and for all to achieve this kind of detachment.

Would Persis have laughed at this? Am I taking her too seriously? Ellen asked herself. What did it matter? The thing that mattered was that that light was gone out of the world forever. This was not something she would ever get over. But perhaps the hardest thing to accept about death is that life goes on. The form doesn't change, though the substance—at least for a few people—the substance has suffered a radical change. Ellen Forbes pushed the bell concealed at the side of her desk and assumed her usual expression of intelligent concern as a disturbed parent was shown in.

In Detroit, Francis' friend, Saul Wiseman who had lost his own mother the year before, stood with the telegram in his hand. "Dad!" he called out, "Dad, this is awful. Francis Chabrier's mother died yesterday."

Mr. Wiseman was struggling with his income tax in the study and called back, "That's too bad."

And Saul went up the big polished staircase, still holding the telegram, and sat down on his bed. It just didn't seem possible. Why, he had been over there only a week ago. That wonderful woman! Saul's first thought was for Francis—what would he do now? Where would he go? Should Saul ask him to come out to Detroit for the rest of the holidays? But how Francis would hate this pretentious house with its bad modern furniture and Dad's unfunny jokes. Should I go back to college earlier? Would he want me to come? These questions raced through his mind, and then suddenly he was very quiet inside. He felt he had no right to the immense unreasoning grief that overwhelmed him. After all, she was not his mother. He had actually never, except once, been with her in a room alone, and yet he knew now how much he loved her, how he had dreamed of doing something great in the world so that she would be proud of him, of saying something wonderfully bright that she would laugh at. He always felt challenged when he went to the house, excited and challenged as if he were to meet a test. And she had liked him. Francis had told him so, told him just what she said (the treasure he took out and looked at), "Saul has something better than a good mind, Francis. He has a sort of natural wisdom. That's rare." Nothing would ever seem as important as that. It was the accolade. Beside it his rows of straight A's, his Phi Beta Kappa key meant simply nothing, except as trophies to bring home to his father.

When his mother died he had gone straight to Mrs. Bradford, had sat in the library—he could see it now, see it all, the bunch of white chrysanthemums on the little table, even the book she had been reading, Bergson's *Laughter,* open beside them, and Mrs. Bradford and her unutterable kindness that day. Before that he had always been a little afraid of her, he remembered, as if that were long ago in another life. He had even thought her a queer cold woman, too bright. But that day he had seen the tears start to her eyes and flow down unashamedly while she talked of her own mother, and of death, and of him. He had found himself suddenly inside her heart without even knowing how he got there, had felt absolutely included as if there were no years between them at all. And when he left the house that day, he knew that something had happened to him of great importance. In a way, he had perhaps grown up. He had felt something hard to define about how life is woven together into one fabric. He had realized in himself what is meant by our being members of each other. And he had been consoled in the deepest sense by feeling himself to be part of humanity and, in another sense, part of her humanity as she was from now on part of his. He had flown back to Detroit that night to meet the weeping and wailing of relatives and his father's closed silent grieving and he had been kind, had restrained all his impulses of revolt, had come through somehow whole.

Could she be dead? Were such things possible? So sudden? So terrible? Where was she now? What does it all mean? Is there a God? The peace of the last year was shattered now all right. The questions poured in and swamped him, the chaos he had not faced when his own mother died, from which he had been miraculously preserved, took hold of him now and shook him bitterly. There was no comfort anywhere, no escape.

I must go to Francis, he thought. I must be there. He's all alone now too, among strangers.

CHAPTER FIVE

FOR THE FIRST TIME since they were children Ann felt shy and awkward when Francis finally called her on the phone that evening.

"I thought maybe you'd like to go for a walk tomorrow—I can borrow the car, that is, if you'd like to—"

"All right." Francis was noncommittal. She could tell nothing about his real desires from his voice. "What time?"

"I'll come by at about ten."

She was relieved that it was decided. All day she had hung around not knowing what to do with herself, wondering about Francis with a curious emptied-out feeling, as if some long story which she had been reading for years had come to an end. Ann knew very well that she had been on the edge of falling in love with Francis ever since they had first gone to dances together when she was still at school. It had always been there, that possibility, a negative possibility in a way in that she imagined, perhaps to comfort herself for being unmarried at twenty-six, that it had prevented her from falling in love with anyone else. Francis had always been there, to take her skiing or to the important dances, to play tennis with—and yet what all this meant and added up to, at least in their relatives' minds, had never happened. They each found a kind of safety in its *not* happening, as a matter of fact. Yes, that was it, they felt safe with each other and perhaps neither of them wished to risk that safety by pushing things any farther. More than once, one or other of them had turned away abruptly at the moment when something might have happened. They lived in a hermetically sealed world of their own composed of childhood memories they shared, of tree-houses, icy swims at Mt. Desert, and later, one or two drunken parties after which they had humorously exchanged data. So far they had held the adult world at bay. Ann had often wondered whether Francis had ever been in love and then brushed that aside as irrelevant. Whether he had been or not, the thing about him was that he seemed curiously intact.

But certainly a part of that safety she felt with him came from his mother. Francis was framed in a background so endearing that it was hard to separate him from it. Ann had felt at home with Mrs. B., as she called Persis, as she never had with her own family. And now suddenly the frame, the background was gone. Francis stood alone and she found that she was frightened of him. She could not, in a sense, place him any more. This was disturbing.

It was not at all that she had ever felt that Mrs. B. stood between them or that now he might be released from the strongest bond he knew, it was rather that Mrs. B. had seemed to supply the warmth and the understanding he lacked. She had surrounded their whole relationship with charm, had made the dinner parties shine with a special brilliance, had felt for Ann, she knew, a tender, half-humorous and searching regard, had kept her always from facing the sense of failure she now faced for the first time, for surely Francis should have fallen in love with me by this time, she said to herself, still sitting in the hall by the phone, her hands in her lap, holding at bay a feeling of absolute desolate loss.

The most noticeable thing about Ann, one would think on meeting her, was her honesty. It simply shone out from her face with its high rounded forehead, wide apart blue eyes and large firm mouth. She was not beautiful, but she was immensely likable. At times when she was feeling relaxed she could be wildly funny with a kind of childish abandon; but her habitual self, her everyday self was chiefly inquiring, curious, honest and, in a way, selfless.

At college she had plunged immediately into economics and social questions and while still at Radcliffe worked at the Cambridge Community Centre and had helped to raise money for their new building. This was one of the things she could talk about endlessly to Mrs. B. but which simply bored Francis. For the last three years Ann had been getting her Master's Degree in psychiatric social work and was now an instructor at B.U. in the school of social work. This involved supervising various students in the field and took her away from Boston one week out of two, traveling to Bedford and Providence and spending several nights a week away from home.

She lived with her parents in a big house on Commonwealth Avenue but had a floor to herself and rarely had a meal at home. She made her own breakfast on a hot plate in her flat. Her parents had not been intimates of the Bradford household. They were a little older than Persis and Alan and felt a great deal older. Her father, connected with Lee Higginson's, never got over the 1929 crash and had been a semi-invalid ever since. Her mother was shy and rather dim and moved in an inflexible pattern of activities which included of course the Friday afternoon symphony and lunch once a week at the Chilton Club with a group of women friends. They were both very proud of Ann, their only child, and followed her career with passionate interest. She had never felt it necessary to break away from home, perhaps because she was not very deeply attached to it. She took her parents for granted, played cribbage with her father in the evenings when she was at home, and otherwise hardly thought about them. In the terminology of her profession Ann Winthrop was a repressed but on the whole well-adjusted person who had learned to function in her environment. Of course, she wanted to marry. But even that had not been a pressing anxiety or no doubt she would have married before this. She had had three or four chances, but everyone including herself took it for granted that she had turned them down because of Francis.

And now, as she blew the horn once softly in front of the house on Mt. Vernon Street and looked up at the windows of the second floor where Mrs. B. had nearly always been until today, she was surprised herself at the violence of her feelings. She was actually trembling when Francis ran down the steps in his lamb-lined trench coat.

"You drive," she said, sliding over. He lit her cigarette and his own and inhaled deeply before he said anything. And in fact he just sat there, as if he could not make up his mind to start the car, for quite a moment, which seemed an eternity to Ann. His first words had become in her mind, long before they were spoken, of great importance, the key to something. And she waited as if she were waiting for a proposal of marriage.

"You're a trump," he said, "I needed to get away." This was their private world again and immediately Ann relaxed. The word "trump" had done it. So everything was the same after all. She was disappointed.

"It must be awful in the house," she said sympathetically.

"Grisly," he admitted, driving slowly down the steep hill to Charles Street. "Alan wanders around like a lost soul. Mary cries all the time. I've been taking the red bows off the wreaths all morning. You're a genius to have thought of this. Concord?" he asked, taking it for granted.

"Yes, Concord."

For the first time in their lives they found nothing to say. And so for the first time, Francis said the usual thing.

"You look very nice in that hat. It suits you. You look like a snowy owl or something."

Ann giggled. "I found it in some stuff Mother was going to give to the Morgan Memorial—I just cut off about half and here it is."

"Much too good for the Morgan Memorial," he agreed with a grin.

But under this politeness, she did not recognize him. Francis, she said to herself, is not here. She looked dreamily out at the cold gray river as they went across the bridge. It was trying to snow. A few gulls sat disconsolately on a patch of floating ice. The trouble was, she surmised, that they could neither of them manage to say Mrs. B.'s name. And until it was said, they would not be able to talk. They would have to be polite.

How polite he was being was proved by Francis asking her about her work. She made an immense effort to talk about it and did not succeed for once even in interesting herself in what she was saying. And after that, they were silent until the car picked up speed on the turnpike out of Cambridge. Now the forlorn fields, the little cedar trees, the whole triste thin landscape began to come into view, interrupted by roadside stands boarded up for the winter, and shining red and white gas stations.

"How incredibly ugly this must look to a foreigner," she said suddenly.

"And to you"

"Oh, I love it." They were passing a group of reservoirs, irregular ponds with low hills standing around them in a casual way. "But it is poor-looking, isn't it, Francis? Worn-out somehow, thin—"

"And you love it," he teased.

Because this teasing voice was his own voice at last, she changed the subject.

"I suppose your mother knew," she said.

"I suppose so."

"She was very brave."

"She was very secretive." The car leapt forward under his foot on the accelerator and Ann was a little frightened as the needle swung up to sixty.

"I don't think I've ever faced death before," she said quietly. And then as he didn't answer she said half to herself, "It's frightful."

"No, life is." She wondered why Francis must talk in this

cryptic way, three words at a time as if he were biting them off, but she supposed grief showed itself in various ways and this might be one. They were old friends but not old friends of grief. This was something they had not shared in childhood. It was undiscovered territory. That, perhaps, was why she had felt frightened at the beginning and felt both excited and frightened now.

"I know, Francis."

Now he turned on her savagely, "No, you don't know. You have a life. I haven't."

"Have I?" she asked lightly. "Some people might think not."

"Well, you know what I mean. You know what you want to do and you are doing it."

"You don't have to be so high and mighty about it," she said crossly.

He pulled the car in to a side road and stopped it.

"Let's walk."

"Yes, let's. I don't like driving as fast as that a bit."

"I'm sorry. I was thinking." And then relapsing into their childhood when he had always loved to frighten her, he asked hopefully, "Did I scare you?"

"Yes."

"That's fine." They found a bitter wind to greet them when they got out, but the road, cut deep just here between two high banks, provided a shelter and soon they would be in a wood. It was a walk they had often taken before and they walked fast.

"It smells like snow," she said, rubbing her nose with her mitten. "I hope it does."

She was disgruntled at her own anxiety. She felt like a school girl who has taken a chance and is going out with "a strange man," as if at any moment something would happen with which she might have to cope.

"Saul Wiseman is coming to the funeral," Francis said, looking straight ahead. It was impossible to tell whether this was considered to be good news or the last straw. She knew Saul, of course, and it seemed rather formal of Francis to use his full name. "Also the cousins from Portland," he said.

"How merry."

"Yes, it's going to be peculiarly grim; the family comes back to the house for lunch, it seems. That is what 'we' do, the funeral baked meats and, I presume, eulogies of the dead. I told Alan there must be liquor or we shall never survive it. But what bothers me, Ann, is Saul."

"Why?"

"I would like to ask him to come back for lunch—but—well—"

"Mrs. Bradford wouldn't approve, you mean."

"No one would approve. They'll all be frightfully polite and make him feel the way I always feel at these family parties, hardly a human being. I can't bear that to happen to Saul. He's sensitive enough about being a Jew as it is. He'll think it's that, you know."

"I don't think he'll want to come."

"But don't you see," Francis said with that nervous exasperation which was so familiar, "I want him to be there. I'll have one ally then at least."

"But that's selfish of you, Francis, if you know he'll be made miserable," she said earnestly.

"God damn it, it's my mother who's dead. Can't I be selfish?"

"Francis!" Ann was really shocked. She knew what most people thought of him and she had always thought that she knew better. But somehow this violence of self-interest, this over-emphasis shocked her now.

"I'm shocking," he said bitterly. "I even shock you."

"Well, it doesn't seem that important," she said conciliatingly.

"What *is* important? Mother liked Saul a great deal better than she did the relatives from Portland, God knows. She hated them."

"No, she didn't hate them," Ann said, determined to be just, "she just didn't like them very much."

Francis kicked a stone viciously, and then ran ahead to kick it again before she could. This was an old game they played by the hour.

Francis was struggling again against the perfectly stupid rage which seized him these days, rage about anything, about nothing. He was ashamed of himself. He too was feeling the absence of the frame. But Ann had been part of that frame and for that reason if no other he clung to their old relationship. He didn't want it to change. He wanted to be with her as he had always been, frank and at ease, kicking a stone up a road. It annoyed him that this didn't seem to be possible—Ann had not evidently wanted to play. She too was edgy.

"All, all is changed utterly," he quoted as he walked back to her.

And with that Boston talent for recognizing poetry, Ann answered, "A terrible beauty is born."

"Yes, that was Ireland. The Irish, I expect, are a resilient people and are perhaps really only happy at a Wake, especially if the death has been violent." Francis chuckled.

They had come into the wood now. Dry brown oak leaves still waved like brittle small flags here and there. Their feet crunched down on the soft leaves underfoot. There was not too much underbrush. It was a wood with no grandeur nor size, scrubby growth punctuated by a few trees which looked incongruous, a limbo of a wood. It suited them in their present mood, perfectly. Far off they could hear a woodpecker tapping. Ann had been observing Francis, watched him relax slowly, stop to listen, become absorbed in their walk itself and she was glad not to talk. But as they walked she thought about him a little anxiously. He seemed an almost intolerably solitary figure.

"What will you do when you're through this spring?"

"I'll go to Paris," he said instantly and, saying it, remembered the stolen letter in his pocket, which he had not after all read, but now didn't know what to do with or about. At the moment he kept it as a kind of talisman. It was one thing he had, apart from all the rest of them. They could perfectly possess his loss, but this they could not touch, for they didn't know it existed.

"Yes," Ann said without hesitation, "I'm sure that's what you must do." Right now, as they walked through the wood so familiar and safe, she felt the peril. She felt the wrench. Would he feel at home there as he never had here and never come back? The perspective of her life without Francis in it loomed up before her, so bare of any hope, that she clutched at the first thing that came into her head to remain inside his life. She said her next words in French. "Tu seras heureux là-bas sans doute," she said. It sounded unexpectedly tender.

He had never heard this tone in her voice before and he shied away from it, answering in English, "I don't know about happiness. I might find some way though of becoming myself—"

"Yes," she said sharply, out of her panic, "you might fall in love."

"Has it ever occurred to you, Ann," he said with heavy irony, "that I don't seem to be capable of that almost universal emotion?"

"I think maybe you've been in love all your life but didn't know it." She was thinking of his mother, but he could not of course know that and she realized it as soon as it was said. He snapped off a branch and held it in his hands, examining it with great interest like a boy.

"I've been a beast," he said.

"Oh," Ann blushed now to the roots of her hair and looked for some escape. "I didn't mean—"

"Never mind what you meant. I've meant, I suppose, to fall in love with you all these years. Maybe you've meant to fall in love with me. It's awfully queer."

She laughed. "That it hasn't happened, you mean?" She knew now exactly why she had been afraid. She had always known that it would be dangerous to talk about this with Francis, that it must be prevented from jelling, so to speak, or it would in fact freeze instead of jelling.

"What is the matter with us, Ann?" He stopped and turned to look at her. She had fallen a little behind to hide her panic and her shame and her sense of catastrophe. Actually she was near to tears.

"I don't know," she said with a vague gesture of her mittened hand. "It doesn't matter." But how much it mattered she had been finding out all day.

"Maybe we're too old," he said thoughtfully. "If you get to be twenty-six, maybe it's too late."

He was, she thought, the most inhuman person she had ever met. Why then did she love him? He was also a little mad, she thought, as the last statement showed, and she couldn't resist taking him up on it.

"Alan seems to have done pretty well at fifty."

"So you know?" Francis turned on her almost savagely.

"Know what?" She was startled.

"How terribly in love he was. I never knew till yesterday—I guess I never wanted to know."

"It was fairly obvious, Francis."

"Do you think she loved him?" Francis hated himself for asking this question and it was, he knew, a final nakedness before her which, under the circumstances, was in shocking taste.

She felt the full weight of the charge. And she did not know how to answer. "It's really none of our business," she said, knowing it was the wrong thing.

"Of course it isn't. But I would like to understand." In the end Francis always won out, she thought, because he tried so hard to be honest. This, she had learned, very few people ever do. It gave him a sort of dignity, in spite of his rudeness and his childish fits of temperament, and this quality came straight from his mother.

"You'll never understand your mother until you get away from her, away from Alan, away from here," Ann said bitterly.

It was, obviously, the truth.

Later in the car, Francis turned to her almost humbly and

said, "We'll always be friends, Ann, won't we? I mean you won't give me up—now—"

"Now?" she would not look at him. "Of course not. Don't be silly. I'm afraid for better or worse we're deeply embedded in each other's lives. And that's that," she said briskly, lighting a cigarette. But what would this summer be like without Mrs. B., without Francis? Of this she didn't dare to think. Her face felt completely frozen with the effort to be dispassionate.

CHAPTER SIX

SAUL WENT STRAIGHT from the station to King's Chapel, checking his bag. It was too late to try to get Francis on the phone; he had just time to walk and was glad of the chance to clear his head after the long train ride. The impulse which had carried him through the decision to come on for the funeral had now had a good many hours in which to spend itself and he wondered if he had been wise to come. It was snowing. The tangible soft veil increased his sense of unreality, wafting gently down between the harsh high walls of office buildings, separating the hurrying office girls one from another. King's Chapel is in the middle of the busiest shopping district, in the midst of life of the most bustling pushing kind. Taxis swooped down past it blowing their horns. Christmas shoppers, weighed down by bundles, hurried along and bumped into the members of the funeral, as Saul ironically called them, as they got out of their long black limousines. One could hear the insistent ringing of a Salvation Army collector's bell. One of the department stores had a loud-speaker blaring out Christmas carols, but luckily this was some-what muffled by the snow. For almost everyone this snow was a sign of Christmas, a sign of rejoicing, not as it was to Saul, a snow for the dead. He stood on the corner of Tremont Street, feeling the throng push its way past and around him, balancing himself between this bustle and the thread of mourners crossing it at right angles. Now, watching these faces break through the crowd, he was aware of the formidable aspect of Mrs. Bradford's world.

He recognized a few of the faces, the editor of *The Atlantic Monthly,* distinguished heron, followed by the hatless solid figure of one of Saul's English professors. There seemed to be innumerable faded intelligent women, under those hats peculiar to Boston, designed to conceal rather than reveal the personality of the wearer. The whole array struck him now, as it streamed into the church and separated itself from the vulgar shoppers, as essence of Boston. It occurred to him that Francis with his overt brilliance, his moods, his violent air, all intensity and conflict, was a real outsider. It was not just an idea he had, as Saul had sometimes imagined. It was not their intention but these people gave the impression of belonging to a secret society, the rules of which you somehow absorbed with your mother's milk. Saul fingered the heavy silk scarf his father had given him for Christmas, and knew it was the wrong thing altogether. For an instant he imagined he would not go in. He would lose himself in the unbelonging crowd, push on downtown, explain that his train was late.

Considering this idea, he glanced up at the smoke-blackened pillars of the chapel. Somewhere in there was Mrs. Bradford, was Francis, the outsider. After all, he had come for them, not for these others. With a quick secretive gesture he slid the silk scarf into his pocket and joined a group going up the stairs, hoping to be concealed by their protective coloring. Inside, the silence was so powerful, it seemed to have a smell. It was hardly credible that just a few feet away the street bustled with noise, carols, shoppers, gaily wrapped bundles. The silence flowed out underneath the organ playing the usual nondescript faded music. It took possession of everyone. Hurried steps fell into a slow walk. There was a moment of hesitation as each person entered the chapel itself from the anteroom, and suffered the discreet glances of the elderly ushers who (Saul thought) separated the sheep from the goats with ineffable tact. He was escorted to a seat in a remote already half-filled pew near the back. This chapel breathed a sense of intimacy, not so much with God as among the people who worshipped here. Saul, opening the little gate of the square pew, felt that he had inadvertently walked into a stranger's drawing room. The only seats still vacant faced the pew itself instead of the pulpit. This was disconcerting, but a quick glance round apprised him of the fact that one could twist oneself around cleverly and so avoid confronting the other occupants. He knew he was being stared at. His mind was such a chaos of embarrassment and self-consciousness that he found it quite impossible to concentrate for some time. He could not see the coffin, so there seemed no center of contemplation, only a great many people and a great many flowers and this monotonous rather sickly music. Mrs. Bradford was dead, but as yet he had no acute realization of the fact. Rather he felt he was at a reception to which he had not been invited. As if he had run the whole way from the station, he felt oppressed, and began to sweat quietly. If he could have left now, he would have done so.

He did not recognize what the organist was playing, but he did feel that this was real music at last, the kind of music Mrs. Bradford would have chosen herself. It was the Chausson piece

Francis had looked up and it was the cue for the family to come in, the beginning of the service. Saul caught a glimpse of Francis' rigidly controlled face as he walked slowly down the aisle beside Alan Bradford. At this moment the distance between him and his friend seemed absolute. And Saul lowered his eyes, suddenly shy at having even looked at Francis at this moment. An automobile horn sounded loudly across the music. Saul, looking deliberately away from the family, suddenly noticed the governor's pew with its canopy suggesting a box at the theatre. Absorbed in this, he was startled by the minister's voice beginning a prayer, and quickly bowed his head.

"Merciful Father, O Thou Invisible but here among us at this moment, help us to understand Thy glory and Thy power as we feel it particularly today, through the life of a woman devoted to all the manifestations of Thy spirit as we see them in music, art, friendship, the love of our fellow men. More than most of us she knew what Thy servant Paul meant when he said that we are everyone members of one another. Help us to feel this great truth with fresh devotion now for her sake. Let us pray."

Saul, who had never attended a Unitarian service, was so amazed by this personal reference to Mrs. Bradford that he found it difficult to compose himself. Besides, like so many of his generation, he had first to battle through a whole series of questions, "Do I believe in God?" he asked himself with his head in his hands, an attitude so unexpectedly devout that it disturbed the old gentleman on his right. It was not usual here to assume such attitudes; a discreet bowing of the head, arms folded, seemed more appropriate to the dignity of man and the Majesty to whom he appeals. "Do I believe in God?" Saul asked himself and then in the few seconds of silence that elapsed before the Minister launched into the one hundred and third psalm, he asked himself, "What would Persis Bradford have thought of this?" He had never before called her by her first name, even in his own mind. But it was hard for some reason now, to think of the dead as Mrs., to think especially of Persis as in any way connected with the diminished figure of Alan Bradford. So much of her life had not been joined to his, it was that perhaps. Or it was that the dead lie alone.

"As for man, his days are as grass: as a flower of the field, so he flourisheth.

"For the wind passeth over it, and it is gone; and the place thereof shall know it no more.

"But the mercy of the Lord is from everlasting to everlasting . . .

"Bless the Lord, all his works, in all places of his dominion: bless the Lord, O my soul."

The congregation rose to sing "O God our help in ages past."

There was a relief from the intense stillness in the shuffling about of the hymnbooks and in the singing itself. Everyone perhaps had been too tense to feel very much. Now the wave of feeling took them all as the coffin was lifted. It looked, Saul thought, the tears flooding his eyes, so terribly small. The organ broke into the first slow chords of Mozart's *Ode Funèbre* and the spacious music accompanied the slow progress of the little casket covered with white orchids, and rose to its triumphant and inexorable climax, and still they stood. There was now no one in the chapel, so they all felt. Persis Bradford had gone.

This, Saul thought to himself, is what funerals are for, so that one may know once and for all that the person is gone. Here in this great room full of people, this reception for the dead, there was nothing but emptiness. They had been held together by the presence of Mrs. Bradford, even dead. Now she was gone, they felt their isolation. The assembly broke apart. It was finished. Somewhere among the crowd the subdued sound of stifled sobs seemed irrelevant. These people would not wail and beat their breasts. They would go home now, Saul thought, with a sort of admiration, and bring out the pale very dry sherry and remark that the funeral had taken just twelve minutes. But what would he do? It seemed quite out of the question to try to get to Francis —he did not even know where Francis was nor whether the family would go on to the cemetery, nor what indeed was the proper thing to do. Once more he stood alone in the moving throng, hesitating at the entry, aware of the discreetly curious glances.

"Oh, Mr. Saul." Mary clutched his arm and broke into a new sob (it was she no doubt who had made the unseemly noise just now). "Mr. Francis will be so glad you got here. He was worried. You're invited to the lunch at half past one when they come back, Mr. Saul. Indeed he'll be glad you've come, the poor boy." She squeezed his arm convulsively and Saul felt she was an island of comfort in this unknown sea. So they went out together and Saul was pleased to have the good idea to take her back in a taxi.

"Such a short funeral," she said rather sadly, when she had given her nose a good blow. "I was just getting settled when it was all over. But these Unitarians," she said confidentially, "have no religion to my way of thinking. What do they do now, do you think, with no Virgin Mary at all? It's a lonely religion, I'm thinking. And did you notice, Mr. Saul, that the minister did not mention our Saviour once during the service? Surely that's a strange way to bury the dead—at least to my way of thinking."

"I don't know," Saul said thoughtfully, "I'm Jewish," he said simply and for once without having to bring himself to say it.

"Sure, and why not? There's no harm in that," she said comfortingly. "But in your religion surely the service is longer?" she asked.

"Yes, I think it is." There was something so charmingly ludicrous in this theological discussion with Mary that he found it difficult to restrain a smile.

"The music sounded grand, that's one thing. And that's Mr. Francis's doing, you may be sure. He's the one," she said with satisfaction.

"I'm having a mass said for her soul," she confided when they were at the door. "But don't tell them, will you? They might be offended—and I wouldn't seem to criticize, you know. Only the Mass will be grand—perhaps you would like to come?" she said shyly.

This time, Saul thought, wryly, I have been invited to the party. He accepted with gratitude and then left Mary at the door, saying he would go for a walk and come back at lunchtime.

"You're sure, Mary, that Francis wanted me to come?" he asked with a sudden fear of intruding. "Isn't it a family affair?"

"And if it is, like, what of that? Mr. Francis needs a friend," she said solemnly. "Good-bye to you now, and thank you, Mr. Saul, for your kindness."

CHAPTER SEVEN

AN UNKNOWN WAITRESS, brought in to help, opened the door to Saul when he finally got up courage to ring the bell at a little after half past one. He could hear the subdued murmur of voices upstairs as he took off his rubbers trying to distinguish Francis', but just then Francis himself peered down the stair well and after one glance ran down so impetuously he collided with Saul rather than greeting him. This broke the ice and they laughed, and found laughing such a relief that they laughed on, they did not know why. Francis flung himself down on the little sofa in the hall and said, "Gosh, it's good to see you. They're all there," he said softly so as not to be overheard, "the whole shebang, even the awful cousins from Newburyport. Lucy and Dorcas." Francis began to laugh again at the names, he did not know why. "Oh wait till you see them. It reeks of Boston up there. Thank God you've come."

"Do they know I'm coming?" Saul whispered back. "I hope you told them."

But Francis had not told anyone but Alan who had seemed perfectly amenable. When the two young men stood in the doorway, there was a general movement, a turning of heads and a prolonged stare to welcome them. Alan came forward quickly and shook Saul's hand. Then he led him, a lamb to the slaughter, to his mother who had chosen, perhaps unconsciously, to sit in Persis' chair by the open fire.

"Mother, this is Francis' friend, Saul Wiseman. He was good enough to come on from Detroit for the funeral."

"How do you do?" said Mrs. Bradford very distinctly as if she were talking to a foreigner. Saul was then led over to the two Miss Brewsters, sitting stiffly on the sofa opposite Mrs. Bradford. He was relieved when he came to Mrs. Thorndike to see someone he knew. Samuel Thorndike finally broke the ice by saying heartily, if irrelevantly, "Detroit is a fine city. Up and coming."

"Yes, sir," Saul said, blushing to the roots of his hair, but he really did not know why.

"Papa once went as far as Denver, in 1910, wasn't it, Lucy? He climbed Pike's Peak," Dorcas Brewster said gently and kindly, as if this might help.

Alan looked wildly around for the drinks and rang the bell a second time with what he hoped was desperate insistence. Francis had now pulled Saul over to the further window seat where his Aunt Alison was sitting. At the other end of the room, the Brewster sisters were replying at length to the polite inquiries about their father, now ninety-five and bedridden for the last ten years.

"He has trouble with his digestion," Lucy said to Mrs. Bradford confidentially. "The doctor thinks it's because he takes no exercise. But on the whole he is doing very well, considering. The death of the *Transcript* was a great blow to him. He enjoyed it so much and the *Christian Science Monitor* doesn't quite do. Those editorials in Hebrew and other strange languages annoy Papa." Lucy turned to Dorcas for corroboration.

Francis took one look at Saul's unbelieving face and coughed to cover up a giggle.

Mercifully the strange maid now came in with a tray of glasses, sherry for the ladies, martinis for the gentlemen. Susan and Mrs. Bradford took martinis. A sort of embalmed gaiety took possession of the room.

"It takes a death in the family to bring us to Boston," Dorcas said cheerfully, after she had sipped her sherry.

Aunt Alison, who had been looking out of the window as if she were deliberately shutting out the room, now turned to Saul who had sat down beside her, trying to keep his martini hand from shaking, and said, "I do think it was good of you to come, Saul. It means a great deal to Francis—to us all," she added tactfully, though that was plainly a white lie.

"Did you get in in time for the funeral?" Francis asked. No one had as yet said a word about the funeral and he was supersensitive about it now.

"Yes, I did. The music was beautiful, Francis," Saul said shyly.

Perhaps unfortunately this remark fell into a silence at the other end of the room.

"What was the last piece they played?" Lucy Brewster asked. anxious to cull all the information she could to take back to Papa.

Perhaps it was the effect of the sherry, but Dorcas interrupted to say with plaintive gentleness, "It seemed just a shade theatrical, perhaps not quite what Mama would have thought Unitarian"—she glanced around nervously for approval—"but of course times have changed. We are such dodos, Lucy and I, we do not know at all what is going on."

"It was Mozart's *Ode Funèbre.*" Francis said flatly.

"Ah? A French piece—I see." Lucy nodded her head as if a puzzle had now been satisfactorily solved.

"Mozart, Cousin Lucy," Alan intervened, feeling Francis' imminent anger, and he repeated, *"The Funeral Ode* by Mozart. My wife was especially fond of it."

Saul managed to whisper to Francis, touching his arm as if to stop him from rushing in, "It was tremendous. It was the whole thing, I thought."

"Of course Mozart couldn't be Unitarian, could he?" Dorcas conceded with a dry little laugh.

Lucy tittered appreciatively at what was apparently the family conception of Dorcas's wit.

They were now fairly launched. Mrs. Bradford turned to her son, "I thought the funeral was quite perfect, Alan. I'm sure Persis would have approved."

"Thank you, Mother," he said with feeling. He too had been apprehensive of this moment.

"Of course," she went on (Alan should have known that this was an opening gambit and what she really thought was still to come), "I did think the prayer a little overwritten, perhaps, a little exaggerated in its inference."

"I thought it was exactly right," Alison said warmly from her window seat.

"Of course, Alison, we were really all too moved to be the best judges," Mrs. Bradford conceded graciously.

Saul, whose ideas of a family reunion such as this were based on his own memories of much embracing and weeping and a great deal of warm loving exchange, almost too articulate, was amazed by the atmosphere here of something like venom. Do these people really hate each other, he asked himself, glancing from Susan to Mrs. Bradford to John Thorndike, standing in the other window? The faces told him nothing. They did not even wear the sign of tears. But if he thought they were as cold as ice, he was of course wrong.

Perhaps it was that, so afraid of love, or of any articulated emotion, so afraid of intensity, they took refuge in superficial bickering as safer. Francis by now had achieved his most remote expression. He was, to all intents and purposes, not there. He had finished his martini while the others were still beginning theirs.

Alan, who was extremely disturbed by his mother's sitting in Persis' chair, hovered about, unable to decide to settle anywhere. The fact that this was an ordeal showed only in his rather more than usual politeness. Now he lit Susan's cigarette, found her an ashtray, and then went about filling up the glasses.

John Thorndike, Susan's son, sat in the window seat near where he had been standing. There was one question he was dying to ask, but he didn't quite dare. Aunt Persis had not been a churchgoer, of course, but what did she really believe? Not able to ask the question directly his lawyer's mind felt around for an oblique way of asking it, "Of course," he said thoughtfully, "I suppose it is a rather Catholic idea to connect a love of the arts with holiness—"

"Certainly not, John," Mrs. Bradford said quietly, "after all we use a great deal of poetry in our services, and music, for that matter."

"Do you think that Aunt Persis would have made that connection?" he asked the room at large. "I was just wondering—because of the prayer."

Francis was for the first time interested and he answered quickly, "I think the guy was in a tough spot. After all, Mother was not, in the usual sense, religious. She never went to church."

"She did not either, in the usual sense, indulge in good works, did she, Alan?" Mrs. Bradford asked sweetly.

It occurred to Susan that never in Persis' lifetime would this group of people have gathered in this room. There was something monstrous, ghoulish in their being here now, as if their piddling little values had after all won, since they were here and Persis was not. Susan caught Dorcas Brewster's dismayed glance at the Picasso drawing on the wall. She observed the two sisters with strong dislike. Obviously they did not realize themselves that they were feeling particularly well today because, though older than Persis, they had managed to survive her. More often than not, she thought with a bitterness made more vivid by her second martini, it's the dead who go on living. Those who had loved Persis, Susan thought glancing around at Alan, at Francis, at her sister Alison, were diminished, withered it seemed in an hour, but those who had not loved her (Mrs. Bradford for instance) flourished as the green bay tree. All this had taken a second and no one had yet answered Mrs. Bradford's last remark. Susan, impelled by her new insight, got up and walked over to the window seat to join Alison. Saul gave her his place, glad to stand. He had been waiting for Alan to answer his mother, but the last thing Alan wanted was to talk about his wife, here and to these people. The back of his neck was dangerously red as he rather ostentatiously went to the back of the room to fuss with the martinis. Saul did not know him well enough to notice this, and in a sudden spurt of self-confidence because he was really moved, he said,

"Excuse me, Mrs. Bradford, but may I ask what you mean by good works?"

"I meant nothing," Mrs. Bradford said airily. She was not going to get into an argument with this stranger.

But Saul having begun, now felt he must go on and make things clear. It could not be left like that, the shadow allowed to fall, the insinuation to rest. "I know she cared a great deal about other peoples' lives," he said earnestly. Everyone now turned to stare again. The atmosphere was definitely hostile at the far end of the room. "She gave an immense amount of time and trouble to young friends like me who can't have had much to give her in return for so much understanding. She opened all sorts of doors for us—she was wonderful," he ended lamely, feeling how out of place this jejeune enthusiasm was.

"She played the piano so well as a young girl," Lucy said. It was the only thing she could think of at the moment, as there had been a sort of gap after Saul's speech.

John had been listening intently. "I'm sure what you say is true," he answered Saul directly, "but I was asking about her life as a Christian, about the religious element."

"My mother was a pagan," Francis said quite loudly and with the deliberate intention of shocking them. "She often said so."

Dorcas gave a loud hiccup and tittered apprehensively. Lucy clutched her sister's arm as if she was afraid of some outburst. Mrs. Bradford looked over at her son to see what his reaction would be to this bombshell. As usual Francis was being rude on purpose. She, for one, was not going to rise.

"I expect she was, Francis," Mrs. Bradford said sweetly, "and that was all I meant to say just now."

Alan had left the room.

Downstairs the imported waitress and Louise were putting the final touches to the table.

"Why, what's the matter, sir?" Louise was startled to see Mr. Bradford standing in the doorway, shaking with what appeared to be an illness of some sort.

"Nothing, Louise. But I think it's time you served, if possible."

"Yes, sir, we're all ready."

"Then perhaps you would be kind enough to announce that fact upstairs. I'll stay here."

Alan calculated quickly how he would seat the guests. Francis at one end of the table with Susan and Alison on his left and right, Mother on my right, Lucy on my left. Saul beside Alison (she'll be kind to him). That puts John beside his mother but never mind. Sam beside Mother, then Dorcas next to Saul. He was quite calm again by the time they were all seated. But he felt so exhausted that he was afraid his hands were visibly shaking. No one perhaps could measure the strain it had been for Alan to face his mother sitting there in his wife's accustomed place. He had fought in himself the rising hatred during the last hour.

"I hope you will enjoy the wine, Mother," he said with exaggerated politeness. "It's one of our last bottles of chablis."

The tension, since they had left the room upstairs, visibly relaxed. Saul, supersensitive to all such things, basked in the evident sympathy between Alison and Susan. Even Francis stared about him less theatrically. Perhaps they all needed food more than they knew.

It was snowing hard outside. And somewhere very far off, as Louise poured the wine and passed the creamed sweetbreads and thin French beans, as the voices rose and fell, Persis was ashes. Death had come and gone.

As they were gradually restored by the food, they all felt this return to life, as if a door had finally closed behind them and they were now in another room. In this room, it was Francis rather than Persis who took the center of the stage. With the possible exception of Sam Thorndike they had all, in the last three days, been living almost exclusively in the past. Now they turned to the young face at the end of the table, with something like relief. He looks almost relaxed, Alan thought, watching Francis lean over to say something to Saul, framed between his two aunts. To see him, for once not moody, was charming. He looked young, disarmingly young and almost handsome. "He has his mother's eyes," Alan said to himself. At first one would not have thought so, as they were set rather differently in his head, but the look he gave Saul, a penetrating very clear look was Persis' own. It was, above all, an intellectual face, in which until now emotion must always have been a disrupting and not an integrating force. He did not have his mother's severe passionate mouth; his was asymmetrical, always bitter and violently willful in repose. And Alan thought, everything depends now on what sort of woman he falls in love with.

It was true that Francis was a stranger among the people at his table, and alone, but it would be less than fair to believe, as Saul did, that this was the fault of Boston or of his relatives. Just now they were, each in his or her own way, thinking of him fondly, wishing him well. Samuel Thorndike, who had been miserable all through the funeral and especially upstairs, and, as usual when he was with the Adamses, aware of the distance they created even between Sukey and him when they were together en masse, was now also feeling a good deal better. He had just caught Sukey's eye and found it friendly.

And this, he felt, gave him permission to talk. He had contained himself until now out of respect for the dead.

"Well, Francis," he said heartily, "we hear great things of you at college."

"You'd better wait till midyears," Francis said with a smile.

"You'll be through this spring?"

"Yes, sir."

"Would it be in order to ask what your plans are then?"

There was just a faint gathering of tension in the atmosphere. Of course they had all discussed among themselves what Francis would do and why he hadn't yet made up his mind, but as long as Persis was alive, no one would have asked the question outright.

"Do tell us," Lucy said sweetly, "Papa will be so interested." As a matter of fact Papa had often said, "That boy must be a queer duck, half-French and half-Adams. My belief is he will turn out badly, but of course you never know." And Lucy and Dorcas had been violently shocked by his remark about his mother being a pagan and by the manner of his saying it. Now they turned their watery blue eyes on him attentively.

Francis had never been as vague about what he wanted to do as he pretended, perhaps even to himself. He was, as a matter of fact, extremely ambitious. Nothing less than greatness, he thought, would be sufficient. But his ideas of greatness had to do more with what one might become as a person, than with what one might become in a profession. At one time he had been tempted by the diplomatic service and had then made up his mind that that would be too easy—his name, his money, he had everything, but just for this reason he had turned the opportunity aside. He wanted now to do something in which being the son of Pierre Chabrier would count for more than being the son of Persis Adams. How young and how arrogant he was, he did not himself understand. He took his time about lighting a cigarette for his Aunt Sukey and one for himself.

"I'd like to take a year off, maybe study at the Sorbonne," he said. "Anyway I shall go to Paris in the spring."

It was no answer that Sam Thorndike could cope with and he drank his wine and looked baffled.

"Yes," Mrs. Bradford said kindly, "of course you will want to see your father's relatives after all these years."

"And my mother's friends," Francis said with his defiant air. Whoever they might be, the tone implied, they were not here.

"Oh dear, Paris in the spring—I envy you," Sukey sighed. "You'll have to bring us all hats back."

"I guess he'll have something better to do than buying hats," Alison demurred, putting a hand gently on his arm. But Francis, perhaps to his own astonishment, was not angry with them now. From the end of the table, he glanced at all their faces, ending with Alan's. He felt suddenly grown-up and as if for once he didn't need to defend himself any longer by attacking them.

"I'll probably waste my time," he said, with a laugh. "Maybe you'd better come over and keep an eye on me, Saul."

As everyone had been prepared for a blow-up they were not prepared for this sudden turning on of charm. They had hardly ever seen Francis as he was now, almost genial, master of the table. They realized that he had indeed grown up at last, that he was (though he would never have admitted it himself) one of them.

And if he needed a reward Alan's slow smile was it.

Mrs. Bradford was slightly disconcerted. This had been Persis' power, to outface a perilous situation with sheer charm. She had not expected to see it in her son and she was too old to change an opinion she had once formed. She had decided long ago that Francis was a rude spoiled boy who needed taking down.

"Maybe we could even have a family reunion next year in Paris," he dared them. "Do you think you could be persuaded to come over, Mrs. Bradford?"

"I don't know about that, but I'll drink your health in French wine in Boston, Francis," she said gallantly, lifting her glass.

"But Alan must come," Francis said earnestly. "Yes, Alan, you must." Francis could afford to be magnanimous now. He had in some way won. And because he had won at last, won over himself as well as them, not allowed the black mood to get hold of him, the mood which would have ended in fireworks, in defiance of them all, in his deliberately setting himself apart from them, he felt again the stab he had felt at breakfast three days ago when he had realized Alan's loss.

"Alan will have to finish his book, won't you, Alan?" Mrs. Bradford said firmly. She was not going to lose him twice, not lose him to this strange stepson as unpredictable as a chameleon.

Reflected light from somewhere caught the diamond on her hand; it flashed out for a second like a warning.

"I don't know, Mother, we'll see," Alan said irritably. The others were all talking about Paris again; Sukey and Sam had spent their honeymoon there and the Brewster sisters had had their coming out dresses made by Worth. Even Alison had her memories of Jaurès.

Saul, quietly watching and listening to it all, registering the atmosphere as perhaps none of the others who were involved in it did, thought "How glad Mrs. Bradford would be if she could see Francis now." Indeed as in a fairy tale, it seemed as if some wicked spell had been broken. In the back of his mind was the idea that death is always a clarification. But he would have to think about this later. Was Persis Bradford's death Francis' great chance, his way out or his way in? Was that it?

For the present Saul watched his friend's face eagerly and rejoiced in his new-found grace. And when Francis turned to talk to his Aunt Sukey, Saul murmured to Alison Adams, "Francis is going to be all right, isn't he?"

"He's always been all right, you know," she answered quickly, giving his hand a squeeze under the table. Why do people say Boston is cold? Saul wondered, filled with happiness, the happiness of being included here where he had most expected to feel an outsider.

The thing is perhaps that Americans almost never feel at home where they were born. To Saul this house, and the life it represented—music, conversation of a kind that would have simply bewildered his parents—was the nearest thing to home he had ever imagined. It was the kind of life he would dream of achieving for himself, and scholarly, gentle, wise Alan at the foot of the table, the kind of person he dreamed of becoming, or Alison with her pure and selfless dreams. They took so much for granted which to him seemed extraordinary and wonderful.

But for Francis the whole image was different. These

amenities, this elegant frame was a prison. What Francis wanted was to extend his personal frontiers, was to break out into what he, perhaps mistakenly, called "life" in his own mind. For him the heart of the matter was personal relations and, with the exception of Aunt Alison, he felt only the poverty of relationship here, the emptiness of it, the fact that he was supremely and above all *not* involved.

While Saul sat silently considering these things, the conversation at the table had broken up. The wave of emotion, which had lifted them for a few moments toward Francis and united them, ebbed. Everyone felt rather tired. Alan had lapsed into absent-minded silence and given up even being polite to the cousins. There was a hiatus in which the only sound was the creak of the dumbwaiter coming up and Louise's discreet passing of the dessert plates.

Francis met Alan's forlorn empty eyes and looked away.

It was a relief when Dorcas Brewster announced that she and Lucy must catch a four o'clock train and Mrs. Bradford offered to take them to the station in her car. At least now, Alan thought, there is hope that this will be over in an hour. They went back to the drawing room for their coffee. They all felt obscurely that something had come to an end. Never again would they be in this room together. And Dorcas, looking around again at all the strange things, wondered but didn't dare ask what would happen to the house now. Would Susan and Mr. Thorndike move in here? Would Francis wish to keep it on in case he married in the next few years? It was a pity that she couldn't take this information back to Papa, but the atmosphere had a chill and one glance at Francis' closed face sufficed to scare her into silence. It was, indeed, time to break up the party.

CHAPTER EIGHT

BUT WHEN they had all gone, it seemed both to Alan and to Francis, that life had come to a full stop. Until now there had been things to do. Now there was nothing to do. They drifted off, each to his own room, and Francis wished he had insisted on Saul's staying. At the last minute he had felt shy, felt that perhaps he should stay here alone with Alan, not shut himself off. And yet, when the front door was closed for the last time and he and Alan stood in the hall, there had been nothing to say, nothing to do but climb the three long flights behind his stepfather's slow tired steps and then leave him at the door of his study.

"I guess I'll try to do a little work," Francis said.

He shut his door and sat down on the bed. For a moment he allowed himself the comfort of realizing that he had not disgraced himself and that it had on the whole gone off better than could have been expected. But just past this and all around him was the terrifying emptiness. Ever since his mother's death he had kept it at bay, this sense of panic, of being left alone with no map and no sense of direction. Now it was there and he had to face it. "What am I going to do?" he asked himself, looking around the walls like a prisoner. His whole life stretched before him and seemed interminable and above all too difficult.

Even grief now would have been something to do, to seize on and to live. But he felt no grief, only emptiness. His mother had, it seemed, actually disappeared. At the moment he tried to, but couldn't remember her face. His head had begun to ache rather violently and he took an aspirin and lay down, unable to find the will to get up and pull down the shades though the light hurt his eyes.

For the first time in his life Francis was meeting an experience which he could not dramatize, which he could not exaggerate as food for his temperament, because it was itself beyond exaggeration, more final than one's most final thoughts.

He must have lain there half an hour before he leapt up and fumbled in his coat pocket for the letter. The address was written in purple ink in a decisive bold hand, Solange Bernard, 18 Rue de l'Université. Without waiting to inquire again of his conscience whether this was permitted, he tore it open and read it through without stopping. Each word came to him so vividly in his state of suspense that he could have repeated the letter by heart after a first reading, but he read it three times, studied the curiously abrupt hand, the very literary sentences thrown down it seemed without a second thought, the erratic spaces here and there where perhaps Solange Bernard had looked out of the window and tried to visualize his mother's face—and was she able to, he wondered? Could she, so far away, see what he could not see? Never had Francis read a letter quite like this before.

Do you remember, darling, how Swift used to call his Stella, *dearest lives?* When your letter came I was transported back as if by magic almost twenty years to the house on the Rue de Vaugirard, to Francis glowering when you asked him to take his book upstairs, to the pale gray dress with a green velvet sash (do you remember, and was it Worth?) you wore at that time and the soft green cloche from which your eyes looked out, such perspicacious eyes, with amused severity—for were you not quite a severe New Englander in those days and a little shocked by my madnesses, or were you only amused? I call you 'dearest lives', cherishing this plural which assures me that you are coming, though I can't believe it, and we shall have another life to share, after all these years. And now that glowering son of yours has grown up, is in love with France, bless him, and will come with you. These simple words as I write them seem to me to be filled with magic, a Proust in reverse, for we shall go in search of time to come. Can it be true?

I have not written for so long because there was too much to say. I have begun so many letters and torn them up, fearing the long journey would deprive them of truth, so you do not perhaps know that André died last year as a result of his years in concentration camp. At least we saw each other again and had almost a year of those simple joys, the only really incredible joys, eating with someone you love, sitting in a garden with someone you love, waking up with someone you love beside you. Now there is only emptiness around and in me. I am surrounded with people, but I am myself a desert. But you, dearest lives, you who bring both the past and the future with you, will make the desert flower once more. I am still Solange, but you I think have become *L'ange.* Do not break my heart by saying this is all a dream.

Reading the letter for the third time, Francis stopped here. Even as a boy he had been entranced by her, her quickness, her shouts of laughter. He had not wished to be pushed out of the room. But she had always had so much to say to his mother—

And now, he thought, she will have to say it all to me.

Had anything been done about notifying these people? On an impulse Francis swung off the bed and went out into the hall. Alan's door was closed. He could see the light under the crack. What, he wondered, was Alan doing? Did he dare interrupt? He knocked very gently.

"Oh come in, Francis. Sit down and have a drink," Alan got up to shift a batch of papers off the only other comfortable chair in the room, and flinging them down on the desk said rather shyly, "You see, I've been pretending to work."

Francis observed this face he had never been willing to see closely; he accepted a whiskey and soda. Alan's face had something of the impassivity of a Chinese god and Francis wondered if he had acquired this opaque and beneficent look or whether it had come naturally to him. He had very clear blue eyes, rather too pale, they seemed, in his bronzed rather fleshy face. He was, Francis had to admit, a handsome man, an attractive man, full of secret gentle powers.

"I was wondering," Francis said, "whether anything definite had been done about the friends and relatives in France—I mean, about telling them."

"I'm having notices printed, as a matter of fact. I hope that seems all right to you."

"Fine."

"If you'd like to go through your mother's address book and make a list, it would be a great help, as some of these people you must know. There may be others you can remember—"

"I'll be glad to."

Alan was somewhat taken aback by this amenable, this almost human Francis.

And he was afraid of showing how terribly glad he had been at that gentle knock on his door, afraid to show anything for fear it would be the wrong thing and the temporary truce come to an end. For Alan, the luncheon had been a great bruise. It had exhausted whatever reserve he had left after three sleepless nights and the complete containment of his grief. And he felt acutely the resilience of Francis, his youth which would, no doubt, absorb the death of his mother and go on, which already seemed well on the way back to life.

"I was awfully grateful for the way you swung things at the lunch, Francis. It was a help—" The eyes in the Buddha mask tried to smile kindly, but it was clearly an effort. Francis was again touched, as he had been so long ago, at breakfast.

"It was pretty awful, wasn't it?"

"I'm glad you've decided to go to France." Alan changed the subject, afraid of his violent resentment of his mother and not wishing to speak of that.

Francis frowned. "Yes, it's the thing," he said absentmindedly. "But of course all I said at lunch was a big bluff—I mean, I don't really know what I'm going for or what it will all turn out to mean. I'm a failure, of course," Francis confessed suddenly, so wrapped up in what he was saying that it did not occur to him that it was strange that he could be saying this to Alan of all people, Alan before whom for years he had maintained an attitude of complete self-sufficiency.

"No, you're not a failure yet. There's still time," Alan said a shade ironically, hitting by instinct on the right tone, Persis' tone that always challenged even while it understood.

"I get frightened," Francis said quietly. "I want to be so much more than I am."

"Yes,—" Alan nodded and was silent.

"There's something terribly wrong here, about us all, I mean. There's something dead in this little bun," Francis laughed, remembering the old joke about the Englishman and the fish cakes. "Aunt Alison, Aunt Sukey, John Thorndike, those Brewster cousins, even Ann—" Francis paused, thinking of Ann and that nightmarish walk, of her face so clear and straight even in its grief, and of something almost wooden at the same time, as if life didn't flow through her towards him but was stopped somewhere or got metamorphosed into usefulness, into humor, siphoned off just where it might have become creative, turned into love. For this reason he hated her to talk about her work.

"Well," Alan observed him curiously, "I can't see very much in common between the people you mention, I must confess—aren't you being a bit arbitrary?" Francis' ideas about Boston had always seemed to him irritating, perhaps even unintelligent.

But Francis was thinking aloud, frowning slightly as he talked and glad to be talking. "There's a short circuit somewhere between them and life, that's what I'm trying to get at. They're detached without any reason for being, out of habit, because it's more convenient—or something—I don't know. Take Aunt Alison, for instance, she's awfully good really, but there's so much she doesn't know. So in a way her goodness doesn't count, is no help. I want to know all the things Aunt Alison doesn't know," and then, breaking off suddenly in the middle he added, "Of course Saul thinks Boston is heaven—but I guess that was because of Mother—this house—"

"Yes," Alan shied away by subsiding into silence. He did

not feel able yet to talk about Persis. With an effort he pulled himself back to the moment and what still had to be done, "About the house, Francis. You're not thinking of getting married, are you?"

"No," Francis said, closing up like a clam.

"I shan't stay here forever, I think. That means that the house will be available. I have an idea that Sukey has her eye on it. As you know, it is jointly owned. If you married, it would, I think, be considered yours if you wished to go on with the arrangement your mother made with her sisters."

"I see." Francis was disturbed by the implications of this major shift in the pattern of life as he had known it.

"I'm not ready to make any such decisions," he said quietly. It was just another piece of the unreadiness for everything that he knew in himself only too well.

"Well, there's time. Maybe when you come back from France—"

"You'd better come to Paris too," Francis said suddenly. "It will be hell here." Ever since his mother's death he had realized that he was in some way responsible for Alan now. He did not want the responsibility, but it kept looming up.

"Oh, you won't want any shades of Boston to haunt you over there. You'll want the pure European experience unadulterated by family."

"You're being awfully good to me, Alan, I wonder why," Francis said with a grin.

"Nonsense, it's rather a relief to find you're human after all." Having said so much, Alan shifted in his chair and then leaned forward clasping his hands and running his fingers over the knuckles nervously. It had been on his mind to speak of the will and he realized that this was as good a time as any. Francis might never again be so tractable. "Francis," he said rather gravely after a moment, "I have to tell you something. It's about your mother's will."

"Oh," Francis unconsciously stiffened in his chair. He did not know it, but this was an inherited characteristic, this inability to talk easily and rationally about money. The Chabriers all had it. Now he bristled quietly. "What about it?"

"Your allowance, three thousand a year, goes on but your mother's fortune, the main part of it, is left to me, with the understanding of course that eventually it comes to you. When you marry you will have six thousand." Alan was suffering. He had been disturbed by the will; he did not want the responsibility and he knew it would cause talk in the family. Only his mother would be pleased. For Francis it would inevitably be a blow. Alan looked across at him now and thought that for once Francis looked stupid. His mouth was slightly open and he was staring into space almost as if he had not taken in what had just been said. Then he laughed a short sarcastic laugh,

"In other words I had better marry—if possible a rich woman." As a matter of fact Francis had not thought about money until this moment. It had not occurred to him that he might have expected to be today a very rich young man. But none of that mattered, what hurt was that his mother had, it seemed, not trusted him. She did then think I was a failure, irresponsible in some way, hardly a man. Francis buried his face in his hands. He was choking with revolt.

Alan was silent. He had not expected Francis to take this well, but he was sorry that he was taking it badly. Around him he felt intensely the emptiness of the house. And he got up and padded softly over to the table where the drinks were, pouring out two stiff ones.

"This was not my wish, Francis, of course," he said gently.

"Of course not," Francis snapped back. "It was Mother's idea. She didn't trust me." His eyes were blazing with anger.

Go slow, Alan said to himself. Anything which touched Persis, the shadow of a doubt about her affected him like a whiplash and he must be very careful not to get angry. It would be quite fatal. Nothing of this showed except that his hand shook slightly as he took a swallow of his drink. He did not answer.

Francis was left with his harsh words to swallow or leave there between them. He got up and walked to the window. "I don't give a damn about money," he said with his back to Alan, "I'm glad it's yours. It's Adams money and Brewster money and I hate the whole tribe."

"Well," Alan said gently, "that's a good way to look at it."

"It's Mother. Why didn't she trust me? Why did she do it?" The third question which was "Did she tell you?" Francis couldn't bring himself to ask. A few moments before he had felt responsible for Alan, deeply sorry for Alan. Now, he saw, the whole thing was reversed. Alan would be responsible for him, would see that he got a fat check at Christmas and on his birthday, would find ways to "make it all right." Whatever else Mother has done, she has found a fine way to keep Alan and me apart, he thought, so bitter now against his mother that he would think anything, and gladly.

"I don't know," Alan said miserably, "she never discussed it with me."

He could feel the slight lessening of the tension, the relief of this.

"Perhaps she didn't believe money was the best means to happiness," Alan went on.

"Well, she certainly didn't believe in happiness," Francis said shortly.

"Only perhaps as a by-product." But Alan knew he would have to come out with it, say what he really thought and that anything else was pure cowardice. "Whatever she did, I don't need to suggest to you, Francis, was reasoned."

"Yes, that's just it," the harsh young voice rapped out.

"She may have reasoned that money would not be the best means to your ends, that it would not be a help but actually a hindrance. You talk now and then about becoming a person. This idea obsesses you—you always come back to it. You talk as if this becoming a person were some isolated process which you can do all alone, without ever coming to a final decision about anything—"

"I know," Francis said softly and flung himself down in the chair again.

"Without taking on any responsibility. In this case money might not be the most fruitful kind of responsibility. Don't you see?"

"It has certainly kept most of our friends from becoming human, if that's what you mean."

"Yes, in a way, I think it has. Security is perhaps only necessary to children. It's possible that she thought you were grown-up enough to do without it, at least on a grand scale."

"A small-scale security for a small-scale person," Francis said but though the words were biting the tone was not. He looked across at Alan almost humbly, a little ironically, "You're trying awfully hard aren't you, Alan?"

But Alan had waited a long time to say what he had in mind, had waited through all the years of his marriage, and now he was not going to be put off. "It's about time, Francis, that you learned to serve something, not just master everything. There is a difference, you know."

"No doubt," Francis said icily. "I never did understand about you and my mother. Now I understand less than I did before," he said very quietly, but Alan could see the angry points of light in his eyes and reminded himself to stay calm.

Francis had always had to hurl words around as other people hurl china in their rages. It was not a very pleasant characteristic and it certainly did not come from his mother who had a great respect for words and used them charily.

"You are a good deal younger than I am, Francis, you know—" Alan said mildly. "There is no particular reason why you should understand everything yet."

"But I want to understand, damn it! Unless I understand my mother, how can I get away from her, go on living, do anything?" he shouted. Alan hoped that Mary on the fourth floor could not hear.

"I'm sorry, Francis, but I can't talk about her," Alan said, "so I'm afraid I can't help you."

"No," Francis subsided again into his misery, "I don't expect you can. Nobody can. You're so afraid of saying anything, all of you, life here is embalmed, some secret process no one is supposed to mention. I shall never know why my mother married you, never," he said half afraid of his own impetus which had carried him a little farther now than he intended.

"Your mother married me because I loved her not because she loved me. Is that what you wanted to know?"

It had been said in a perfectly clear cool voice. Francis groaned, "God, I'm a rat. Forgive me, Alan. If you can."

The shame of the elation he felt now welled up in Francis and covered his face. How can I be myself and behave so badly? What is it in me, this poison? Whatever I touch withers.

But Alan was not angry. He was full of pity for children and parents and this most binding and difficult of all relations. Persis had tried desperately to leave her son free and yet he was bound hand and foot. His own mother had done everything in her power to bind him hand and foot and only ended by making him hate her.

"You're not a rat, Francis. I'm sorry you've had such hell. But you did from the beginning make it impossible for me to talk with you— I might have been able to help years ago, at the very beginning."

"No, I just raged for years. No one could have helped. Mother didn't even try—she knew it was pure poison and had to be lived through, I guess. I stayed away as much as I could. We've all had too much Freud," he said suddenly, "poisoned by that too. No one can be natural anymore. We're all so busy analyzing ourselves and each other, looking for the fatal flaw. Who lives his own life now? We watch ourselves living out the old myths and hate ourselves and know we're in a trap."

What can heal this bitterness, Alan thought? Or rather, who can heal it? Not Ann evidently, not patience, honesty, perfect good will such as hers. What then?

"Mother didn't hurt other people," Francis got up and walked up and down, his hands in his pockets, as always talking his way out with an ease that astonished Alan, this flow of words, this expressiveness which seemed strange in one so intense and so confused. "I watched how she made them feel more themselves, Saul for instance, and that boy—what's his name?—she used to play with. She knew just how to do it." He stopped walking and stood at a little distance from Alan looking at him intently, but without seeing him, it seemed. "I was always outside that magic circle."

"You didn't want to be in it, Francis, really did you?" Alan asked gently. The immense tiredness he had felt after the funeral was there again like an illness. He had waited years for this hour when he and Francis could talk at last, but now he was too tired. His emotional muscles had gone slack. He felt dreadfully old again and wished to go to bed, wished to go back to the room where he and Persis had slept and to go to sleep at last by her empty bed. Her face now came between him and Francis' like a mirage. In a moment, he thought, I shall be able to remember it all, every moment we ever had together, every word she ever said, as a dying man is said to remember. This was all he wanted.

"I don't know," Francis bowed his head. "I don't know."

"It may be, Francis, that now you will find peace about all this, now that war is really over."

"Yes," he flung himself down in the chair and leaned his head back looking up at the ceiling. "It may be that the death of one's mother is the great release, the only way one is born again."

His eyes felt like wounds and the tears that poured down his cheeks, might have been blood from those blinded eyes.

"It's all right, Francis," Alan got up and laid one hand very gently on his shoulder, "it's all right."

CHAPTER NINE

OUTSIDE IT WAS SNOWING hard, thick soft flakes that blew small drifts into the corners of doorways and already had changed the public gardens into a fairyland. Saul had been walking for over an hour and finding himself on Commonwealth Avenue, tired and longing for someone to talk to, he decided on an impulse to ring Ann's bell. Once inside the door, feeling the warmth, blinking in the light, he felt disheveled and awfully wet. His feet were soaked through. The maid, having telephoned to Ann's flat, told him to go up two flights. Now that he was here, he wondered why he had come. He hardly knew Ann. He had seen her once or twice at parties, at Mrs. Bradford's more often, but never alone. Would she think it very strange?

"I'm a wreck," she said at once, "but come in, if you can bear it." Her face was blotched with tears.

"I—I shouldn't have come. I've been walking around for hours and—well—"

"Of course you should have come. Oh Saul, it's dear of you to have come. I've been feeling so lonely I could die."

He looked around the very large room, finding it difficult to feel at ease here. Ann had brought her college furniture back and it looked incongruous—the sad little daybed, the low bookshelves, a Van Gogh reproduction on the wall—and over it all the immensely high walls, the intricate moulding on the ceiling and the over-ornate chandelier. It looked as if Ann were camping out in the room, didn't really live here. In one corner there were piles of Christmas wrappings and boxes. The desk was a muddle of papers, some of which had fallen to the floor.

"We'll have some tea," she said, her voice high and bright, "that'll do us good."

He was rather glad to be left alone while she puttered about in the kitchen which no doubt divided this from a bedroom at the back. Saul sat down in the only comfortable armchair and waited passively. It hardly seemed possible that this was still the same day. The exaltation of the funeral followed by the curiously trivial lunch at the Bradfords', Francis and his elation. It all was to Saul quite unreal. Only during his walk alone in the snow, he had felt real again and had been able to realize the full extent of his own loss. The fact was that the world seemed an entirely different place now. The substance of life had altered. Even his relation to Francis had altered in the last hours. He almost resented that self-control, the ease with which Francis had seemed to carry things off. He felt very far from Francis now, cut off. So, in a way, the sight of Ann's honestly grieving face was the first comforting thing he had seen. He simply couldn't understand the atmosphere of the lunch. It seemed to him shocking and for the first time he felt critical of Boston and Boston manners. The whole thing had been unnatural, all except Aunt Alison, he thought, unnatural and cruel. He thought of the way Persis Bradford had talked when his own mother died, the way she took grief for granted, her own and his, and felt with him to the limit. Death, he thought, should bring people together—it's the only way to go on living.

"There," Ann said pouring his tea rather awkwardly, "I hope it isn't too strong."

"It's wonderful." The very smell was restoring, though Saul had not been brought up in a tea-drinking world. He took his time, sipping it slowly and once looked up shyly to smile at Ann.

"It's awful to cry so much. It doesn't do any good," she said apologizing again, for it was really appalling she thought to be seen like this. "And I feel like an old woman."

"When my mother died everybody wailed and wept like anything," Saul said, "and at the time I thought it was awful, but after that cold smiling lunch at the Bradfords' I've decided it's better to wail."

"How is Francis?" she asked quickly. All day she had wanted to run to Francis, bury her head in his shoulder and tell him that she loved him. But he might have been in another country for all the good that did.

"Francis was in a way wonderful. He was almost gay at the lunch and talked about going to Paris. I don't understand him," Saul said almost angrily. "The family, I think, thought he behaved splendidly. He didn't seem like an outsider at all—you know, how he always talks about them. The only person there who showed that he cared was Alan."

"Yes," she said thoughtfully, "I know. One can't bear to think of Alan."

"He seemed to be in a dream, very polite and not quite there."

"Saul?" she asked, looking absent-mindedly out of the window into the dark. Here on the third floor she never pulled her curtains.

"Yes?" The question came obviously from another room, another dimension.

"Do you think Francis has any heart?"

The question made Saul uncomfortable. It was, perhaps, too direct, like Ann, and he was not ready for it, quite. He didn't answer.

"I think something happened to him when his mother married again, something awful. I don't think he will ever get over it. It's very bad when the worst thing that can happen to you happens so young—you may get cut off, permanently cut off. He's always talking, you know, about becoming himself. But it's not that—" she interrupted to turn back to Saul, "Do you mind if I talk a little? I've bottled all this up inside myself for years?"

"Of course not. Francis is my friend. I love him," he almost added "too" and stopped in time.

"Well, I think he lost himself, the real self when that happened. He felt rejected. Ever since then he has been at war with his mother— I always felt he was trying to conquer her, to make her admit something about him, about herself. Sometimes I wished I weren't there when they were talking."

"Yes, I know what you mean," Saul considered. He remembered once at least a sort of jeer in Francis' tone, and Mrs. Bradford's sharp quick answer. He had forgotten even what they were discussing but he remembered the tone, as if the words had had no importance, were only a means of communicating tension.

"There doesn't seem to be any balance in him—between too much love and too little, but maybe we are all like that," she ended, feeling she had talked too much already, "maybe that's the way life is, only none of us can admit it so we go on bungling."

"But," Saul said quietly, "Mrs. Bradford didn't love too much."

"I wonder—"

"You think she did?" Saul sat up, amazed. He had until now taken it for granted that Mrs. Bradford was beyond criticism. He didn't count the petty remarks of old Mrs. Bradford, of course. But among people who appreciated her, who loved her, perfection had seemed the premise.

"I think she was afraid. I think she fought Francis off because she was afraid of doing him harm—and I wonder if she was right."

"I don't understand, quite."

"Well, she was everything to him except a mother—she was a marvelous teacher, a provocative stimulating friend, everything but—a mother."

"Yes, I see what you mean. So in a way, she could help everyone except Francis. For instance," he confessed, warming to this chance to speak at last, "I date practically everything from two years ago when Francis first took me there. She changed my life, Ann—somehow everything seemed clear at last. I knew what I was doing."

"I know."

"And for Francis it was maybe just the opposite. She expected so much of him; she dug so deep into him—for him, I suppose maybe all this is a good thing."

"I think so," Ann said quietly. "I think that's why he was elated at the lunch—he's relieved. He must be terribly relieved to have it over."

(But a half mile away Francis lay now on his bed, weeping like a child, a small child who has lost his mother, weeping for all the love he had needed and never had, weeping though he didn't know it for her failure as well as his, weeping for the lack of love, the terrible lack of love, the tears of deprivation. And at last weeping the tears of relief; though he did not recognize them as such.)

Saul, disturbed by this new insight into Mrs. Bradford, looked at Ann with respect, a little shyly. Here is a person, he thought (and how unconscious she was of her effect upon him, of the shift in his attention), who is so honest that she must often seem insincere. Francis of course would be put off by this kind of honesty, would be frightened of it. He supposed that it was her training in psychology that made it possible for her to be so objective, an objectivity in amusing contrast to her face, disarmingly young, after all the tears. Saul would have liked to put an arm round her now, but he was much too shy. Instead he went on talking on another level,

"It's possible, I suppose, that now Alan and Francis will get to know each other at last."

"It's possible," Ann agreed, "but I think Francis is hardly here now, for any of us. He's in Paris—he's just taken a leap over everything here. We don't exist." The full bleakness of this statement and what it held for her, Saul felt intensely, but he knew it was true. He did not therefore tell her that he would be going to Paris with Francis. It seemed kinder not to mention that, just now.

"I wonder what makes him so endearing," Saul asked himself as well as her, thinking of the way Francis had run down the stairs to meet him and their incongruous laughter in the hall.

"He's selfish, violent, irresponsible, everything irritating and destructive, but he has some fierce power inside him—as if he were overcharged," she said quickly. "I often feel sorry for Francis."

"I never do. I envy him," Saul said simply and then added with a smile, "He's such an actor really."

They laughed with the pleasure of recognition. "Yes," Ann said almost happily, "and at the same time he's so disconcertingly honest, savagely honest. How can one deal with such a person?"

"He isn't to be dealt with," Saul said gravely, "that's just the trouble. He refuses to yield an inch of himself."

"He's scared. Who isn't?"

"I guess you have to be pretty sure of yourself not to be scared."

"How do people grow up?" Ann asked bitterly. "It seems to take such a hell of a long time."

Talking together in this way, feeling the sudden intimacy and rejoicing in it, they had succeeded in all the desolation in creating a small temporary island of peace and of safety.

"Gosh, you were good to come, Saul," Ann said after a short silence. "I guess I was pretty nearly in despair."

CHAPTER TEN

AT ELEVEN O'CLOCK it was still snowing and the city was hooded in silence. Saul and Ann had long since parted; even Francis was asleep, exhausted by the day. The roar of a snow plough charging down Charles Street made Alan lift his head from the cards he was checking over and pause for the first time in two hours. He was preparing the final synthesis of the chapter on the Sung Dynasty. But the sound interrupted his concentration and now he remembered. It was like coming back to a strange room, which is now no longer strange because one has unpacked in it, gone out and come back to find oneself there. So it was, he discovered, with grief. The room was familiar, almost homely and so he felt released from the almost overpowering tension of the last days, and able to recognize and feel. How often in the last years he had lifted his head like this, hardly knowing where he was, and rediscovered his love for Persis, always there like a charm, stretched his cramped legs and arms, and softly gone down the stairs to find her reading in bed. Sometimes then he went down to the kitchen to bring up glasses of milk and sandwiches Mary left ready.

And this late and somehow secret meal had been the best time of the day, the really intimate time when he and Persis talked quietly and enjoyed each other. Always then the night seemed to him to open like a flower, to give back the lost sense of time which all the affairs of the day interrupted. As long as the lights were on, it held a great sweetness. He loved to see Persis like this, a soft white cashmere shawl flung across one shoulder and her face without make-up touching in the extreme simplicity of its lines, an ageing, a wise face full of the purity of youth, and her eyes so deep and clear. How much they had laughed together! How much they had had to say to each other, always! Often it was one o'clock before he put the glasses back on the tray and turned out the light.

What followed was his affair, not hers. In the dark on many nights he had lain awake till dawn, when he could see the outline of her head on the pillow, the perfect tranquillity of her breathing, her infinite remoteness. And worse, on the nights when, having clasped her in his arms, he knew that she was not there, had never been there for him.

With an effort, Alan got up. It was time now, before his thoughts carried him any deeper into that misery and that fire, to go down to the room where he had not been for four days and nights. Very softly he went down the stairs, down through the intensely still house, surrounded by the intensely still night. I might be a ghost, he thought, half-amused, or a burglar for that matter. He opened the shut door and walked over to the windows without looking back. There he stood for some minutes, watching the halo of light around the street lamp and the thick-falling snow, and one light high up in the house opposite. Then he drew the curtains and felt his way to the table between the beds. The light sprang into the room, dissipating all gentleness in an instant, making every object fearfully distinct. Persis' white shawl lay across the foot of the bed. His pajamas and slippers were laid out and his own bed turned down. From where he sat, he looked at the back of the silver frame which held Chabrier's face.

At least it would not haunt him again. He took it in his hands and looked at it one last time, startled by the resemblance to Francis as he had looked at the other end of the dining room table, smiling across at Alan. It was the face of a man both full of clarity and full of tension, with a deep line almost like a wound between the two eyebrows and it looked out with piercing intensity as if to say, "I'm alive, not dead, believe me." Or as if to say, "Even if I never finished my work, my life, I am here, not to be forgotten." Tomorrow, Alan thought, I shall give this to Francis.

Then he got up and undressed, laying his clothes on the usual chair, his watch on the night-table. He noticed that there was phenobarbital by the bed and remembered saying so to Sukey long ago. It would be wise, no doubt, to take one. Instead he lay with the light on, his arms under his head, wide awake, as if he were waiting for someone and would not sleep before she came—came in from a party, perhaps, a party where he had refused to go preferring to work, came in all shining with the evening air, tossing her little fur cape on the bed, coming to kiss him and tease him and tell him all about it, to ask how his evening's work had gone, to be charmingly malicious about the people she had just left, or more often to tell him, "I am worried about so and so, Alan. He's working too hard," or "Nancy is drinking too much. There must be something wrong.

I must ask her to lunch one day soon and see if there's anything we can do." Or, with a delighted mischievous smile, "That old Mr. Bowers is a shocking flirt. You should have been there, darling, to protect me from his not very subtle advances." Or "Alan, what do you think about treason? How does the Pound prize compare with the stupid business about Gieseking? Are we right to absolve art from political responsibility? We talked about it for hours. I think we Americans are more savage, being less involved. The French are crowding the theatres to see De Montherlant's plays—is that lack of moral values, or magnanimity or just curiosity?"

He was alone, but she was there, would always be there, he knew now. The dead do not die and one's feeling for them never changes. Only the living change and die in oneself. So he began to understand about Chabrier and Chabrier's power. Now in the last few days, by dying, Persis had separated him forever from his mother. Such is the power of the dead, who act as pure entities beyond will or good and evil, for Persis had done all she could do to keep Alan's feeling for his mother intact, admiring her vitality, praising her love for him, careful that Mrs. Bradford should often be included in their dinners or informal parties, always charming to her. But in dying she could not conceal the truth as she had when she was alive, putting a screen of words between him and it.

And it was strange to come to admit as he did now, that he had in the deepest sense, not lost Persis, but had lost his mother. There is nothing better as a preservative he thought than a completely selfish life. Had his mother ever for a moment entertained the idea of guilt, blamed herself, even questioned her own motives? Her delightfully smooth pink and white face had never, it seemed, been furrowed and ploughed up by life. But Alan deliberately turned away from these thoughts, bitter thoughts. There was no point in bringing his mother into this room. With an impatient gesture, he turned off the light, but not before he had said to himself, "Whatever happens I am not going to live with her."

At first he had wanted to run away, leave this house, leave Persis' clothes hanging in the cupboards, her books in the bookshelves, leave them all and never look back, become a wanderer on the earth if necessary, but never come back here, above all never again sleep in this empty room. But that was four days ago and in four days, he had grown old and very tired and in four days he had realized that he would always find Persis here, here and nowhere else. Instead of wishing to leave, he now felt that nothing on earth would ever make him leave, unless he should be forced to, unless Francis married.

For how many nights had he lain like this in the dark, wide awake, in the last ten years? Outside the snow fell, the silence fell and here in his bed Alan realised that the only wall which had remained to keep Persis and him apart was gone forever—that insurmountable wall of his passion for her. Now that she was dead, he possessed her at last, because he was free. Peace and love flowed in and soon Alan slept.

PART TWO

"Fill'd with her love, may I be rather grown
Mad with much heart, than ideott with
none."

JOHN DONNE

CHAPTER ONE

FRANCIS STOOD on the bridge, looking down at the olive-colored Seine, then lifted his head as if to remind himself of what he couldn't yet believe—this space all around him, these great perspectives, the soft gold of the Invalides Dome against the veiled blue sky, the immense square of the Concorde, and then turning back, his eye drawn down the green aisle of plane trees to the ancient island where the square towers of Notre Dame rose and stated the Eternal theme. It was as if for years he hadn't known how to breathe and now he could breathe. He was not a tourist but a man come home from long exile, recognizing the powers in and all around him not as magical or strange, but his own.

Now it was all blue and white and gold and green, all soft and shining, gently horizontal after the perpendicular American cities. The evening before, at his arrival, it had been veiled in a hyacinthine light, damp that never became rain, but stayed suspended over lavender streets, and he had had the sensation of dreaming, of walking in sleep through what was remembered and strange, familiar and fresh. He had sat for a long time in a bistro across the river from Notre Dame, drinking brandy, trying to sort out all the sensations. From there he had phoned Madame Bernard; now he was on his way to see her.

It was four o'clock in the afternoon on the tenth of June. His examinations were passed. He was through with all that, through with studying, through with the long suspense since December when everything focussed to a distant point, to the day and the hour when he would stand in this place, alone and free. But cities, like hearts, are haunted by human faces. The distant point within Paris was a single person, and that person was Solange Bernard. For the last months he had lived on her letters. He felt now that he knew her well, but his image of her was still a child's image, and so he was afraid. He had been walking for an hour, unable to stay in his room, unable to concentrate, and yet held in a suspense so vivid that he thought he would never forget a single face he had met on his walk, nor a single shadow of a single tree, nor the wind blowing the spray from the fountains in the Concorde, nor the massed clouds, the play of the sky for which the whole city seemed at times only a stage-set designed by genius.

All his anxieties and troubles of the last months had been washed away one by one on the long dull sea-days when he had walked round the deck with Saul, hardly speaking. There on the boat he had been haunted by Ann's face when they had said good-bye; had imagined he was tearing up her roots with his in a single ruthless gesture by leaving her now. He had worried about Alan. He had worried about himself and what he was really coming for, had tried to prepare for disappointment like a man who has just bet his whole fortune on a horse and is sure suddenly that it won't win.

But Saul had almost persuaded him that all these doubts and fears were just the reaction to the strain of exams and of leaving. And it did seem that at some place in the middle of the Atlantic his mind turned from facing toward Boston and faced the other way. It was not a deliberate act, but an unconscious change brought on by the empty days, sleep, boredom and the steady throb of the motors that carried him to France. Now Saul had gone on to London for three weeks and would come to Paris later. They planned to find a flat and, if they could afford it, to hire a car, but all of this Francis felt to be unreal, as nothing was real except Solange Bernard in whose single person he was seeking his father and his mother, his childhood and himself.

Was this too great a burden to lay on one human being? Can one expect so much, demand so much and receive more than a crumb? Francis, looking down again at the water, so quiet it hardly seemed possible that it flowed, had an impulse not to go, to put it off another day, not to risk everything yet. For, he thought, whatever she may be, whatever happens, I am not prepared.

And then he turned away from the questions and the great open perspectives and made his way into the familiar narrow streets where human dwellings rather than sky must provide the answers. Number eighteen Rue de l'Université was a vast door opening into a courtyard. The concierge directed him to the stairs at the opposite side and he glanced up once nervously at the windows on the second floor. Was he being watched? Was he early? Late? He was filled with embarrassment, wondered suddenly if he would be able to speak French, wondered in perhaps the first moment of real humility in his life whether she would be disappointed: she would be looking for a person worthy of his father and his mother. But by then he was at the door.

The bell tinkled very far off but he could hear no sound inside. When the door finally opened he was met by a fat Breughelesque servant who beamed and told him he was expected. At the end of the long dark hall he heard laughter, first a man's deep loud laugh and then a lighter one, harsh and light. As if he were breaking open a world, Francis opened the door.

At first he hardly saw her, confused by a roar of welcome from the old man who embraced him on both cheeks and shouted, "Francis! Well, here he is, the prodigal child—let me look at you!" and held him fast in two surprisingly strong hands and stared at him with laughing black eyes, his mouth open like an ogre's, then turned to the woman lying on a chaise longue by the windows to say with unexpected gentleness, "Pierre's eyes."

"My poor dear, you will think us quite mad. Come here and kiss me and let me introduce you properly to Jean-Marie Fontanes, your father's dear friend and mine."

Francis found himself kissing a cheek he had not yet looked at, aware of a smell of perfume, of a small brown hand cuffed in lace, clasping his warmly, and then of the room itself, rather dark, old-fashioned, he thought—formal, too. He found himself sitting between them, commented upon, admired, teased ("He's terribly serious, Solange") until he had only one desire, to escape. He had never imagined that there might be a third at this meeting, especially such an overwhelming third as this old man. He must be someone important, Francis thought, trying to remember what his mother must have said about a person called Fontanes.

"But you haven't even looked at me!" The voice from the chaise longue accused him.

"You see," Fontanes confided ironically, "she is used to being looked at. She expects to be looked at, in fact she demands to be looked at, which is not a very subtle way of getting peoples' attention, you know, Solange." In the glance they exchanged of perfect intimacy, Francis had the opportunity at last to lift his eyes.

The first thing he thought, with the cruelty of youth, was: she's older than I imagined. The second thing was: she's not beautiful at all. And the third was: what an extraordinary face. Her eyes looked brilliant blue for she had on a soft blue dress; her nose, a sharp and delicate beak, a little too definite for beauty; and her mouth, mischievous, subtle, changing every instant and showing very white almost wolfish teeth. All this sharpness, brilliance was casqued in quite gray hair. Francis thought, she's like a gray fox, a little gray fox who's always managed to escape the hunters and even laughed at them. He was charmed, but not in a way he had foreseen. Here was no statue of poised beauty, no quiet shrine where he might find understanding and compassion. Here was a living human being, almost painfully alive.

His glance, these thoughts, took a few seconds, but evidently something in his expression changed, for Solange pounced on him (this suddenness, this daring frankness he suddenly remembered), "Yes, you are young for your age and I am old for mine, little Francis. But we must try to fling a bridge across all the years, just the same, eh?"

Ever since he had come into this room he had felt attacked, prodded and now he lifted his head and looked at her full in the face with irritation. "In America we are taught not to make personal remarks and I am, after all, half American—you just bewilder me, both of you," he said, smiling now because they looked so contrite, so surprised.

"Solange, we are unmerciful," Fontanes said gravely and turned to Francis with a complete change of tone. "Now, Francis, let's be serious. Boston must be a very serious place. What is it like to come home after all these years?"

"It's home," Francis answered, "that's all." He could hardly tell these two strangers more than that. He was not going to pour himself out at their feet as they seemed to expect.

But after tea was brought in and delicious little cakes, he found himself after all talking a great deal, describing the ferocious old maid who ran his pension, telling them about Saul, and finally about his own vague ideas about his future. Whatever his first glance at Solange had intimated, like a premonition, was now dissolved and forgotten as he relaxed; by the time Fontanes rose to go, she had become, or so it seemed, an old friend. Almost he felt at ease here.

"Now I've found you," Fontanes stood with one hand on Francis' shoulder and looked him fiercely in the eye, "I am going to hang onto you. You had better come and have dinner with me tomorrow night. Next week I'm beginning a new play and shan't have much time. All right? That's decided?" Then he took Francis' chin in his hand as if he had been a small boy and said, "It's good that you've come. We need you here, little one."

"What an extraordinary man!" Francis turned to Solange as the door shut behind the elephantine figure. "Who is he?"

But even as he asked the obvious question and listened to Solange's answer, the transition was as complete as when an aeroplane bumps along the earth on landing. At last they were alone.

"Where to begin? Fontanes was your father's best friend. They were fellow officers in the '14 war, Fontanes in some sort of ground job and your father of course as an aviator. But you must know Fontanes!" she interrupted herself to exclaim, while Francis wandered about the room, picked up a silver snuffbox on a little table, opened it, shut it, put it back absently, then stopped by the desk to look at a row of photographs, his back to Solange. "The theatre director—you must have heard his name! He is one of the pioneers of theatre in France . . ." Was he listening? Apparently not, for Francis, taking a silver frame in his hands, sat down and said,

"My mother. My mother as she was when you used to come to see us in the Rue de Vaugirard. She was beautiful, wasn't she?"

"Beautiful, I don't know. She was herself, something more than beauty—don't you think beauty is rather overrated, in people, I mean?"

"I don't know much about it."

The tone was so bitter that Solange smiled, "My dear, you sound like a man disappointed in love."

"I've never been in love," Francis answered.

"Ah?" She caught his eye, looked at him half seriously, half mockingly, "You *are* a child."

"Yes," said Francis as if he were confessing to a murder, had crossed half the world to confess to this woman that he was a murderer, "I am."

"Have some more tea," she suggested irrelevantly.

"You see," Francis said frowning, with the effort, "I was always at war with my mother. I didn't know it until she died but now I see it. And it was a very absorbing war. There was hardly room for anything else. Now I only want peace."

"Why were you at war with her?" Solange asked gently.

"Because—because I suppose I wanted her to admit—to admit . . ."

"That she loved you, yes." Solange nodded her head as if she were thinking aloud. "I can see that very well. And she was afraid. What miserable creatures we are, even the best of us. What mistakes we make. How we hurt each other . . ." She lifted her face and looked out of the window as if she were saying a private prayer.

"Always when you came it meant that I was sent upstairs, sent away, and even all those Jules Verne books and chocolates hardly made up for that," he said wanting to bring her back from her thoughts toward him. "No, no more tea, thank you. I was frightfully jealous. Now when Fontanes left, it seemed strange that I could feel this relief to be with you, you who always until now have been—well, what?—I suppose, a threat." He laughed. "Well, now here we are."

"Yes, here we are. It is strange, Francis, you know. I shall have to get used to you little by little."

"Yes," he frowned, "of course you were expecting my mother." Very deliberately he got up and set the silver frame back on the desk.

"I was expecting you. I've been expecting you all these months," she protested.

"And now I'm not here?" he asked with an acute sense of his lack of everything she might admire.

"I had not expected someone so alarming," she hunted for each word, "savage—afraid. Why are you so afraid, Francis? It isn't like your letters."

"Oh, letters," he said brusquely, "you're not like your letters either."

"There, you see, that's what I mean. Of course you are disappointed, but why say it so brutally, in such a tone of voice?" she asked softly and almost impersonally. "It's rather rude."

"But you're alarming, too," Francis said almost angrily, "I—I'm not used to being talked to like this or talking like this to people I hardly know. It's disconcerting." He got up and walked up and down restlessly. He felt like picking up the little silver box and flinging it down on the floor.

"Come here," she commanded, "we are both being very foolish. Come and sit down on the end of my chair—there" —she pulled him down— "Now that's better. I've been clumsy. I felt I knew you so well we could just plunge in and be old friends. It was stupid of me." But having granted so much, she attacked again, "But of course you can't have peace, not yet. You've got to live, Francis. Good Heavens, how old are you to be talking of peace?"

"Twenty-six."

"Twenty-six," she murmured, but whatever she thought she kept to herself this time. "Now," she said firmly, "first of all we must plan about theatres and things. It's too late for the best, but there are one or two things, Claudel's *Partage du Midi,* for instance. That you and I must see."

"Lesson number one?" he asked ironically.

"If you like, yes."

Francis had come to learn but he resented a little being put at once in the position of a pupil. Standing on the bridge on his way here he had been rather pleased with himself and the world. Now he felt like a cat whose fur has been rubbed the wrong way, ruffled and on edge. He got up rather clumsily and said he must be going. Now he wanted to escape, to get off by himself, to find his own Paris, to get away from those slightly mocking eyes that looked at him quizzically, critically.

"I've frightened you away, wild creature that you are. How like your father. He was such a sudden man and people often thought him rude. But he was also a dedicated man, he was always running away to work, so one forgave him."

Later Francis would remember those words, but now he remembered his father. "He used to take me for walks in the Luxembourg Gardens. And then when we got there he would forget all about me, and begin to walk much too fast, not saying a word sometimes for half an hour. And then he would stop suddenly and make me look at a tree as if I had never seen one before. He would pick a leaf and show me how it was formed, make me feel the trunk with my hands. I loved him, but sometimes I got tired of always being taught something. I wanted to talk to him about *my* things. He wasn't very human, was he?" Francis asked, standing at the end of the chaise longue, looking down at Solange.

"I think your mother made him human, and that was why he loved her. Tell me, Francis, before you go," she said, taking his hand absent-mindedly and looking at it, "what is he like, this Alan Bradford?"

It was a question he had expected but it was a hard question to answer; his hand stiffened in hers so that he found he was clasping it. Startled, he withdrew, sat down again with the strange sensation that his hand had gone numb or been left behind in her small dry warm one, as if without meaning to, he had given a part of his physical self away. He was so disturbed that he didn't answer for a moment and Solange went on, "Your mother wrote me when she married, wrote of his kindness and the great work he's doing—a history of China, isn't it? But he never seemed quite real to me."

"I think Alan is a very good person," Francis said then.

"Good? What does that mean exactly?"

"Well, maybe that's not the word," Francis lit a cigarette, forgetting to offer her one and leaned forward intently. "Maybe I mean, pure. And it's curious because Alan has lived all over the world, in China, the Near East, knows Europe well—but there is something in him that has remained absolutely itself, untouched—how can I say it? You see, when he married my mother I think it was the first time he had ever really loved anyone."

"A man of fifty?"

"That shocks you, does it?" Francis looked up and smiled.

"No, it seems strange—"

"Yes, I suppose it does."

"And you and he get on well, then? In some way you are alike . . ."

"Heavens, no! You see Alan is enormously gentle and understanding," he said unconscious of the humor, or the self-criticism implied, "I never knew him really. I just ignored him until Mother's death. Since then we've become friends. I'm trying to persuade him to come over this summer. He needs to be distracted, to get away from his devil of a mother."

Solange laughed, "Americans always have mothers, don't they?"

"It seems to be a biological necessity," Francis answered, laughing outright, a loud boyish laugh. "Oh, you don't know how good it is to be here, to be able to talk like this. I feel as if I'd been in a strait jacket for years. It will take me awhile to get used to this, to move about freely. Solange," he said turning to her with simple conviction, "you don't know, you can't know what it is to live among people who have no juice. And they're all so terribly *good,*" he ended, "all except me. I have become a monster really. I'm only half-human. You've observed that, no doubt?" he challenged her.

"Perhaps," but she refused to make a judgment, "you are a lot of things and people all at once and not one person yet—that's my guess. But don't believe a word I say, Francis, except"—she looked down, for the first time shy—"that it's lovely to have you here, lovely that you've come. Since André died I've been a desert. But for Fontanes I should have died." Remote, withdrawn she seemed now as the moon, and at this moment of her drawing near to him with words, Francis felt that he could never reach her, that it was not for him to make this mysterious desert flower, though he wished devoutly that he could. He was silent.

"Fontanes is a terrible friend, really, terrible and wonderful. He demands so much—you'll see. He just won't listen to defeatism. He'll fight you back into the front line inch by inch, if you try to run away. He can be cruel, can Fontanes. Well"—she turned on Francis suddenly—"there is a man I would call pure, pure fire."

"Can fire be pure?" Francis asked pointedly.

"That's a question for philosophers or chemists not for poor women to answer. What do you think yourself," she demanded, "you who have never been in love?"

"I think it has something to do with detachment. Mother was like that, you know. She helped people. She demanded a great deal too."

"Yes," Solange sighed, "your mother was an angel."

The silence which had been in the air for the last half hour fell. Francis didn't dare move, didn't dare look at her. And all the time the silence kept growing like a balloon, softly growing and getting larger and larger until before it could burst, he got up and said, "Now I really must go."

When Solange lifted her head, he had gone. She saw him walk quickly across the court without looking up at the window.

But once out of sight, Francis stopped, stood in the street without knowing where to turn. It was quite beyond him to make a decision, until a passerby, seeing his lost look offered to help him on his way. Only then he turned to the right and walked toward the Luxembourg Gardens. Once he stopped to look curiously at his right hand. Once he stopped for several minutes before a bookseller's window, but he could not have named one title he had seen when he turned away. His mind was blazing and yet he had no thoughts. He was empty and full at the same time.

He heard his own words repeated senselessly, "I have never been in love. I have never been in love." And he ached with loneliness.

CHAPTER TWO

SOLANGE HAD BEEN so absorbed in trying to encompass and understand Francis that she hadn't thought of herself in relation to him at all. In a way he was frightening, this young man with his shy piercing glance and his stubborn mouth, his air of passionate disdain. Would she be able to help him? At the moment she felt tired and old. And she was glad to be alone again in this room where she had fought out so many things by herself. Under her façade of charm and gaiety, Solange hid a deep melancholy, hidden from everyone but Fontanes. He knew that after her husband's death she had been near to suicide for months. He had beaten her out of it, forced her to take a job reading manuscripts for Gallimard where he knew one of the editors. He had refused to pity her, had challenged her at every point of weakness. When he saw the traces of tears—for at one time she had fits of weeping which came on her like seizures in the Métro or walking in the street—when he found her weeping, Fontanes swore at her, even shook her physically like a child, would have none of it. His very simplicity acted like a tonic. It was impossible to fight Fontanes, one had to give in, give in to being saved, to being pushed back into life.

And, she thought gratefully, Fontanes will help this boy. He will know what to say. He will break right through the brittle façade, the little defensive attitudes—Oh, that air with which Francis had said, "I have never been in love"! Was it true? Or was that too a defense? For a second he had looked disarmed, at a loss, and hating her for forcing him into a corner. Well, she had not meant to. And now she wondered if there were not some young girls to whom she might introduce him. He was certainly an excellent match and she thought it would please Persis if he married a French girl. Yes, that was it! Solange felt relieved at the very idea, so relieved that she was startled. Was it really that she didn't like him—this puritanical young man who asked so much, with his violence, his self-pity, his self-absorption?

Thinking these harsh thoughts, she was taken aback when a messenger arrived with a spray of yellow orchids. The card said simply Francis Chabrier. She was touched. She was going out to dinner and the orchids would look lovely on her gray dress. But the aptness of it, a flower arriving at just the right moment startled her. She had not expected this sort of thing from Francis at all. And she was embarrassed by Eugénie's exclamations, as she held the delicate spray in her thick red hand.

"Madame will be beautiful this evening."

"Hardly, Eugénie," Solange answered crisply, "one can't hope for that at my age."

"The young man has been charmed."

"Don't talk nonsense, Eugénie," Solange was in no mood to respond to this sort of thing.

But Eugénie shook her wise old head and smiled a secret

smile. It was obvious that Madame was nervous and she had not been nervous like this for years. Eugénie was delighted.

Francis ran through the next days like a horse who has felt the spur. He got tickets for Claudel's play and telephoned Solange to tell her so and to arrange to have lunch with her the following day. He had so many plans suddenly and definite desires that he did not even try to see her immediately. He spent the morning buying books, all he could find of Bergson, of Maine de Biran, of Lachelier, Ravaisson, Boutroux, these names which he knew because he had heard his mother speak of them because they had been the strong influence on his father's thought. It was strange until now that he had felt no curiosity to explore his father's mind. He had shied away from his father except as a flat symbol around which gathered his revolt against New England and Boston. He carried his pile of books back to the pension and lay down on his bed, forgetting all about lunch till half past three, read as if he had never read before in his life, as if he could never catch up with all he had to learn.

When he went out into the street looking for a café where he could eat something, he was astonished by the quality of the light, this European light which didn't bounce off the buildings and dazzle, but seemed to penetrate everything, so the long row of identical housefronts became strangely luminous and transparent. Everything seemed new; he stopped for a moment by a vegetable store to stare at the baskets of leeks, carrots, Spanish onions, rows of damp lettuce and large bunches of Belgian grapes lying like flowers on beds of cotton wool.

"Can I serve you?"

"No—no thank you." Francis walked on to the end of the

street and out onto a Boulevard which he didn't recognize. He bought the *Figaro* and sat down in the nearest café to eat a ham sandwich and drink a glass of beer. He found himself examining every face that went by as if he could penetrate to the roots of an existence in a few seconds. How alive they looked, these worn, often old faces, each so entirely different one from another! A boy and a girl, deep in conversation, went by arm in arm. The boy had on an orange shirt open at the throat and thick fair hair that hung down over his forehead, small blue eyes and a rather silly moustache. The girl was bare-legged in sandals, her hair cut short, and Francis was struck by the happiness in her face. She looked at him absent-mindedly, but meeting her eyes gave him a slight shock. And when she smiled, not at him, he gathered this smile like a present. Was it hunger that made everything so vivid?

He sat on for more than half an hour, smoking, reading the paper or pretending to read it, but chiefly filled with an immense unreasoning happiness which made him long to give someone a present. He wanted to talk and laugh and to be forced somehow to define the ideas which bubbled up inside him at every instant. On an impulse he crossed the boulevard finally to buy a notebook. In this he imagined there would be all sorts of things to write down almost at once. Armed with a map and his notebook, he felt like an explorer.

The first thing he saw as he sauntered along in the sun, was a barrow pushed by four men with something very white, dazzlingly white upon it; as they came nearer the white object proved to be a huge plaster statue of a woman naked to the waist, sitting cross-legged with a baby in her arms—no doubt on the way to a foundry to be cast. The plaster was so fresh it looked as if it had never been touched by a human hand and the whole figure like a secret truth shouted in the streets. The men in their dirty pants held together by string seemed like dwarfs or creatures in purgatory bound to drag Beauty along forever for all to see. Francis stood still and watched them go past, entranced. In America, he thought, the large white object would have turned out to be a Frigidaire. He laughed with pleasure and walked on.

When he came to the Seine and the bridges, he stopped again to take in the full expanse of sky, to see what was being played today in that theatre of clouds. But today the sky was perfectly, uninterruptedly, blue. There on his left was the absurd arrogant gesture of the Eiffel Tower, the grown-up Meccano toy. This too was Paris, this and Beauty carried naked through the streets, this and the dank smell of the river, and Mademoiselle Violette, the incongruously named old maid who ran his pension with the fiercest economy and considered toilet paper a superfluous luxury.

The leaves of the trees along the Seine were perfectly still, folded one upon another like painted leaves, except that Francis felt they were breathing quietly. In their very stillness they were alive, intensely alive against the formal stone balustrade of the Tuileries. Then, wishing to be as close to the still olive-green water as possible, he walked down the stone steps to the Quais themselves. Far above him Paris went about its business, the taxis swerving in and out blowing their horns, the great palaces and museums, the golden dome of Les Invalides, the fountains of the Concorde stating and restating their silent music. He was very much aware of all this, but at the same time he was now in another world. He saw the remains of a little campfire, and here and there a stone arch boarded up, a pile of sand and bricks as if long ago some work had been begun and forgotten. He passed a knot of ragged-looking men who watched him with hostility, forcing him to walk faster and disappear in the shadow of a bridge. Now he was approaching the Ile de la Cité. But still he kept his eyes on the life around him. There, lying quite unselfconsciously side by side on a burlap sack, a couple were reading, as absorbed in literature as any bourgeois couple under a red eiderdown in some run-down hotel on the upper level. Further on two women laughed uproariously as they tugged a great sack of rubbish to hide somewhere. These destitute people evidently had here a world of their own. Francis was a man from the upper world of taxis and fountains and cafés and hotel rooms. They did not envy him, they disliked him.

Thinking about all this, wishing he could penetrate into this river world, sleep on the stones, bake potatoes in the warm ashes of a fire, and above all share their enormous jokes, Francis did not realize that he was just under Notre Dame. He looked up and met it full in the face, standing high over him at the top of a very steep stone wall entirely covered by green vines. More than ever from here it looked like an immense ship come to port, anchored in the heart of the city, looked tremendously high and great as he did not remember ever thinking when he stood on the upper levels. It was majesty itself. And this, he knew suddenly, is the third level of Paris, the level that soars above the buses and people, the eternal level which makes an immensely worldly city also a holy city. Francis sat down and dangled his legs over the dyke and smoked. He took the time to look at it all quietly and at length, till from the whole first impression he began to be aware of the many details, above all of the delicate spire which really soared, he thought, as the Eiffel Tower, so much higher in fact, never could.

When he got up to go, he laid his almost full package of cigarettes down as an offering to the gods of the place.

The warm light was beginning to flow away from the stone like a falling tide, and Francis thought he had better remember just how to get to the Rond-Point where he was to meet Fontanes for dinner. But first he walked slowly round the great ship, moored in stone, supported by the taut bows of the buttresses so that, he saw now, the spire was made possible by the coming together of many strains in balance, springing like an arrow. And there at its base as he came nearer, the three angels his father had pointed out to him many times as a child, came clearly into view, walking quite sedately down the steep angle of the roof, one with a trumpet in his hand. It seemed extraordinary that they should still be there, should have been there all this time, suspended in light and air.

If Francis was an explorer, he stood now on a certain height, this height of memory and experience which made it possible for him to look back as well as forward. He was, after all, free now of some things. How bored he had been by those paternal walks on Sundays, listening, half-listening to all his father's wisdom! Now he knew that he would never be bored again in just that way. His eyes were open. It had taken a great many years to open them, but as he looked up a last time at Notre Dame he knew that he could look and look and never come to the end of seeing.

CHAPTER THREE

FONTANES was standing outside the restaurant with a bulging brief case under his arm, his huge black hat at an unintentionally rakish angle, when Francis hailed him from far down the street, running the half block that separated them.

"Well, that's good," he said, taking Francis' arm, "you are five minutes early."

"But you looked as if you had been waiting—I'm sorry."

"I am always ten minutes early. That's the theatre. It teaches one a rigid sense of time. But as long as you are a five-minutes-early person we shall get on very well. It's the ten-minute-late people who ruin my meals and give me indigestion."

When they were settled on a bench inside, while Fontanes took out his glasses to read the menu, Francis had a chance to look at him. Now that he was frowning, for this business of the menu was obviously a serious matter, he looked quite formidable. Everything in the face was cut in large shapes, the huge nose, the mobile mouth which looked like an ogre's mouth when he laughed, the jutting eyebrows and the bright young eyes under them. His forehead was massive, so massive that one could not tell that he was bald.

He gave the impression of a giant though he was not really very tall, but he dominated by the sheer power of his head. Reading the menu, murmuring certain magic words tentatively "la raie au beurre noire," "le filet mignon à champignons," "côte de mouton vert pré" he looked like a prophet, Francis thought, or, more curiously, like a clown of genius.

The waiter now suffered an inquisition about each item and after some five minutes of discussion Fontanes gave the order, and added with a flourish, "a carafe of my wine, Charles. You know," he confided to Francis, turning toward him with a broad smile, "I have a vineyard near Bordeaux. That's why I brought you here to this only passable restaurant, so we could drink my own wine. You see, they have it here. And it's not a bad wine, not bad at all—you'll see—" and then without a break as if he were still praising his wine, Fontanes put an arm round Francis' shoulders and said, "Dear heart, what it is to have you here! Can you defend yourself?" he said severely, "for we'll devour you if not. You will have to be savage."

Francis smiled, "I'm rather good at that."

"Like your father." Fontanes looked at him half-humourously and laughed. "No, I think you on the contrary would rather like to be devoured. Only then you must be careful whom you allow to devour you. It's a serious matter. I, for instance, am perfectly safe. I'll devour your time and your energy, but I'll leave that little soul you guard so jealously perfectly free."

It was Francis' turn to laugh. "And what if I don't have any little soul?"

"A monster, eh?" Fontanes teased, pouring out the wine and

tasting it with great attention. "Not bad," he said hopefully. "And now, to Francis Adams Chabrier!" He lifted his glass and drank, then set it down hard. "But what in the devil is that 'Adams' doing there in the middle of your name. It's disconcerting."

"Very," Francis agreed, laughing again.

"You are not going to have an easy time getting the pieces of your name into harmony. But it will be interesting. I shall be very interested in the result."

"So shall I . . ." and Francis added lightly, "but for the present I think I shall be just Francis Chabrier, if you don't mind."

"You are glad to be here, really glad, deep down inside you? Yes," said Fontanes, his eyes reading Francis' face with a curious bold glance, "I think you are. Tell me what you've been doing all day. Tell me everything in great detail."

"I've been reading Bergson," Francis said cautiously.

"For the first time?" Fontanes lifted his eyebrows. For someone twenty-six who pretended to be educated not to have read Bergson was amazing.

"Oh, of course I had some vague idea what it was all about," Francis said, blushing.

"I suppose you read Sartre instead, eh? It would be hard for you to imagine the effect Bergson had on the Paris of my youth and your father's. It turned our world upside-down, inside-out, it came to us like a religious revelation, almost. It became a key like all the real keys which once discovered one cannot imagine ever having done without. Poetry, the novel, even music were not the same afterwards. We ourselves were not the same."

"You knew Bergson, I suppose?"

"By sight. I met him once or twice, yes—so, you are reading

Bergson," Fontanes said, half tenderly, half mockingly. "Not a bad idea for your first day back in Paris."

Fontanes cast a lugubrious eye on the hors d'oeuvres and told Charles to take them away and bring them pâté maison instead. "Have another glass of wine," he said apologetically. "You see, the trouble is that the Patron's wife is ill. No one comes here any more for she was the cook. And it's sad, sad for the old man. I'm afraid he is having a hard time. So that's why I come here. How is the Patron, Charles?" he asked when the pâté was laid before them.

The waiter shook his head and pursed his lips, "Ah, Monsieur—you know—things are not too good. The Patron had a great shock when Madame was taken to the hospital. He is not the same."

"Neither is the pâté," Fontanes said brusquely as if perhaps he was afraid of being too moved.

"No, Monsieur, I regret—"

"All right, Charles." And Charles withdrew. "Now, before we get any deeper into philosophy and all that, tell me where you had lunch, what you had and what you have been doing since."

Fontanes was distressed by the ham sandwich and the glass of beer.

"Well, you *are* an Adams Chabrier after all," he roared. "A ham sandwich for lunch. How do you expect to live on that? Is it money?" he asked, taking out his wallet in real concern.

Francis was touched. "No, no, I have plenty of money. Only it was three o'clock and I was too excited really to be hungry or bother with a restaurant."

"Well, all right, only never do it again," Fontanes said severely.

And so Francis found himself describing his walk in great detail, almost eloquently.

Fontanes listened in silence and then pushed the pâté away half-finished and began to make designs with his knife on the tablecloth. Francis wondered if he had been listening. Or had been bored, but after all, he had asked for it. He had an impulse to smoke and then realized that a cigarette between courses would seem to Fontanes even worse than a ham sandwich for lunch. Already he was a little flushed by the wine, warm and slightly hallucinated so that now he would have liked to talk about Solange only he didn't dare.

"You are a different person from yesterday afternoon," Fontanes announced suddenly, "and nothing you have told me explains why."

"Have I turned green or something?" He could see now that Fontanes was a dangerous friend, because he saw too much, too quickly, and perhaps this was what he meant about devouring people.

It was lucky that the soup arrived just then and Fontanes' face cleared. "Now, you don't get soup like that in Boston, I'll wager."

"Well, you know, Mother learned to cook in France."

"Oh yes, of course, your mother," Fontanes had to admit, visibly disappointed.

"Still, it's excellent soup." What was it about this man which was so terribly endearing? Francis watched him with fascination. He was rather like an elephant really, only much more impatient than elephants are credited with being. But if one were inside an elephant as Bergson would point out, what looks like patience from a human outsider measuring it against human patience might be the wildest impulse taking several years to achieve momentum. Francis smiled to himself.

"Now you look like your father—that was just his secret smile, when he would wander off somewhere alone in the middle of a conversation."

"I was thinking," Francis said, aware of the incongruity and enjoying it to the full, "about the impulses of elephants and their conception of time."

Fontanes threw back his head and laughed the rich loud laugh Francis would come to associate always with him, a laugh which included the universe, it seemed, so gigantic it was. "But that is just like your father! It's exactly the sort of thing he was always saying—elephants—why elephants?" Fontanes asked, laughing helplessly, and wiping the soup from his chin.

"I don't know . . ."

"Well, now, what has happened to you since yesterday?"

Francis dived into his steak hungrily and wondered what on earth to answer. Was he so different? "I don't know," he said after a moment, "I seem to have developed a vast appetite for almost everything. I think it's Paris. I feel liberated." He was being entirely honest, because he had no idea himself what was happening to him, what had in a sense already happened to him.

"And how long do you plan to stay, Francis? A year? Two years?"

"I don't know. I know nothing. I'm just what Gide calls 'available.' I'll have to see what happens. But you know, I shall have to decide what I'm to do, what I'm to be, sometime," he ended. "So I expect I shall go back."

Fontanes watched him curiously, this young man who quoted Gide, had never read Bergson, didn't know what he wanted out of life and at the same time seemed extremely definite, almost theatrically definite about everything. There is something, Fontanes decided, that I don't know. I do not have the key. "You don't think I should go back?" Francis asked after a short silence. "I must say, it fills me with dread."

"I can understand that. But you know, Francis, what I think —whatever you do, it must be something where your total self is engaged, can come into play. There's no point in choosing to be one thing or another, choosing mechanically—you are French *and* American, Adams *and* Chabrier, after all. There is no escaping that and so what you must do is discover a way of being both at the same time, of using all that. It's all very well to talk about being available, but it's dangerous—you know that of course—" Fontanes interrupted himself to eye Francis severely, "you may fall into the heresy of Gide."

Francis was puzzled. "You mean, heresy against the church."

"No, no of course not," Fontanes growled, "heresy against life itself. Availability is all very well, the prerogative of poets and lovers, but it's pretty cheap without responsibility, eh? To whom, to what in the long run are you responsible? That is the question, it seems to me."

Francis smiled. "I'm irresponsible, that's evident," he said without resentment.

"While you are here," said Fontanes almost crossly, "you had better learn something about yourself, as well as about Paris."

"I fully intend to." Francis was a little irritated by Fontanes now, probing to the heart of matters he preferred to conceal, even perhaps from himself. He had not, he thought, run away from Boston, from Aunt Alison and all the curious forms of conscience to be confronted here by the word "responsibility."

For the first time since he had arrived in Paris he felt the cloud of his own confusion and doubt settling down on him, that atmosphere of disguised conflict in which he had lived for so long.

"Well, well," Fontanes put an arm round him gently, "I'm a violent old man, but I must tell you that, unlike a great many people today, I believe in America. I think you are the only hope for civilization. That's all," he ended as if they had talked seriously long enough, "and now we must have some coffee. Is the coffee drinkable, Charles?"

He talked then about his new play, about which he was very excited, as he had discovered the author, a young Belgian, and had high hopes of him. He described the devil of a time he had had raising the money for the production. He had sold a painting of Vuillard's to do it, a painting he loved. "But never mind," he said with a slightly guilty expression like a woman who has sold a jewel, "it is worth it."

All during the dinner Francis had held down the longing to speak of Solange, to hear Fontanes talk about Solange. Now while Fontanes waited for his bill, in the silence of the cigarettes the compulsion became too strong to resist.

"I am going to see Claudel's play with Madame Bernard," he said suddenly. And he was aware that calling her Madame Bernard to Fontanes was in itself a slight deception. In the second after he had spoken it dawned on him that he was involved more than he admitted to himself. Was all this new aliveness and excitement that he felt, the beauty of the trees, the sense of Paris itself, his sudden longing to be human, human enough to share in the life of those tramps under the bridges, all this nothing but what is known in New England as "a personal emotion"? Recognition flashed through him, but there was no time to examine it yet.

"It is very good for Solange that you are here this summer," Fontanes said seriously. "You see, for her your mother's death just when she had been looking forward so happily to seeing her, was a final blow after too many others. You will bring her something of the future, you know, something to look forward to. I have been worried about her."

"She seems so alive, so gay—I don't know—" Francis stumbled on the words—"radiant."

"Yes, yes," Fontanes interrupted impatiently, "that is the way she seems, but all that light has its deep shadows, you know. And sometimes the shadows come too close. We are all ill, here in France, since the war—the last war bled France nearly to death. But this was worse, this war poisoned the very sources." Suddenly Fontanes' own face looked old. Francis noticed the deep wrinkles, the sagging throat, the physical heaviness of the man for the first time. And he was silent, because he was ashamed to speak, he who had suffered nothing, knew almost nothing, had spent the war chiefly bored almost to tears, imprisoned in a uniform and a routine without meaning since he had never got into the fight.

"And for those of us who believed, who in our own way, resisted—you know, of course that Solange worked for a secret press—[but Francis had not known] this descent into party politics of the most violent kind has been even worse. You come here and feel the beauty of Paris," Fontanes went on wagging his finger accusingly at Francis, "but for us Paris stinks. Go and walk through the Rue St. Honoré. Look at the faces. Look at the people in the big American cars. It will make you vomit."

"New York is just as bad, worse maybe," Francis said appalled at the flood of bitterness.

"But New York was never Paris. New York is still on the way. Paris is a city of monuments. Here only the dead are pure."

And Fontanes whose changes of mood could be violent seemed now to have forgotten to whom he was talking, seemed in a hurry to go, nursing his rage.

"Tell the Patron to come back," Fontanes said to Charles. "Tell him things are not the same here and he is needed," he admonished Charles. "And you, Francis," he said at the door as if he were Napoleon giving orders to a general, "go and see Solange. Cheer her up. If you must have a responsibility, there's one for you."

Francis watched him hail a taxi and get into it, and stood for several minutes on the pavement, thinking of all he had heard. It's not possible that Solange needs me, he thought. There was a whole night and half a day ahead before he would see her. Already behind the real figure an intangible figure, the figure of his imagination, was forming itself, the secret person the lover creates and who is perhaps not there at all, the person the lover creates out of his own need and to his own dimension.

CHAPTER FOUR

FOR THE NEXT WEEK or so Francis lived this new vivid life of wandering about Paris, reading philosophy and exploring Solange whom he saw nearly every day. They went to the Orangerie to see a special show of mediaeval German art; they went to the theatre and got into a long argument about the Claudel play which Francis hated (it was an atmosphere to which he had no key, this atmosphere of passion). So Solange gave him the *Soulier de Satin* as an antidote and teased him about sacred and profane love. They sat in the Café des Deux Magots, drinking chocolate, making malicious comments about the Americans all around them, and watching the light slowly change on the face of the old church; they sat in the Luxembourg Gardens under the cool green umbrella of a chestnut; every day had its special flavor and every day was a holiday. Perhaps, Francis thought, with a new warmth about his heart, Fontanes is right and I am being useful in distracting her, so he even felt justified for all this joy, that it was not stolen but given, and that he was giving instead of taking, himself. Meanwhile his notebook became full of her comments which he studied as if he were studying a map. He had to discover her on his own for she told him very little and avoided anything personal. But once she had said, "Only really passionate people know anything about detachment" (they were talking of his mother) "because they are forced to learn it or to die; no one comes willingly to detachment."

They were sitting in the Tuilleries Gardens in the small patch of shade afforded by a huge stone urn on a pedestal. It was a hot day and Francis remembered the expanse of dazzling sand and the pool where the children sailed their boats. He remembered two young men half lying in chairs, their shirts open at the neck looking drunk with sunlight. He had envied them and felt suddenly impatient and tired of all this talk, felt a hunger for darkness and silence, for something he couldn't define, obliteration. Solange sat beside him in a pink dress, in a large black hat. She looked very charming. But she had gone on talking, inexorably, while a part of him refused to listen. He thought he would never forget the light, the air, the pink tobacco plants which seemed rather incongruous and floppy in the formal parterre behind them, and yet he couldn't remember just what she had said. It was strange. For he imagined afterwards that what she said must have been a key and now he would never find it. What he would remember forever and ever was a pink dress, a black hat, a woman whom, in a flashing instant of wild anger, he would have liked to strangle into silence.

He had never touched her since she took his hand so absentmindedly that first day. And in fact he went out of his way not to take her arm when they walked together, not to shake hands when they met. But when they were together he was acutely conscious of every part of himself, his feet, his hands, his neck; this made him clumsy. When he shaved in the morning he looked at himself with immense distaste. His mouth seemed small and pinched and his nose too big. It was as if he had no face as yet and looked out of himself as animals look out of their faces like spirits caught and wishing to get out.

He was beginning to find it difficult to concentrate; he no longer felt like reading. There was a heat wave which didn't help. And once Solange said sharply, "You aren't listening, Francis!" It was true that his attention wandered from her words to her throat, to her amazing subtle mouth, to her clear eyes which he had thought were blue, but he knew now to be gray, piercingly clear, devastating in their clarity.

Solange herself refused to admit what was happening. She pushed aside the mounting tension and told herself that they were both enervated by the heat. "I'm taking you to Madame Clermont's," she said. "It might amuse you to see that Paris—you know, the Avenue Foch, all rather grand. Would it amuse you?" she had asked almost tenderly, lowering her eyes before his insistent gaze. "I think it's time we saw someone besides ourselves—otherwise you will cease to listen to what I say, become bored—and," she added with malice, "I shall become bored too."

Then she left him to go to work, left him in the Luxembourg Gardens where they had taken refuge in the shade, left him to think how dusty and dry the leaves looked, how parched the flowers, now that she was gone.

The next day he waited for her in the salon, on a wave of rising excitement. Partly he was excited and a little nervous at being launched into society. But he waited for her to come in as if he were a whole audience in himself waiting for the entrance of a great actress. What would she wear? How would she look?

Was the red and white camellia he had brought and asked Eugénie to take in to her, suitable? Francis wandered restlessly about this room which had become so familiar, as he always did, a little as if he were trying to find here some lost object which he half remembered. Often, as he did now, he went over to the desk and looked at the row of photographs, his mother's serene face looking out seriously from the silver frame, Fontanes in profile looking like someone dead a long time ago and nothing like himself, and the bland secretive face of André, her husband, to whom he had taken an intense dislike, and who looked on the contrary, very much alive, smiling an ironic smile which Francis took irrationally as a personal comment. When Solange spoke of her husband as she often did, prefacing a sentence by "André used to say," or "When André and I were in Brittany," Francis cut her short, or pretended not to hear.

"You are not interested in André at all," she had said rather crossly only the other day.

"No," Francis said shortly. And she had lifted her eyebrows and changed the subject.

Solange had tactfully changed her dress so that she would be able to wear the flower, and that was what made her late, so when she came in she was in a hurry and said, almost brusquely, "Tell me, does it look all right?"

"Perfect," he said laconically after one swift glance at her.

"Come along then, I want to get there early so that I can introduce you properly to Louise Clermont—you know, she adored your father. She is very anxious to meet you."

"She'll be disappointed, I expect." Francis felt cross. He was upset because in the one glance he had given Solange, unaccountably brilliant and distant in her black suit, in her absurd fashionable hat with a little veil, he felt the whole power of the society they were about to enter, standing between them. She herself, for once, seemed not quite at her ease. She talked very fast when they had captured a taxi and were safely on their way and talked about things which irritated him, for instance the fact that although she had had this suit entirely remade it still was not right, about an argument she had had that morning with an editor, and all the time he was half listening, he looked at her gloved hands and would have liked to pull off the gloves. Her face for the moment was just a worldly face, but hands never conceal anything. There she was, enveloped like a mummy, he thought bitterly, in all the multiple bandages of the world while he himself might as well have been stark naked so ill-armed did he feel.

The taxi swung round the Arc de Triomphe and Francis looked out, taken by surprise as he always would be by the height of the arch, by the sheer grandeur of the great wheel of avenues. Here there seemed always to be the echo of trumpets and drums, the inexplicable sadness of parades, all that the French mean when they use their word, "La Gloire," with its tragic overtones of the eleventh hour at the Marne, of De Gaulle's first broadcast, or of the small plaques which Francis had noticed all over Paris, sometimes with a faded bunch of violets or roses beside them, noting that here a Resistant fell during the liberation. They turned down into the splendor of trees, the broad sandy paths of the Avenue Foch and stopped, much too soon he thought, for he had been enjoying himself. Solange paid for the taxi because he had been absent-minded as usual. She gave his arm a friendly squeeze, "Here we are, Francis. Are you nervous? You haven't listened to a word I've said for the last few minutes."

"I'm sorry. But you know, I have to get used to Paris. It

takes me by surprise—and I hadn't been up here before, this time."

For a moment they stood under the trees and looked down the long perspective to the soft blur of St. Cloud. Then it was really time to go in. The elevator crept slowly up five stories. There was just room for two; to be suddenly and for purely mechanical reasons standing so close to Solange, without being able to move, suspended in the air, helpless, made her nearness seem intolerable. Francis was immensely relieved to come in out of the dark into the large sunny drawing room, to be swept into the embrace of Louise Clermont, an old woman in her eighties who led him triumphantly around the room to introduce him to an Ambassador, a Countess and several other ladies. With the last of these, who looked like a brilliant-eyed almost human monkey, and wore a great many jewels, he found himself cornered by a tray of champagne glasses. Solange was at the other end of the room now, talking to the Ambassador. She did not catch his eye. Out of nervousness he drank his champagne too fast, choked on a small strawberry tart and, without having said a word to the woman at his side, suddenly disappeared onto the balcony through the French windows. For the moment he was safe. He took a deep breath and saw where he was, the magic of this balcony floating in the air high over the soft green mounds of the chestnut trees. To the right he could catch just a glimpse of the Arc de Triomphe and to the left the long velvety sweep down to the Bois and further off the unattainable paradise which St. Cloud seems to be from here.

"So you've run away," the cracked old voice teased. "But you can't run away. You have got to come back with me and be polite. Do you know," she said, delighted with him it seemed, "that is exactly what your father did the first time he came here, more than twenty years ago. I had to bring him back and plant him in front of Valéry before he would say a word."

"You are very kind and I am very rude," Francis said humbly, because he liked this old woman immensely.

"But I forgive you, because it's lovely, my balcony, isn't it? It's my treasure, this view. It keeps me alive and it makes me wise, too, that is what is amazing."

"I think Paris makes everyone wise," Francis said, and he laughed suddenly with happiness. "Even I feel wise here."

"No, you are too young," she said as if she were unwilling to give him all the presents at once, "I am eighty-three and so I have a right to be wise. But you perhaps only have the right to be foolish—or mad. How mad are you?" she asked pointedly.

"Completely," Francis said seriously.

"Oh, that's very good. That's all right. Then you had better come back in. You might fall in love with the moon—or that lady opposite on her balcony, drying her hair," she said maliciously. And Francis did not have time to point out that it was broad daylight so he could hardly fall in love with the moon. But he was glad to follow her, to find his hand clasped rather roughly in her ringed fingers and to be brought back.

"He is quite mad, so he assures me," she announced to the room at large, "but I think quite safe—and very charming. Now, first, you must talk to this man. His name which you will forget no doubt is Descharnes, but you will not forget him. Monsieur Descharnes adores the memory of your father. There, I'll leave you two together," she said with a satisfied gleam in her eyes, and made her way to the other end of the room to greet a group of newly arrived guests.

"You are in Paris for some time?" M. Descharnes asked politely. Francis noticed his very thin face, thin and transparent so the skin stretched like silk over the bones, his pale blue eyes, his rather large ears which gave him a look of perpetual surprise. He was dressed impeccably, no doubt by an English tailor, and looked as if he washed his hands every half hour. All these things Francis noticed while he explained that he didn't know how long he would stay, that for the moment he was simply taking a vacation after his exams and that later on he would decide about the winter.

"So—you are marvelously, fantastically free," M. Descharnes answered. "And you are young. And you are American. Isn't this to be as near to a god as a human being can hope to come? I envy you, Monsieur." It was hard to tell whether in the pale blue eyes there was a shadow of a smile. "The question is, how long will you be able to keep this divine freedom, how long will you be able to stand out against it all."

"All what?" Frances asked, his eyes searching for Solange. She must have gone into the other room, for he didn't see her. He began, while they talked of freedom so glibly, to feel a wild impatience, to wish to go in search of her at once. But he controlled himself and lit a cigarette.

"All what?" M. Descharnes asked, obviously enjoying himself, "well, to begin with, all this—this delightful prison of social relations, social obligations."

"I doubt if I ever get into that prison," Francis said ironically.

"Ah, that's what we all begin by saying, and then we find ourselves coming back to certain rooms, at certain times, because, for instance we know we shall find a certain person there, and this process extends itself gradually to two or three people, and becomes a net, at first a very delicate net, but one morning we wake up and find we are no longer free. The little blue book is full of engagements."

"You can't frighten me," Frances said, amused, for none of this had the slightest relation to any reality he knew or would ever know.

"Or else—" M. Descharnes smilingly continued, "on the contrary, the little blue book contains only one name, and then you may be sure we are less free than ever before."

Solange appeared in the doorway between the two rooms and Francis, lighting up suddenly, made her a sign to join them, but she turned the other way, toward the monkey he had abandoned and greeted her effusively. Had this been deliberate?

M. Descharnes was speaking less lightly now. "Eventually every choice we make diminishes our freedom until, perhaps in spite of ourselves, we find that the future is already designed, and the very freedom we imagined we had, cast a long and definite shadow which was some sort of inescapable responsibility. That, as you recognize, was one of your father's ideas," he said looking intently at Francis now. "But I envy you because for you apparently all the choices are still to be made—be careful," he said, half-mockingly, "it's dangerous to be a god. Gods too cast long shadows."

But why did she turn away? Francis was asking himself while he half listened and now he didn't dare even look at her, under the clear gaze of these blue eyes, of this curiously charming but very perspicacious man.

"Did my father cast a long shadow?" he asked, refusing to answer for himself. And in fact what was troubling was that he sensed that they all talked to him in a way as if they were talking to his father, to someone they knew very well. But he did not have that advantage. He not only had not known their fathers, he had not known his own—or himself. In fact he knew nothing. An idiot would have been closer to the truth than a god.

"Very long," M. Descharnes said seriously, "I have been working for twenty years on certain ideas of your father's and I haven't come to the end of them yet."

Francis was drinking another glass of champagne. While he listened, for these things were important and he was really listening now, he wondered how many of the people in this room remembered his father.

"You see," he said after a moment, "I was too young when he died, to know anything about him."

"I'll tell you a curious thing about Pierre Chabrier," M. Descharnes went on, "he was only happy in action. He hated to think. All the last years I felt he was like a tiger in a cage pacing back and forth in his mind, trying to find the way out. That is why this idea of freedom haunted him—"

But just then, and as Francis, deeply stirred, would have probed farther, Madame Clermont pounced again.

"Don't take him away," M. Descharnes said, "I have just begun to get his attention," and after this parting sally, Francis was dragged off to the corner where Solange, Madame Beauregard (that was the monkey's name), and a Monsieur Tangère were talking apparently about Sartre. Solange refused to catch his eye and since this was suddenly all that Francis wanted in the world, he paid no attention to what was going on. He fell into a complete silence.

"Does he ever speak?" Madame Beauregard turned to Solange, with an air of amusement. "Just now when we were introduced, he stood beside me for five minutes and did not say one word. Then he fled."

Francis hated her with a savage hatred.

"Perhaps if you ask him a direct question . . ." Solange smiled, cruelly, Francis thought.

"But then it will have to be such an important question, after such an important silence," the monkey said, her jewels glittering and her eyes glittering all at once, as if she had discovered a new and amusing game.

They treat me as if I were an animal, Francis thought, clenching his teeth.

"You see, I am an idiot, Madame," he said very quietly.

"An idiot," she giggled suddenly, "but he has wit! He's charming."

Francis looked desperately at Solange.

"I'm afraid we must be going, Madame," he said addressing her in an icy voice.

For a second she hesitated, and he thought she would say, "Not at all, it's early." But she turned to the monkey quite coolly and said, "He's right. Alas, we are due somewhere else. You will have to ask him that all-important question some other time." He was saved. She had saved him. Francis blushed to the roots of his hair with gratitude.

They stood by the elevator, having made their polite farewells to Madame Clermont. They stood, silent, listening to the slow glide of the ropes and waited and waited as the elevator crept up the five stories toward them. They got into it in silence and went down in silence. Very carefully Solange put on her gloves. Only when they were standing in the street, at the very place where they had stopped happily on their way in, did she say gently, "Why do you have to be so rude, Francis? You really are difficult."

And now the tide of emotion, of tension that had been rising in him through all these days suddenly pulled him forward, far beyond where he intended to be, forced him to say, "Because I get so angry with you, with myself—because—I love you, don't you see? And I can't stand it any longer."

It was the wrong thing to say, the wrong moment to say it. Francis now felt emptied of everything, hopeless, lost.

"Don't talk nonsense," she said sharply, angrily.

"You, you . . ." His hand clasped her gloved one, so hard his own hurt. "Solange—" He forced her to look at him for just a second, forced her eyes, only amazed, now, frightened to look for a second at his, whose whole being had become a consuming question.

"But you're mad, Francis." And then as he dropped her hand and ran off into the street, "where are you going?"

"Taking you home," he called back. She watched him run across the street to catch a taxi going in the wrong direction. Should she refuse to go with him, in this wild mood? But suddenly she was trembling so much that she was glad to get into the taxi and sit down, as far in her corner as possible, entirely withdrawn.

This time neither of them looked out and after what seemed a very long time, she said in her usual voice, "I am going to forget what you just said, Francis. And you must forget it. You must," she underlined the last word almost harshly.

"Now you're talking nonsense. One doesn't forget such things. Take off your gloves," he commanded. Suddenly he felt full of power, a god, M. Descharnes said, and Francis, who for the first time in his life knew exactly what he wanted, felt like a god. His anger, his uncertainty, his tension, his nervousness had all fallen away. He was there, in his whole self and he knew that she couldn't deny him.

"Certainly not," she said coldly. "Why should I take them off?"

"As you please," Francis smiled in his corner of the taxi. At this moment of extreme danger, he didn't even know he was in danger. He felt, for the first time in his life, perfectly safe.

But Solange knew and she was afraid. She was afraid of herself because she was troubled and had to admit that she was. Francis in the last two weeks had displaced a great deal of atmosphere, had managed to invade her days and even her nights, in a way she would not have believed possible. There were hours when she had felt happier than she had for years, watching his closed face open little by little, watching him blaze up and grow, change before her eyes. She had been devoutly grateful for all he had brought her of youth, that fierce intensity, even the rudeness which she had grown to love as it was part of him, the suddenness, the honesty, the torment. She had felt a tenderness well up inside her which she imagined to be not personal but a tenderness for life itself and everything that must grow and change in order to live. More, she had imagined that she was useful. Now, in one second he had smashed these illusions. Now, she thought bitterly, I shall only hurt him and wither all the young green shoots—even if . . . but here she spoke again in order not to think.

"You told me once that you had never been in love, Francis. Was that true?"

"Of course it was true," he answered, reaching over once more and taking her hand, firmly now, without the slightest hesitation as if it already belonged to him, always had belonged to him. Yes, indeed he had grown up. In the last few moments he had become a man, and as a man a formidable antagonist. Solange felt a sharp pain just under her heart. No, she thought, desperately—no—

Only he was in an entirely different sphere now. He turned a shining face toward her and said gently, "Look at the trees, Solange, they are all on fire."

"My dear," she smiled, in spite of herself, "you may be on fire—I must believe you since you say so—but I can assure you that nothing else is, not the trees"—and now she forced herself to add—"not me."

She was relieved to see that they were nearly home. Once they were out of the taxi, the spell would be broken. She would escape. She would be able to think.

Just now she could feel his eyes on her face like hands and she shrank from them, for it was not a caress, this look, it was an attack and she answered it in the only way she could, by turning her head and looking him straight in the eye, but withholding everything from this look so that it was a perfect blank.

"There, little Francis," she said, smiling, "you see, you have made a mistake. I'm sorry."

The taxi swerved into the Rue de l'Université and for a second she lost her balance and leaned against him, and was annoyed with herself for withdrawing as violently as if she felt a physical repulsion. "And now you must leave me here. Shall I see you tomorrow?"

"I expect so," Francis said.

"Come to lunch, then. We might go and see some pictures."

"We might."

While Francis' back was turned as he paid the taxi, she fled. It was an ignominious flight and she knew it.

CHAPTER FIVE

THE WHOLE APARTMENT felt strange and empty when she went in. She sat down with her hat still on as if she were in someone else's house and looked around, but if she had hoped to find some friendly ghosts here she had been wrong. All she found was a desolation of emptiness, and the half-smoked cigarette butt Francis had left in the ashtray. There was now an enmity, she felt, between her living body and all the things in this room. She was no longer at home here, nor safe, even here. For this room was filled with the past and she had in the last half hour been forced to take an immense leap into the present, a present she had imagined no longer existed for her, would never exist again. She was deeply shaken. It was not a question, she saw now of right nor wrong, but of what merely was possible or not possible. From now on she would be the hunted fox, keeping a few steps ahead of the hounds, perhaps but at what a price! With a sudden gesture of rage she got up and went into the kitchen, "I'm going out, Eugénie. Never mind about supper," she said coldly as if poor Eugénie were in some way at fault. And that, she thought, bitterly, is what this madness does—drives me out into the street to eat in a strange café and hurt Eugénie's feelings. It was ridiculous, stupid. And, she thought, I'll have none of it. I'll go away. Yes—the immense vista of freedom opened before her, the sudden realization that no one could force her to stay here.

But at the first corner, she saw Francis drinking a pernod and, as if nothing had happened, reading the paper. His smile, as she drew nearer, ran to meet her without a shadow of doubt or fear and touched her like an embrace. She sank down beside him, without a word, and ordered a coffee.

"You're cold," he said, surprised. "You're shaking with cold. Why ever did you go out without a coat at this hour?" he said severely as if she were a child.

"You've upset me, Francis!" It was a bleak admission. But he accepted it as if it had been the one saving word he had waited for all his life.

"Darling," he said, "don't be upset. Don't worry and be anxious. Be happy, for my sake if not for your own. Can't you imagine what this is to me? This being alive suddenly after all these years? Of being free after all the years in prison? Don't feel you have to give me anything, if you can't—" (Oh these lovers' gifts which are always taken back, she thought, for from now on his very presence would be a demand and he would not be able to help it.) "I feel marvelous," he said so loudly that the couple at the next table turned to stare.

She giggled, "The people at the next table are listening."

"What do I care? I'd just as soon climb the obelisk in the Concorde with a megaphone and shout, 'Listen! I'm in love! I'm in love! Poor people, you have no idea what it is like. But I know.'" He was laughing now himself.

"Don't, Francis, don't—" she begged. "I can't bear it."

He watched her sip her coffee; in the midst of the unresolved tension between them, he felt only an immense peace. He was quite content to sit here beside her forever and to watch her sip coffee.

"Let me keep this happiness a little while. It's so new," he said gently.

She would go on protesting, but from the moment she saw him so unexpectedly in the café, she had known that there was no longer a decision to be made. Life had made it. Still, she must protest. She must warn him. She must say all that had to be said first.

"I'm a desert, Francis. I'm not what you think—"

"Well, let me walk beside you in your desert, that's all I ask."

"You're too young," she said because it seemed kinder to them both than to say, "I'm too old." But that, perhaps was the truth. She observed him now, gone down into himself, as if he hadn't heard what she said, entranced. Finally as if there had been no silence, no interval between her remark and his answer, he lifted his head.

"Yes, I'm young, but I know about the desert. I have been there for years. I have always been there until now. That's what you don't understand. Oh Solange, don't try to be detached"—and she knew that the sardonic emphasis on the word "detached" came from real suffering, from his mother—"Come with me. I need you so much."

"My dear, come with you—where?" She knew that her voice was saying something else than the words and that her voice was saying, "Anywhere, I'll go with you to the end of this journey," but she couldn't help her voice, the creature of her body. She was already transported into regions where reason has no place, wrapped in the mysteries no one will ever understand.

"To all the places you know and which I don't know where people can love each other in peace. Oh, I need peace so much," he ended and she knew that it was true and that for a little while at least she could give him peace. "What a beggar I am!" he said and it was wrenched out of him, bitterly. "Don't say anything," he begged. "Just be quiet."

She looked at him, fully and deeply, allowed him to feel his way down into the depths of her eyes, entirely open to his glance.

Francis saw the spirit of the woman shiver there, for a second, and took possession. He was full of awe. So this was love, this opening deep deep down, this gift of something one did not know one had in one's possession, this obliteration of the self in another self.

And all this had happened in a few seconds, sitting in an ordinary café on an ordinary evening. The people at the next table didn't even know it had happened. But he would never be the same again.

CHAPTER SIX

THE NEXT DAY they did after all go to see pictures and what had been a threat when Solange said it and had meant we shall go to see pictures and be sensible, now became something entirely different, became we shall go to see pictures together because every familiar painting in the Louvre must be seen again now, because it has become something entirely different, because we ourselves are not the same people we were yesterday. They walked arm in arm, full of a secret tenderness for each other's bodies, content to walk down the long formal galleries in a dream, stopping here and there and especially before the Chardins, the Pieter der Hoochs, and the Vermeer because such ecstasy needs simple objects to rest on, a loaf of bread, a fish on a plate. Every now and then Francis looked at Solange, just to be sure it was true, to receive again the slight shock, the tingle of something like fear as he realized again that he had entered into a universe he had not known existed and which was his to love, cherish, learn by heart. But this was not to be talked about, only felt. They talked instead about what they looked at, drawing each other's attention to some detail, sometimes laughing suddenly when in their state of mastery of all around them they concluded that a certain painting was absolutely false or ludicrous. Occasionally they disagreed.

"Darling," said Solange after half an hour of this sort of looking, "I shall have to sit down. I'm dead."

They went back, searching already for a past, to the same two chairs under the stone urn where they had sat a few days before.

"I didn't know when we sat here before," Francis said happily, lighting a cigarette and passing it to her like a present. "Oh, the things I didn't know," he laughed. And then, "My love, my love, how did I ever find you?"

The pink tobacco plants behind them waved back and forth hysterically in a sudden gust of wind. Clouds they hadn't noticed covered the sun and Solange shivered. The bubble of happiness she had held so lightly in her hands, burst and she was filled with forebodings. She turned to him, and saw he was still there, smiling his secret smile, his brilliant wilful reality taking all this for granted already. Whom would he marry? What had she stolen in one night from a young girl—some young girl she would never know, perhaps waiting in America?

"Why are people so afraid of happiness?" she asked him and asked herself. "Why is it always slightly suspicious? Why do we turn it round and round looking for the flaw?"

"But you are happy?" Francis asked, disturbed by this change of her mood as if she were reflecting the sky. "You have no regrets?"

"No, dear heart." For a while at least, she thought, let us believe we are angels even if we have to become monsters to ourselves later. So they sat hand in hand until large drops of rain forced them to run out to the street and climb into a taxi.

"Do you know where we're going?" Francis asked.

"No, do you?" She was out of breath from running so fast.

"We are going to Notre Dame."

So do all true lovers wish to bring their love to the highest and holiest place for a blessing. Solange recognized his impulse and was grateful. It was a strange poignant pleasure to watch him discovering one by one all these things she had known for years, known and almost forgotten. She had come here with Jacques twenty years ago, Jacques, the cruel, the devastating, the Jacques of those days when she knew Persis, Jacques of whom she had never breathed a word to Francis. Had her moment of fear in the Tuileries just now been a reminder from the ghost of Jacques (as if she needed reminding!) that passion is a poison and always someone dies of it, someone is cruelly hurt?

But Francis at that moment took her hand and kissed it, each finger and then the palm and she felt the sweetness in him flowing into her like a balm. Why look back or forward? Why question?

If only I could kneel and really pray, Francis thought when they had pushed open the leather door and stood in the silence. Why can't I? When his mother died his whole existence had seemed in question. Nothing had any reality and yet he had felt no such hunger for God, for prayer. But here in the first day of his love, of his passion, in the first newness of himself, already unappeasable hungers were planted.

Solange had wandered off down the right aisle and he followed her. Then they sat for a short time before the strangely worldly Virgin, each locked in his thoughts.

Francis had felt impelled to come here as if he had a burden or an offering to lay at the altar, as if perhaps being conscious of the full power and glory of his own body he wished to give thanks. But now that he was here, sitting uncomfortably on the low chair, it was not after all possible to make his offering, to lay down his burden, simply as he had laid his head on Solange's shoulder last night. He was unable to kneel, unable to give up a parcel of his own consciousness of himself and of this woman who sat beside him suddenly a stranger as strange as the Virgin holding the Child on her flowing hip. He was a modern man dressed in a gray suit, not a spirit given the world of flesh to inhabit, the whole earth as his possession, the mountains and rivers, the soft hills and valleys of her unimaginable beauty as he had been last night. Now he felt small, diminished, afraid of this silence which seemed to have parted him from Solange, not brought them together solemnly in the presence of God, as he had intended. She looked distant, wrapped in her solitude. So he whispered, "Come, let's go home," and very quickly almost as if they were running away from the candles and the incense, they walked out.

It was raining hard, one of those sudden harsh rains that fall out of the sky without a warning. There was no taxi in sight on the whole wet square. And where should they go? At the Rue de l'Université Eugénie would be there (thank Heavens she slept at the end of a long hall and Francis had dressed and gone out before she woke, at six o'clock that morning).

Could he face Mademoiselle Tonnerre as he called the waspish old maid at his pension, could he ask Solange to face her inquisitive black eyes, her malice? Where, where could he take his love now? And she was saying,

"Take me back, Francis. I must do some work. And you must go and find your own little peace until suppertime. That is what's wise," she said firmly, sensing by the pressure of his arm what very different ideas he had at the moment. But now she felt exhausted, and she needed to be by herself.

"Don't be wise, not yet," he pleaded. "It's so lonely in the rain. Or let me bring my books over to your place and read—I'll promise to be quiet."

They were still standing in the doorway. Time flowed past like the rain. Had they been here a few moments? An hour?

"All right." What else could she say? When he found a taxi and they rattled off on their way first to his pension to collect the books and then to the Rue de l'Université, she sat withdrawn in her corner, leaning her head against the cold leather seat, her eyes closed. Now she was back in the human dwellings again she realized that though her desert had been terrible it had had the advantage at least of freedom. Whole areas were blocked off now. Almost, she felt she was in a prison.

Francis sensed the distance and was unaware that he had himself created it by his demand to come and share her peace. He became very tense, watching her for some sign, some explanation. Was she thinking of André? The idea made him sit bolt upright and stare out of the window where he still saw her face frozen as if the image were photographed on his retina. The delicate slightly taut line of her chin and throat haunted him. Perhaps he had fallen in love, had desired her physically the first time she had turned her head away from him and looked out of the window. He remembered she had been saying how glad she was that he had come, she had been saying that she was a desert. And he had known in that instant that she was not to be possessed, that some part of her would always escape him, that there was too much behind her, too many faces he didn't know, too many other— "Come along, here we are," he said harshly, gathering the books together. "You run while I pay this man, or you'll get wet."

She was talking to Eugénie when he finally rang the bell.

"Monsieur will have his tea in the drawing room, Eugénie. Will you bring me mine in the bedroom? I must do some work."

So, he was banished. Francis was filled with rage, with amazement. What had happened? What had he done?

Already, Solange thought bitterly, I am withering the green shoots, but I can't help it. He will have to learn what is and is not possible. I must be allowed to be myself. But the very fact that he was there in the next room, with only a wall between them, made it impossible for her to be herself. She lay down on the bed with a pile of pillows behind her, cigarettes, an ash-tray, and the pile of manuscripts she must read, and sighed. Everything was the same as usual except, she thought ironically, the pillow is rather crumpled. Eventually, she supposed, Eugénie would have to know. It was a disturbing thought. The telephone rang. Absent-mindedly she picked up the receiver. It was a shock to hear Fontanes' rather loud rasping voice (he always shouted on the phone as if he imagined he wouldn't be heard). She felt guilty all of a sudden, as if she had betrayed him.

"How's the play going?" she asked, knowing that he would try to read her voice, her mood and afraid of just that.

"Terribly. I got into an awful rage with that little Le Monnier—he's so conceited. Of course it didn't do the slightest good. He has the hide of a rhinoceros—and eventually he will be perfect in the part when I have managed to enrage *him,"* Fontanes laughed.

"You sound just like yourself," she laughed too.

"And why not? And how are you, my little blessing? Working too hard I expect? When do I see you?"

"When you like—this evening for dinner, for instance." She was amazed at the relief she felt at the idea of not having dinner with Francis.

"I'll come and get you at seven. Look as beautiful as possible. How is our little Francis? I've tried to get him three times on the phone. He is never in."

"He's here at the moment, reading in the salon."

"And where are you?"

"Working on my bed."

"What strange ideas you have of entertaining people!"

"No, it is they who have strange ideas of entertaining me."

"You are cruel," Fontanes said slyly. She could feel his smile at the other end of the phone.

"Am I?" and with that, and an "au revoir until tonight," she hung up.

She half regretted her decision now. She had just made things difficult for herself and for Francis, more difficult than they needed to be and she saw with perfect clarity that they would be difficult, remembering the tone of Fontanes' voice that first day when he said, "Boston must be a very serious place." Francis would throw himself complete, whole, with all his demands, needs, questions, doubts into the next weeks or months. He would, she foresaw, analyze, deepen, extract the subtlest meanings from every moment they would have together. For, she knew already, she divined that he was that most redoubtable of lovers, the mystic, who would try to make a religion of love. This was his father speaking through him clearly. He did not have an ounce of his mother's saving grace, that ironic sense of reality, that blessed detachment—but he's so young, she reminded herself. How many times would she have to remind herself of this fact? For she saw she would have to be detached. She must be wise, since he could not. When the sharp knock came at the door and Francis appeared, smiling rather shyly, with the teatray, she was glad to be faced with a human reality instead of her tormented thoughts.

"Can't I have tea with you?" he said. "Eugénie agrees with me that it is very cruel to make me have my tea alone . . ." In a single look at his face she saw that he had been suffering—already.

"Of course, darling, come in and sit down."

Shyly he glanced around this room in the daylight while happiness flowed through him like a liquor. He poured out the tea, rather awkwardly. He sat on the end of the bed, sipping his with a spoon like a child, looking up at her now and then as if he were tasting her smile as well as the tea. How Persis must have adored him, she thought—and yet she too had made him suffer, had withered the green shoots.

"What are you thinking about?" he asked gently. Her face, which he studied like a foreign language, kept teaching him new words. This word was tenderness, but he did not recognize it. He thought she looked sad and wondered why.

"I was thinking about your mother, how she must have loved you when you came and drank tea on her bed."

He froze and answered stiffly, "I never did." He sensed the danger, the transposition to another key of what had been last night great and fierce, the tremendous opening to a place where they were more or less than human. He did not want her tenderness, not yet. He pushed it aside violently. "Don't think about my mother," he said harshly.

"Darling, why not?" She sat up, amazed.

"Because—because—I'm not a child any more. I grew up last night. I became at last something other than her son—don't you see?" His eyes were black. In that instant the bridge, the physical bridge which had been down now for hours was set up again between them, the steely tension. Sitting across from each other on the bed, they were actually locked in each other's arms.

"It will never be the same. Every time will be different," he said with triumph in his voice, "worlds within worlds within worlds. I want the night!" he cried out, and then in an altered voice, "Do we have to wait?"

"Yes," Solange said, deliberately breaking the tension between them. "And darling," she went on ruthlessly, "you mustn't be cross, but I'm having dinner with Fontanes. He called just now."

"Oh" and then after a moment's pause, he put his teacup down on the tray and got up and went to the window to stare out at the sad courtyard, the balconies opposite, the pot of geraniums in a tin can on a window sill. "I suppose," he said carefully, "that you will have to tell Fontanes—"

"About us? Of course not."

Francis chuckled, "Fontanes told me that freedom without responsibility was immoral and he told me to take care of you, so there. 'Let Solange be your responsibility,' he said."

"He did?" They exchanged a look of heavenly complicity, and the moment of danger was past.

"Why? Would he be furious?" Francis said, coming over to sit beside her where he could take her hand, turn it over and look at it.

"No—I don't know—perhaps . . ."

"I suppose he's in love with you himself," said Francis with the happy arrogance of the accepted toward the rejected.

"Heavens no. He looks on me as his most difficult child. He loves me, yes, as I love him. But it's not this," she said, bending over to kiss the hand that held hers.

"And what's this?" Francis asked, on the flood of his happiness, because now he wanted words as well as everything else, and did not yet know how dangerous words are.

"This?" she said lightly, "is madness of course."

But at the moment it was not madness. They sat side by side on the bed and hand in hand and knew that love was also there, flowing between them, and that it was not madness, and that it was good. Again Francis felt in the depths of himself that he must find some way of giving back all this, giving it back to what? To life perhaps. Whenever they were at peace like this—for so he had felt when he woke up and looked at her early in the morning, asleep, turned away from him and strangely innocent and lost—he knew that love at best is the communication of goodness and so implies responsibility. At present his only responsibility was to her and so he did the one difficult thing he could imagine and got up.

"I'm going to let you work," he said, "so you won't be cross with me later. I'm going to leave you. But I'll come back."

"You're an angel and I love you," she said lifting her face

to be kissed. Why had she been afraid? What was there to fear? Francis was not Jacques. Francis would not need to hurt her to prove his power. Suddenly she felt the tears rush to her eyes. "Bless you," she said as he turned at the door to see her once more.

Of course she didn't work. She lay for an hour on her bed, half awake, half dreaming and it seemed to her now too that the night was far off, a long journey. And she was terrified of Fontanes' perspicacious eyes. So much so that she didn't wear the dark red rose sent by messenger a half hour later. She put it in a glass by the bed. It was difficult enough to make up her mouth and she did it three times, as if to hide the vulnerable curve. "But my face hasn't changed after all," she told herself, grateful that she looked quite forty-five, quite hard and clear from the outside at least.

Francis was relieved to be alone for a few hours, free, and he felt a need to go and look at the river again, to see what was happening out of doors, to the trees and the light. Every hour, he knew, was bringing him something and at the same time taking something away, since his love changed every hour and so it was necessary to have time to think, to realize each thing as it happened to him. His whole relationship to his mother had shifted as a kaleidoscope shifts, for one thing. And when he thought of his father, he felt a physical identity with the man of whom he had never thought as a physical being like himself. He could conceive of how violent action might be like this, a consuming hunger and release. His father must have felt like this about flying—yes, he thought happily, I am beginning to understand you, Father. He looked at his mother now with a man's eyes, his father's eyes, Alan's eyes. I suppose, he thought, that there are many kinds of love; it made him immeasurably happy to realize how much he had to learn, and to think that before he died he would give and receive love in many shapes and forms.

Just now it appeared to him suddenly in the way the wind moved through the leaves of the plane trees along the Seine, how it took one tree after another and gently shifted all the poise and the pattern, and made it flow.

Later in his walk he saw it again in the V-shaped ripple that spread from the wake of a barge, widening and widening its range until it broke softly against the stone embankment. Everything he looked at had a message and he thought with amazement of all he had missed; for the message had always been there, only until now he had not known the language nor how to read.

CHAPTER SEVEN

TO CELEBRATE Saul's arrival from London Solange was giving a dinner party for him and Fontanes; there was something gala about this meeting between Francis' dear friend and her own. It seemed altogether a happy occasion, for Francis too, for he had been a little afraid that when Saul came there would be a subtle change in the magic circle he and Solange had drawn round themselves. But actually he was learning that there is a very special pleasure in seeing someone one loves with others present, of sharing a private secret. He stood at the mantelpiece looking at the room and at Solange who lay on the chaise longue in a pale green evening dress with long sleeves which Francis had never seen. Each time she wore something new, it changed her into a new person, a delightful stranger whom he must reconquer in every dress, in every mood.

"All you need is a unicorn," he said out of his contemplation of her.

"What are you talking about, Francis?" she asked, charmed to see him like this, charmed by his slightly formal air, leaning on her mantelpiece in his dark blue suit, playing the host for this evening.

"The lady of the tapestries who was someone's only desire . . ." Where in the whole world is there anything as beautiful as your throat, he thought?

"Darling," she said half laughing, "you really mustn't look at me like that. It frightens me." She could feel her heart beating absurdly where his eyes had rested. Lately she had found their love a real miracle. She had rested on it. She had never imagined that a love affair and especially this love affair (since she was inside it) could be happy. But she knew that it couldn't last, mustn't last, and so there were moments when it all became almost too poignant. It was immensely tiring, as if they were living on air or fire.

"It's time they came," she said sitting up.

"Yes, but it's lovely just waiting here. . . ." He looked around the dear room into which he had stepped long ago to endure her probing questions and finally to raise his eyes to her face. It had been another world, long ago when he was young and unhappy and knew nothing.

When the bell rang sharply, they both jumped, unprepared suddenly to meet the friendly eyes. Francis ran to the door to open it himself, filled with excitement and joy at this meeting of all he held dearest in the world.

After the introductions, when they were seated, and the comfortable silence had arrived and Francis passed the Dubonnet with a serious and responsible air, Fontanes beamed and, including them all in a look, said,

"It's nice to be here, among friends. Let us drink to Solange who makes us happy and makes us feel human again—"

Everything that had been missing in Boston after Persis died is here, Saul thought gratefully: the warmth of Fontanes' greeting at the door when he realized who Saul was, the inquiring affectionate glance Solange gave him and above all Francis' own air of being at peace with himself and the world. His thoughts were interrupted by one of Fontanes' sallies.

"So, Saul, you are in love—"

"Am I?" Saul laughed. "I'm glad to hear it."

"Of course you are. All Americans fall in love with Paris. It's the *coup de foudre*. Can you deny it?" he teased.

"No, I shan't try."

"He just lives at the Bibliothèque Nationale," Francis said. "I can hardly get him out long enough to go exploring."

"Well, I'm not in love with the Bibliothèque Nationale," Saul said, "though it's great fun trying to track something down, provided you have the patience of Job."

"And you have that patience? Extraordinary character—a patient American! Not like this one here," he said giving Francis' shoulder a pat, "this one who wants to turn the world and himself upside down in the first few hours."

"And who does," Solange said gaily with a tender glance at Francis. "And who does!"

"I suppose you've swallowed Bergson whole and are on the lookout for another whale—did you find Bergson digestible?"

So they talked, and what they said did not have very great importance to any of them, but the fact that they were here together seemed to have an importance.

Much later when they had had dinner and sat on at the table finishing a second bottle of champagne, Fontanes, his fierce eyes grown tender, began to talk to the boys seriously about America. Saul realized that he had almost unconsciously assumed the self-deprecatory air that intelligent Americans assume among Europeans, as if he took a certain inferiority for granted, so he was surprised, and almost ashamed of his humility when Fontanes said gently,

"You see, I love the Americans. I always have. It's not like England, complete in itself, sealed to outsiders. No, the American is just man."

"Perhaps," Francis said, "but not the Bostonian American."

"But that's just a tiny little corner," Saul answered quickly. From this small rather dark dining room where the glasses sparkled against the purple velvet curtains, he saw in a new perspective the immense plains of wheat, the isolated bare farms, the rather touching poverty everywhere in spite of television sets and big cars, and every secretary with a mink coat. He realized how deeply he loved his country, and even perhaps Detroit, big and brawling and brassy with young power. They had turned to listen to him, sensing the flare of emotion in his quick answer, waiting for what he would say next. "No, what I feel is the immense possibility, the sense that everything is to be done, all the inward growing, I mean, all the civilizing if you will. It's exciting to be in on that. To know that you are responsible—" and then, embarrassed by their close attention, Saul smiled. "I never knew I felt like that before. It must be the champagne."

"Americans have everything except souls." Francis was lit up with excitement, looking across at Solange now and then with a leap of joy inside him so violent, he could hardly contain himself, so now he felt he must talk wildly, exaggerate everything so as to conceal the one thing which could not be exaggerated.

"But really, Francis," Solange asked, enjoying the argument, "you can't talk about a country as if it were a person—or lump Americans together—isn't it only that a very few people exist in the world anywhere whose 'souls', whose inner life, whatever you want to call it, really come into play, emerge, are tangibly there? Would you say France has a soul?" she asked turning to Fontanes.

"Certainly I would say so. Of course we have betrayed it a million times since Chartres was built, and even then people were betraying it. How restful it must be to live in a country which is still just making its soul not in a country where it is a matter of digging down under layers of filth, centuries of disgusting selfishness and lack of faith."

Out of such anger and self-disgust France has grown to be what it is, Saul thought, enviously—out of such passion—and that is what I miss in America.

"No," Francis broke in, "I think it's not a matter of countries—at least we know that now—but my whole generation is the dispossessed. We start with nothing, whether we're French, German or American. Fontanes can growl about faith because he knows what faith is, faith in France for instance. We never had it. The young Frenchman of our age, Saul, was twenty or so when France collapsed. You and I are pretty cynical about the great American dream. We know too much, that's the trouble, and it's dangerous to know so much when you have no faith. We don't even believe in the goodness of human nature any more

—after the German camps. Most of us have no religion. What is there left?"

"Personal relations," Solange said promptly.

"Yes," Saul interrupted, "but surely good personal relations need a frame, a frame of manners at worst, of belief and standards at best. Where is our frame?"

"There is nothing we can take for granted," Francis said, "don't you see?"

Solange and Fontanes exchanged a glance of understanding, of compassion.

"Take Gide—" Francis went on, "I suppose the root of everything for him was being a Protestant in France, was in breaking away from that frame. We are in the opposite position of searching for a frame, desperately—or if you will, being completely available as Gide would say, we are looking for something that will force us to be responsible. Communism, Catholicism provide it, provide that frame—I don't see anything else that does. What we all want, of course, is a religion. We want to be possessed," he ended savagely, looking down and not at any of the people at the table, as if he were engaged in some bitter battle with himself. "And as it is, we don't even possess ourselves. We are nothing."

"Champagne is a dangerous drink," Fontanes said after a moment, because they all felt the empty space around them and were afraid.

"We'll go into the other room." Solange got up. "Eugénie must be dying to clear the table and get to bed." She slipped an arm through Saul's and led him out, so he had a chance to say, "It's so good for Francis to be able to talk like this. He works everything out by talking, you know, he must express it all—it's wonderful that you are here," he said gently.

"You are wise, Saul," she said warmly. "How are you so wise?"

"No," he shook his head, "it's just that I don't expect so much. Francis makes great demands on life, on himself."

"And on everyone else," she said with a smile.

"You talked about responsibility the other night," Francis said turning to Fontanes, when they were back in the salon and Solange had stretched out on the chaise longue. "But to whom are we responsible? Why?" he asked.

Fontanes lit a cigar and smoked in silence for a moment. He looked majestically rooted and sure of himself, like a great tree. "I think we are responsible quite simply to everyone we meet, even by accident on the street, that we are wholly responsible to each other, in every exchange, even the least important. That may seem a rather indefinite responsibility to you, Francis, but if it were universally accepted, we should have a fairly decent world, it seems to me." For once Fontanes had laid away all his mannerisms. It was quite clear that he was expressing in words the essence of his own life, so the words seemed real, the first real words to be spoken.

"No wonder my father loved you so much." Francis looked up to catch not Fontanes' eye but Solange's because he was moved. "No wonder he envied you."

Fontanes puffed his cigar, ashamed of the tears in his eyes. I am getting old, he thought, my skin is getting so thin that everything touches me. That is getting old.

"Tell me," Francis went on out of his silent exchange

with Solange, "wasn't Pierre Chabrier a man who felt alive only in danger? M. Descharnes at that party said that he hated to think, that he had to force himself to work—"

"And yet," Solange said thoughtfully, "he was driven to it. It possessed him, as you would say, so it can't have been entirely hateful. It was a hunger too—"

"Like the hunger of an unbeliever like me for God." Francis frowned. "How is one to know what is real in oneself?"

"Ah, but the conflict *is* the reality," Solange interrupted quickly. "Don't you see, without it your father would have been an ordinary philosopher, not what he was at all."

"Of course," Fontanes said conclusively.

"What is your conflict?" Francis challenged him with a smile.

And then they all laughed because it was so evident that Fontanes lived in a perpetual state of war with himself and with everyone else on almost every subject.

"I'll tell you a secret," Fontanes said almost shamefacedly, when the laughter had subsided, "my real conflict is the theatre. Come down to a rehearsal and you'll see it played out on a grand scale."

"Could we?" Saul asked eagerly.

"Of course. Why not?"

They talked for a while about the theatre, about the plays they had seen and then Solange, who had been thinking all this while, had to go back to say, "About your father, Francis. I must just say this. I believe it was a question of responsibility—your word, Fontanes—Pierre thought the danger was that men of action are apt to be irresponsible and thinkers incapable of action. He wanted—his hunger, if you will, was—to make a synthesis and in that I suppose he could have been called an existentialist."

"He wanted to give it back to life, that excitement, that sense of wholeness." Francis stood up, carried to his feet by this break-through toward understanding. "I felt it in his relation to me always. There was so much in him that he had no way of giving—it was that—" They all sensed the tension in him and waited as if Francis were at that moment fighting an angel or a devil they couldn't see. It was true, Francis was in the midst of a struggle, was on the brink of finding something out which he desperately needed to know. The conversation of the evening had brought it sharply into focus, what Fontanes said about the American being just man, for instance. And all the last days and nights, especially after making love, he had been pursued by the idea that he must find some way of using the love, the power, the awareness which he suddenly held in his hands.

"And you, Francis," Fontanes asked as if he could read Francis' thoughts, "how are you going to give it all back, you, the dispossessed?"

"Well—" Francis sat down again—"the dispossessed are not looking for glory, I can tell you that. My father had a great hunger for glory, I understand that now. He wanted to possess man himself. That was his hunger."

"And yours?" Fontanes challenged.

Francis laughed as if he were amazed at himself. "It sounds ridiculous after all this. But I think I want to be a teacher." The last was said very quietly and with great conviction. "You see," he went on turning to Fontanes as he might have turned to his father, "what we have left is human relations, as Solange said.

And just because it's all we have, they have to be so good. How shall I say? It seems to me that in America our human relations are poor, undeveloped. We don't ask enough of each other, do we, Saul? We're afraid."

Saul leaned forward. "You have to be something to ask anything. We hardly know yet what we are."

"I want to be as close to the roots of life as I can be, as close to reality in the deepest sense as is possible, never to forget human beings, not theories of human beings, but each person in himself. I guess it sounds crazy." Francis pulled his ear half-humorously like a clown. It was to hide his joy, his immense joy at having at last come out to the place where he could see the meaning of his life.

Solange got up and laid a hand on his shoulder. "It is a real celebration tonight, dear Francis."

"It takes the Americans to make us feel young again, eh Solange?" Fontanes said reaching for her other hand. "I haven't had such a conversation for years."

"I thought it was because we were in France," said Saul, smiling his slow smile.

CHAPTER EIGHT

FRANCIS CAME BACK to Solange much later, long after twelve, when he had said goodnight to Saul at the door of his room, slipped in with the key she had given him and tapped softly at her door. He came back with all of himself, with all his power and love close to the surface, and this deep new joy, and he did not guess yet that she had done now all that she could for him, had opened the door into his real life, had brought him through to the place where he must in the end go on without her. But Solange knew.

It was a strange night for them both. In the dark, in the very closeness of the embrace, Francis sensed that she was detaching herself from him, and because he sensed this, for the first time he was driven to use sex as a weapon. The serpent is always there (Solange knew it well) but he had not yet bitten. Their love-making had been until now pure of poison, the poison of possession, the poison which drives a lover to ask more and more, to demand of sexual passion the one thing it cannot give, the communication of one person to another, the real deep meeting. Over and over again Francis reached out to Solange and forced her to come to him, but by the end of the night they had gone far beyond the place where the sexual act is the inevitable overflowing of love to where it becomes a frightful and exhausting battle which no one wins, which no one can possibly win. And this, if Solange and Francis could have had a child, or come through at the end to the place where a life together begins, might have had its own meaning. But as it was, when the dawn came, they lay apart, empty and exhausted as if love itself had been poured out and was finished.

When they woke at nine, they hardly dared to look at each other for fear of what they might see. And it was strange that it was on this morning that the fates had chosen that Solange be forced to admit the affair to Eugénie. She decided that they would have breakfast in the salon on trays. There, in another room, in the normal sunlight, they might find their way back to themselves.

Eugénie showed no surprise, which was a blessing. No doubt she had suspected all this for some time. But Solange dreaded the time when they would be alone and Eugénie would congratulate her, smile at her, nod her head, as if she had won a prize in a lottery, and not, as she felt, that she had lost something irrevocably.

The whole extraordinary devastating night which seemed now like a journey in itself, had passed almost without words. Now, as they sat opposite each other, wounded, words came into play again.

"Well, little Francis," Solange said, deliberately putting the distance, the years between them, "how does it feel to wake up knowing what you want to be, to do?"

Francis stared at her as if he had never seen her before, with an almost hostile look. He drank his coffee down in one gulp and lit a cigarette. "What happened last night?" he asked her. "Something happened. I think it was my fault." His tone was icy cold and she imagined for a second that he hated her, but then she knew it was not that. It was shame.

It was necessary now to be honest. "There are limits," she said carefully, "perhaps we went beyond the limits."

"It was like rage," he said almost to himself.

"Yes."

He looked at her with a sudden frightful pity which had nothing to do with love—at the dark circles under her eyes, at her pure throat in the loose wrapper she wore, at her hands and strong delicate wrists. And he felt a deep shame as if he had done something monstrous. Before he had always felt as if they were both flowering in the night and the morning had held a particular sane and simple happiness. He had wanted constantly to catch her eye, to exchange a half-amused half-tender glance like a confession, to say over and over, "I love you." Now he hardly dared meet her eyes.

"I have a great deal to learn," he said humbly. "You must forgive me." Until now it had seemed to him that every night brought its new revelation, and that one could go deeper and deeper, touching the heart of a new mystery with each union. Now for the first time he was aware of the tragic undercurrent of all passion that can lead nowhere but back into itself, that cannot in the end be used, be translated back into life, a shared life where love will open again all the doors that this raging desire to possess and to be possessed has closed.

He wanted Alan now, Alan in all the world because Alan must understand all this. Could a woman ever understand it? Had his mother understood it?

"It's all right, Francis," Solange heard herself saying because in the last few minutes she had become his mother, and this one thing which he had known would be fatal and she had known would be fatal, had happened. Either she hated and fought him now, who threatened her in the very quick of her senses, or she became his mother. "One has to learn these things. One has to experience them. I couldn't tell you—at least not until now . . ."

"No," he groaned, a heavy groan. "Can't we go back? Yesterday, the day before, it was so happy—can't we go back?"

"To love, darling, yes," she said quietly, "I love you very much, you know."

He got up and walked up and down restlessly, energy pouring back into him through the very force of his emotion. "I felt all the time as if I was fighting death last night. It was death that was taking you away from me—and I couldn't win, could I? No one can. It was that—"

"What a romantic you are!" She caught his hand and held it a moment in hers very gently. "To think that Pierre and Persis could have produced such a romantic," and she laughed.

"Don't laugh at me," he said very quietly, "I couldn't bear it."

"My dear, sit down." She pulled him down beside her on the chaise longue. "You mustn't be so distressed. It's just life, you know. You want to be human. Well, remember, this is human, all this. We aren't gods, even though we may think so for a little while."

"M. Descharnes said I was a god because I was an American and perfectly free and didn't know what I wanted to do," Francis smiled suddenly, "but he didn't know."

"What are you going to do today?" Solange asked. "I think it would be nice to go to St. Cloud and walk around, look at the trees. Why don't you go back and read or work at your place and have lunch with Saul and then come back for me about four? We'll pull ourselves together and everything will look different by four o'clock, you'll see."

"Will it?" Francis asked eagerly.

And then, Solange said kindly, "You had better tell Saul about us, sometime. I think we can trust Saul."

But when Francis had left and Solange sat, very straight at her desk, writing letters, she no longer felt kind. She realized that she wished above all that he would go away. She dreaded the next weeks. It was not lack of love now, but fear of the future. Until last night they had been friends as well as lovers,—this was what had made her happy all the last days. Now since last night they were at war, however much tenderness might try to conceal this fact. Oh, there would be moments, even hours of truce, but the fire Francis had seen burning the trees was burning too fiercely and already the blackened branches were beginning to show.

The only hope was in withdrawal, gradual withdrawal to some safer region. But this would involve suffering, especially for him. And she could not bear his suffering face, not yet. The thought of it drove her to work and to forget. And yet even when she was hard at work, his voice came back to her, she could hear him saying with such conviction, "It was death taking you from me," and she had not contradicted him. But in her heart she knew that it was life, not death, which was parting them inexorably—and so soon.

By afternoon the sky had clouded over, but having decided to go to St. Cloud they were carried by a kind of inertia into going, even if it rained. Solange wore an old raincoat and took an umbrella. They decided to be extravagant and to take a taxi for once, all the long way past the factories along the Seine and over the bridge, to climb the hill and leave them at last far above the city, in this great formal garden. The atmosphere of the day was their own atmosphere, subdued, gentle, making no demands. They hardly spoke.

And when they were walking along one of the winding paths through the trees, having left the panorama of Paris behind them, Solange invented a game. "How many trees can you name in French, Francis?"

"I think almost all—you see, I used to come here with my father once or twice a year on Sunday afternoons." And as they walked, he amused himself at the way the chain of names remade itself in his mind, a litany of trees.

Later they stood at the center of several paths, looking down the high leafy walls, the perspective which always moved Francis strangely like music, perhaps because this was a thing never seen in America, requiring centuries to come into its perfect form, requiring care and forethought carried on for many generations.

"But why is it so sad here?" he asked slipping an arm through hers for the first time.

"Because you are sad, my friend," she answered, taking his hand and clasping it into hers. It was icy cold.

"Tell me about when you were a child, what you were like,

tell me everything, about your parents, your school," he asked as if this was one way of finding her again. But it was strange how as she talked, he felt lonelier and lonelier, jealous of all the places, people she had known before she knew him, driven on by curiosity to wound himself again and again on all these things they could never share, dreading even her sudden laughter as she told him how she used to climb down the fire escape at her school and run wildly through the streets at night, just to escape, just to be free.

They were walking now across a little wood and came to a clearing where a woman was teaching a group of twenty or thirty small children to play one of the immemorial games which are handed down from generation to generation like the clipped avenues of trees. This game had a song which the children sang in their high reedy voices, interrupting themselves to indulge in spasms of giggles when the time came to choose partners. Then they made a grand tour of the clearing arm in arm. It was beginning to rain.

Solange and Francis stood in the shelter of the trees and watched without speaking, smiling, but at the same time filled with sadness. Yes, why was it all so sad, this summer afternoon with the rain coming, and the grand old park all around them? Francis shook himself deliberately out of this mood, for he was afraid of it, as if he were sinking into wild tears or, worse, some savage irritation against the passive beautiful woman beside him, with her rather vague smile.

"There is something lovely," he said, to say something, "about formal places, open to the public, about ordinary people wandering about framed by the gardens of palaces never planned for their enjoyment. I'm glad we came," he said almost defiantly.

But actually he felt lost here, lost everywhere, feeling his way like a blind man. And so hungry for some gesture from her of real tenderness and love that he could have cried out, "Help me."

"Are you going to be able to afford a car, you and Saul?" she asked having been following her own thoughts, as they moved on, "you really should see some of France, you know."

They walked quickly now as if something was finished, as if there were nothing more here for them, driven on and away by the children and their innocent game upon which they had made no comment to each other.

"We're getting a car next week. I think we may go down to Chartres and the Touraine for a few days," Francis said shortly. He had restrained the impulse to turn on her and ask bitterly, "That's what you want now, isn't it? To get rid of me, to have me go away?" His tiredness was so extreme that he stumbled. It was the tiredness which a pilgrim feels at the beginning of his pilgrimage—for the only place where Francis could imagine laying his head, the only place where he would ever rest again, was, he thought, on her breast, this woman who walked beside him and was not there.

And in the taxi he said, because again he thought of Alan with a sharp sense of recognition, of something like fellowship, "I think Alan may be coming over after all. You know, I've been writing him steadily to tell him that he must. Only he is in the middle of a crucial chapter and won't make up his mind to leave till it is done. He talks now of perhaps getting over by mid-July for three weeks."

"Ah," she sighed, "I would like to meet Alan."

Immediately Francis was sorry that he had spoken. For he saw with extreme clarity that everything now would be a threat, even Alan, to whom Solange would no doubt talk. When Solange slipped an arm through his amicably, he drew away. He would have liked to scream, "Don't touch me."

And then as the taxi bounced along over the bridge, his head fell to her shoulder as if the force of gravity itself pulled him down and all his virility was gone, was falling, just so that he could lay his head on her shoulder like an exhausted child.

Very gently she caressed his cheek, and he knew by the very delicacy of the caress that as deeply as he was moved, so deeply was she withdrawn.

"Hunger," he said in a strange throttled voice. It was the only word he could find.

CHAPTER NINE

AFTER THAT WALK Francis' life changed. It was no longer possible for him and Solange to talk. Every path they chose ended in a barrier or a large sign saying "Detour". Every current ended in a short circuit. They were glad when Saul was there because they were afraid of being alone together. Solange had decreed that for the time being at least they should have a pause and he was not to come to the apartment any more at night. Francis had accepted this decision as wise, but under his silence she felt the pressure and whenever they were alone together she resisted by closing herself up, refusing to catch his eye. It was cruel but she could not help it. Francis' intensity, his brusqueness which had amused her at first, then charmed her and finally conquered her, now irritated her profoundly. In her heart she knew very well that when one begins to want to change a person it means that one has ceased to love them. But still the flowers came, the messages, Francis' voice a little blurred on the phone, veiled in anxiety, demanding her love and her caring, calling her out of herself, trying to break her will, which was not even will but compulsion.

During these days she turned more and more to Saul who had become the only bridge between them, whose presence was almost a necessity, Saul who seemed so poised, so wise, so complete in himself. But above all she longed for them both to get off and to leave her alone. She imagined that she would be able to write to Francis, that they might get back to a real communion by letter.

There were hours when she longed with an almost physical longing for Persis, when the need to talk to someone, to justify herself, to be reassured was overwhelming. At night she lay awake rehearsing her whole life which seemed to her now a failure—at least wherever she had loved most, she had failed, except with André at the end. But that was because then tenderness itself became a passion. How had she been able to forget him, even for a night? The cruelly misshapen body which had come back to her from the German camps. She saw vividly the thick knobs of his knees and elbows, the wrists, the fearful nakedness because it was a nakedness not even of flesh but of bone. After he died she had refused ever to think of this terrifying weakness because it would have been a betrayal of the man himself. But now ridden by guilt, she could think of nothing else. She could hardly see his clear blue eyes and his extraordinary smile. The photograph which Francis hated so much had been taken years before and was of a different person. The person who had come back to her after the war was her secret, and their love itself a secret, the sweetness, the poignant sweetness and radiance of the last months when they had sat for long hours in the garden of the clinic where he was, reading poetry, hardly talking, holding hands, amused and amazed by the simplest things, the flight of a bird close to them or the shadow of a leaf. It had had the taste of eternity. That was what she had wanted to tell Persis and no one else. Not Fontanes who had wept so bitterly the first time he saw André and who would never speak of him after he died because he cared too much. But Persis. Persis would have listened, would have understood.

And André would say to her now, "Be gentle. Be kind. Do all you can to help." Oh why why, do we torture those we love, and ourselves? What is it that brings the furies to the window? Is it because at such times we forget God or love another human being as only God can be loved? Who punishes and why? These were the questions she asked herself through the long nights.

But seeing the Solange of every day, dressed if anything with greater care, wearing a flower he had sent her, always smiling and teasing him, never yielding to a moment of real kindness, how was Francis to know of the torment she was in? How was he to read, when all he knew was that he was being shut out?

It was rather like being ill and having hours of respite from pain. And if he managed to get through an hour without thinking of her, he felt it a triumph. He made himself work, wrote letters to America about a teaching job; he took over the business of renting a car for their trip to Chartres; he tried to read seriously again, but his magic power of concentration was gone. All the façades he built up between himself and his desperate love never entirely hid it. These days were a truce.

"When we come back from Chartres . . ." Francis told himself as if some miracle would happen in the interval.

But when the bell rang at half past nine on the evening before Saul and Francis were to set out, Solange who was fortunately not in bed, but reading in the salon, a cup of tea beside her, knew at once what had happened. She had known that the storm must break sooner or later, now that nothing was natural or sane between her and Francis. Very deliberately she closed her book, looked once round the peace of the room, the big white peonies standing on her desk, breathed in its familiar silence as if to arm herself, and went to the door.

"Come in, Francis," she said coldly. "Come and have some tea."

He sat down, heavily in the chair opposite her and waited while she went to get another cup, hardly aware it seemed, that she had gone out and come back. The fact was that he was so charged with revolt and anguish that even if he had looked at her, which he deliberately did not do, he would not have seen her. She had in the last days ceased to be a person at all, she was simply the point where all his pain converged and became intolerable, a magnet of pain.

"Well?" she asked when the silence had gone on long enough.

He started violently as if woken out of sleep. "Did I say something?"

"No, you've said nothing, that's just it. Is it good, the tea?" she asked as one might speak to a sick child.

"Very good, thank you." Now he was here, for he had stood for more than ten minutes at the door, without the courage to ring the bell, now he had finally arrived, it was becoming more and more difficult to speak. All the speeches, the violent accusing speeches he had designed in his mind when he lay awake at night, had left him. He only wanted to lie down beside her and say nothing and go to sleep.

Solange had been prepared for a scene, would have almost welcomed it as a chance to get things clear, once and for all. But the man who sat opposite her sipping his tea very carefully as if he were afraid of dropping the cup, this man who had not lifted his head since he came in, who sat in front of her like a heavy weight she must somehow lift and send to bed, this stranger she had once loved, now frightened her.

When finally he raised his eyes all she could see was the wound; she was appalled at what she had done. Quickly she spoke, quickly to bind the wound with whatever she could lay her hands on whether it made any sense or not, "My dear, I think we are both exaggerating a little. Aren't we?"

"Are we?" he asked with intense bitterness. Every word now would act like sandpaper on an abrasion, and Solange felt this and resented it. She felt hemmed in.

"Please be sensible, Francis." His tragic look seemed to her almost indecent.

"You're quite a sadist aren't you, in your charming way?" he said putting his cup down on the tray and getting up. For a moment she imagined that he was going to do something violent. But instead he took out the inevitable cigarette and lit it.

"I can't talk to you in this mood," she said quietly. "You know very well that isn't true." She was afraid of the anger she felt rising in her, the anger that rises up when someone is hurt in spite of anything we can do, when someone makes himself our victim of his own will.

But now he sat down beside her and took her two hands in his and held them very hard, so hard that it hurt, but she said nothing. "Let me stay here tonight—please—" he said, letting her go then to lean forward, his head in his hands.

"Very well," she said after a moment, "but first let me try to tell you a few things, Francis."

So great was his relief that in a little while he would be able at last to lie beside her that he hardly listened to what followed. It is possible that in hell one of the torments is a total lack of communication. People talk to each other and do not hear what is said, but only hear themselves talking. So Solange said what she needed to say and he heard what he needed to hear and these were at opposite poles in reality.

"I am forty-five," she said to herself, "and you are twenty-six. That means that my past is almost twice as long as yours, and your future is more than twice as long as mine. This is one terrible difference."

"It's why I love you, don't you see?" he interrupted.

"Dear Francis, it's also why I can't be with you as you want me to be. There's no real meeting because in reality we are moving in opposite directions. It's so strange, but in the last days I have felt the past opening more and more vividly. I've remembered things I thought I had wholly forgotten—and this you have done, and yet every one of these intense memories blurs the present just a little, so in a sense the more deeply you move me—and you must know, little Francis, that I have been deeply moved—the farther I go away from you. Oh dear," she wrung her hands nervously, "I am not saying what I mean. It is too complicated for words. But don't you see, when I hurt you, that too drives me away—" she ended, helplessly. "It's too much. It's too great a weight. I haven't that kind of love to give any more. And if you force me to give it, then I resent you as I did that night . . ."

But what penetrated in all this was the one sentence, "you must know you have moved me deeply." Much later perhaps he would hear the rest when someone else opened in him the buried truths. Now his physical suspense was too great. The present was too imminent, his whole being tensed towards one thing and one only. He lifted her off the chaise longue in his arms and carried her to the bedroom. She was not prepared for this, and when he had laid her on the bed, she turned her mouth away.

"No," she said, "no, you haven't been listening," and then as if to soften the blow, she said matter-of-factly, "Your pajamas are hanging in the bathroom. You get undressed first."

Later he lay with his head on her shoulder, quite still, wide awake, trying to touch the peace he had imagined all these days would be there without question if he could ever again lie down beside her and rest his heavy head where it rested now.

But there was no peace for either of them, only words whirling in their heads, disconnected from the powerful heartbeat each sensed through the other like a machine out of control that goes too fast. Very quietly, as a nurse, as a mother she drew him to her finally. But she had broken the fierce tide in him and now their love-making was only the binding up of wounds, the giving of sleep to a child. If she had not resisted him at the moment of his pure fire, if she could have given her love to him then, all might have been well. They might have come through to the tenderness they both needed so much from the other. As it was, the great wave broke in tears instead of love. Francis fought the sobs in his chest as if each rib were cracking, rending sobs as purely physical as sex itself, and finally the awful shameless tears. Even while he cried, he felt the wall growing higher and higher between them, the wall of her pity, the wall of his impotence. Now he could never take her again without the memory of these tears between them like a curse.

"My darling, don't—don't—" she murmured, "I can't bear it."

"I'm so sorry"—his teeth were chattering—"I can't help it."

Finally she brought him a glass of red wine and made him drink it. They sat beside each other in the bed, sipping from the same glass.

"What was it, Francis? Why?" she said when the dawn finally came and they had found no sleep.

"I don't know. Don't ask me," he said. But what good was pride now? He was stripped down to nothing, to a child, or a monster since he was not a child. In his heart he knew and she knew through the masks of tenderness that whatever they still had, they had lost in that night. For real tenderness, flowing out of real communion had been violated twice, once by her refusal of him, again by his breakdown.

They slept in each other's arms, but they were strangers now.

CHAPTER TEN

JUST BECAUSE he was so tired, numb with tiredness, everything seemed extraordinarily vivid to Francis when he and Saul set out for Chartres the next morning. They started early and there were hardly any cars on the road. It was a still hot day wearing a faint blue haze, and Saul, who was driving, slowed down often to look at a house or a tree, or in Versailles at the immense flight of stone steps which seems to mount straight to the sky. When they passed a grove of poplars set out in straight lines, the light trembling like raindrops on the leaves, he said,

"What I shall miss most when we go back is the trees . . ."

"And the old stones, Saul. Do you realize how angular and sharp everything is in America by comparison—the roofs don't sag, the stones look as if they had just been cut—"

So they talked and looked and rejoiced in this new freedom of having a car. Paris already seemed far away. For Francis the relief from tension, even these few miles of space between him and Solange, acted like a beneficent drug. He relaxed. And as he relaxed he began to remember. He saw in his mind's eye the salon where he and Solange sat the night before, drinking tea, saw it in perspective, the Louis fourteenth chairs, the little silver box, the big bunch of white peonies on the piano, all this atmosphere of quiet elegance, of repose, and in the center of it Solange herself whom he looked at as if she were reflected in a mirror, one step removed from reality. From this brief distance already she was becoming a myth and it was not to be believed that he had ever held her in his arms. Now that it was too late he overflowed with love and homage. He imagined that when they came back, he would be a different person, wiser and calmer and more worthy. Lost in the paths of the imagination, he really believed this and so found peace.

In a little over an hour they came out into the plains of the Beauce, the rich pattern of fields unbroken to the sky, open to the wind so the green rippled now and then and flowed in gentle waves. Some of the fields were shot through with daisies and poppies and bachelors' buttons and looked like stained glass, or the blue-green was interrupted by a square of bright yellow mustard. All this was shining, rich and peaceful. They hardly expected to see suddenly rising above it, alone, the two amazing spires of the cathedral, like magic spears of some heavenly wheat themselves. Then they agreed that it was time to stop and breathe the air, to stand with their feet on the earth for their first look at Chartres.

"I guess a cathedral is the only thing that could stand over a field of wheat and surpass it."

"I don't know," Saul remembered his own country, "the grain elevators are rather grand. It's not the same thing, of course, but they are splendid, you know."

"But surely, Saul, you don't feel compelled to get closer to them. They're static. They're not magnets. Look at those spires, they're magnets." Francis was uplifted by his joy.

"Yes," Saul said reflectively, "and they've been magnets for such a very long time. That's what's moving. We're two out of so many, for so many centuries. It makes one feel part of an endless pilgrimage—" he ended, looking up rather shyly to see how Francis would take this.

"I'm glad we're together," Francis said, "it's nice, isn't it?" and he gave Saul's arm a fraternal squeeze. And then as if everything that touched him deeply must include his love, Francis said, "Sunlight—wind—all this—it should be enough. What more can one want? I think it's finished with Solange," he said getting into the car.

"Oh," Saul drove on slowly.

"In one sense finished. I've really been like a thief trying to steal or borrow someone else's life, something already made. But it's not my life is it, Saul?" he said, turning to his friend. "It's too easy."

"It doesn't seem to have been exactly easy," Saul answered with a smile, and then with a slight thrust, "You're such a romantic, Francis. It all has to be so important."

"It's my life. That's important—at least to me," Francis answered quickly.

"Do you ever think about Ann?" Saul asked, because driving in a car it is possible to ask certain things one couldn't ask anywhere else. The spires had disappeared behind a grove of trees. They were alone again.

"Of course. I write to her every week or so," Francis said briefly. He did not like to think about Ann. It made him uncomfortable.

"Ann is not complicated, subtle, difficult, and twenty years older than you," Saul said, keeping his eyes on the road.

"Ann is like sunlight," Francis said, but at the instant he said it, he remembered her pinched masklike face the day of their disastrous walk, the thin snow falling, the meagre air everything had. And in a flash he realized that something of what Solange had done to him, without meaning to, he had done to Ann.

"What more do you want? As you yourself said just now," Saul pursued pitilessly.

"I suppose I want the moon. I don't want Ann." He was annoyed with Saul for bringing this up just now. He looked out at the old rich country all around them and thought, This is what I want.

Beside Solange Ann seemed like a child. She could not teach him all the things he needed to know, the secret, the strange things, all that gaiety rooted in sadness, all that beauty haunted by eternity just because it could not last. "I suppose I am a romantic —Solange says so too—but is that a crime?"

"Not necessarily. It depends on what you do with it."

"My dear man, one does what one can," Francis said moodily. "One doesn't choose to fall in love. It happens."

"Yes, but one might also say, it happens because of certain choices one has made or not made," Saul said.

At this moment the spires came into view again and they were silent. Now one could see clearly the plain denuded spear and its Gothic sister.

Francis was glad to become absorbed in less personal thoughts. Already his peace of the morning, his lucid peace was troubled. Already he was eager for reassurance, for some word from Solange—she had promised to write. The brief respite from tension was at an end. But now they were drawing near to the town and the cathedral stood over houses not wheat fields, and then disappeared as they began to climb the narrow streets.

When at last they came out into the square and the small magnets had become huge triumphant fingers pointing to the sky, when they had stood craning their necks, when they had parked the car, they instinctively made their way inside, hardly stopping to look at the grave stone saints that greeted them at the door. They hurried in, not prepared, full of curiosity, and separated at once.

The immense height, the glass flowering and blazing above his head, the stillness, this huge shell which was filled every day and night with the presence of God made Francis sit down, at first hardly daring to look around him, as if it were sacrilege to stare rather than to feel. Human will, even the will to understand a piece of architecture, at first seemed to have no place here. Francis put his head in his hands and said the Lord's Prayer because it was the only prayer he knew.

Saul, less vulnerable, more learned, for he had studied the cathedral in photographs, walked slowly around in an ecstasy of recognition, it was all so much more beautiful than he knew, and yet all familiar. The windows were as unlike the colored reproductions as a living face is unlike a photograph. Here the light became music, sounding through the stone like music, repeating itself in long shafts that laid their flowing carpets on the floor.

Saul made no prayers but he was filled to the brim with joy. How Persis would have loved this, he thought, and wondered how many times if ever she had come here. This reminded him to look for Francis, whom he found exactly where he had left him, sitting quite still, lost apparently in his own thoughts.

Then they walked all around the cathedral, once together, without saying a word.

For the first time since the evening at Solange's when he had suddenly known what it was he wanted to do with his life, Francis felt that some answer was given him, that his feet rested on a firm foundation. Here where so many others had found the strength to rededicate themselves to God, after his single and rather mechanically repeated prayer which he made in deference to the place, Francis had felt a new certainty about his vocation. Nothing but the essential person could stand here, or kneel here if he had the strength to kneel. And if Francis prayed at all in the true sense of the word it was his half murmured "Help me to be more human." He did not that first time see Chartres at all, but he was penetrated by the spirit of the place. Even in their slow walk round, he really saw nothing. But he felt everything.

It was strange to come out into the sunlight, to the disgusting smell of gas from the exhaust of an old car, to people talking in what seemed like loud voices, to life not stripped down to its essence, but clothed again in its complicated rather sordid clothes.

"I was thinking about your mother," Saul said as they got back into the car to look for a hotel.

"I wish she knew what I am going to be," Francis said. For the first time since the funeral he saw her clearly as she had been the last days, free from all his own feeling about her, free to be herself for him, and apart from him, as if a cloud had been dispersed between them.

"She was such a teacher herself," Saul said, "I guess that's where you get it from. She taught me everything, I sometimes think, just by being what she was."

"I'm nothing yet," Francis said, "but in there just now, I

thought I knew what I can be. What I want is to make a bridge between all this and what it means, all the old riches, even Solange perhaps, and what we have in America, not to be one thing or the other, as I always thought I would have to be, not to make a choice, but to be what I am, part of both and so perhaps able to make a bridge. We need all this so much, don't we Saul?" he said looking out tenderly at the base of the spire which he could just see from the car. They had stayed where they were, deep in this conversation.

"Yes—and it doesn't need us," Saul said. "That's the point isn't it? Even about Solange. It's all finished here, and we're beginners. On the whole I'd rather be a beginner, you know."

"I would too. It's harder," Francis said quickly.

"You old Puritan," Saul laughed and with that they drove down the hill again to look for a hotel.

For the next days they spent hours buying reproductions, books about Chartres, studying the cathedral together, then going off in the car for picnics in the fields, happy in each other's company. But Francis never again found what he had found the first day. Such collisions happen only once.

A beam of sunlight fell across the page of manuscript Solange was reading and dazzled her eyes. All morning she had held off the thoughts that pressed at the back of her consciousness, she had forced herself to work. But the beam of sunlight bringing another dimension to the flat printed page made her stop reading. She lifted her eyes and looked out at the court which the concierge had just sloshed down with water and which now reflected the sky in pools of blue. She pushed open the window and smelled the fresh summer air. It was going to be a fine day.

But she could not enjoy it, she was too sad. Ever since Francis had left, she had been warding off this sense of oppression, and now it was there. It was useless to go on reading. Her mind registered the words but not the meaning and the thoughts burst through, the thoughts she must face sooner or later. For once she lit a cigarette, pulled out a piece of notepaper from one of the pigeonholes and opened her pen. She had promised to write and now she must do it. She must try to find the words, to tell him—what? Nothing but the precise truth would do, the rational truth. The time for allowing sense or feeling to show the way was past. But even as she formulated one sentence after another and cast it aside, she realized that there was no pinning down such things in words. Her feeling about Francis was confused, multiple, every statement could have been followed by its opposite. And at the bottom of it all lay a fierce resentment. She had built up a small reserve of peace and joy in the last three years. She had managed to remake something of a life, after all. Now all this had been thrown open as if it had no value, thrown open, invaded and sacked. Oh, it was all very well for Francis, he was at the stage in life when he could use everything that came his way. Emotion was the motor force which would drive him to think, which would light up his whole world and where even disaster in the end would only be grist to his mill. He is so masculine, she thought, bitterly. Does he have any idea, I wonder, how different love is to a woman, what a price women pay for love, rooted as it is deep inside them, not a mere release of excess energy, but something to be contained, received, and always involving human responsibility? She did not want to be responsible for Francis. She resented being responsible. She resented the demands he made upon her, resented being forced to give more than she had to give.

No, it was quite impossible to write him the kind of letter he expected. And hating herself for what she knew would be anything but balm she wrote quickly and without stopping.

Only people who are foolishly brave or simply foolish dare to write real letters. The risk is too great. Only the inexperienced believe that people say what they mean in writing. Unfortunately Solange was too wise to be able to write to Francis simply from her heart and Francis was much too inexperienced to read between the lines. He weighed each word as if it were an immortal substance, the exact equivalent of Solange's feeling. As such, it seemed to him incredibly cruel, a deliberate blow.

> "Dear Francis," he read, "you have been gone two days and life begins to have its normal proportions again. I have been getting through a load of manuscripts, and as usual wondering how there can be so many bad writers, so many people who go through the labor of writing and yet have nothing to say. I can't help resenting too the influence of American literature on ours at this moment. Have we been so nourished on violence and hatred in the last years that we cannot taste any more the discreet, the reserved, above all the expression of anything except violence and filth? It's almost as if writers had to vomit out in their books what they can't stomach, get rid of it. Granted that human nature is a mixture but surely it is time we stopped isolating all the elements of brutality and impotence? What do you think? It seems to me that we have talked very little, you and I. Fontanes says to tell you he expects you to be back for the dress rehearsal of his play, as you are probably the only person alive who will see what he sees in it! He has grown very fond of you, you know. That is all the news. It is a lovely day here and I imagine you and Saul (you must look up Péguy's poem on the Pilgrimage to Chartres, by the way) wandering round the dear old town and going into the cathedral at all hours, to see how it changes in all the lights. Don't be sad. I hate it when you are sad. Be happy and know that I am yours, with much affection, Solange."

Unfortunately Saul had gone off by himself to study certain things in the cathedral. Francis reread the letter in their room. He had waited for it with a rising impatience that became like an obsession, hanging round the desk whenever a mail was due, ashamed of his eagerness, filled with love, and a humble sense of inadequacy, wanting to pour over Solange the little source of goodness and patience which he had found in himself the last days—and now, there was nothing in him but a black rage. The image his imagination had been so busy building of her, which had almost concealed the real person, was shattered. This, then, was the real person, incapable of generosity or understanding, "a bitch," he said aloud, with satisfaction. His anger was a protection against the hurt, the awful hurt in this letter. Am I mad? he asked himself. Did I dream all the rest? He remembered her sleeping face, so beautiful in sleep, in the early morning and the wild tenderness he felt when he looked at it. And then he rememberd his tears of that last night and the shame of those tears. How could she?

"With much affection," "Be happy," they were stabbing words. Without a moment's hesitation because his only deep need was to be in communication with her, on any level, and quickly Francis began to write.

"Dear Solange," he wrote, the words tumbling off the pen, "You can imagine the joy with which I saw your handwriting at last. But this letter sounds so far away, so unlike you, I am staggered. What does a word like "happy" mean? How can you expect me to be happy now? Or for a long time to come? How can you use such a word unless you use it only as a weapon and to wound? It's just now that I need your love. I know that something irreparable happened that last night, but don't you see, just because of that, I need some reassurance, some word that comes from your heart? It's all very well to talk about literature, to suggest that we have some conversations when I come back, pleasant intellectual conversations—I can just imagine them. I may be a fool and a child but I am not absolutely without feeling. I love you. I am willing to do almost anything, even to go away, but not for nothing, for a few cold little words. Do all our nights and days and the trees on fire end in your "affection"? Please believe me, yours faithfully—Francis."

Without rereading it, Francis closed the envelope and tore out to the post office. There was no voice inside him to say "Wait", to say "be careful. You can't do this sort of thing to love which is always and at every moment of the day and night endangered, in peril." He did not know. He imagined that one can write letters as one talks, walking up and down in a room, where what remains is a stream of emotion, and not a series of imprinted hieroglyphs which will be deciphered at the other end by the cold clear eye of the intellect. If he did not tell the truth to Solange, to whom could it ever be told? Pride between lovers seemed to him irrelevant. And he was delighted when the letter was safely posted.

CHAPTER ELEVEN

FRANCIS WAS GLAD that he would see Solange for the first time with other people, at the dress rehearsal of Fontanes' play, that he would see her with Fontanes whose presence always seemed beneficent, for she hadn't answered his letter. Saul and he were both eager to get back now. They felt they had been away a long time and Paris seemed like home. Just once they stopped in the open fields to take a last look at the cathedral. Then Francis raced the car forward—how had he been able to stay away six long days?

"I suppose in a way work is a drug," Saul said when they were almost there, driving along the Seine past the Renault factory. "Holidays are dangerous because they show one exactly where one stands, inwardly speaking. I shall be glad to burrow in the library again."

"You've been depressed, haven't you?" Francis asked, for Saul had been rather silent for the last days, but he so rarely wanted to talk about himself, Francis had hesitated to probe.

"Yes," Saul said with a shy laugh, "I suppose you might call it depressed. The real trouble is that I like it too well here—I never want to go back. It worries me."

"I wouldn't worry yet," Francis said in a fatherly tone of voice, "after all, you may feel differently at the end of the year. Meanwhile for heaven's sake enjoy yourself and don't acquire an adopted New England conscience."

"I'll try . . ." but Saul could never express in words his loneliness, his sense of isolation. He would never be able to go back to his own roots, such as they were, to the country club fake Tudor house, to the bridge and business life his father led. He knew that he was intellectually justified in making a complete break, but he was frightened of the vacuum. What he really most wanted was the sort of life Francis had been given by the gods, all that the house on Mt. Vernon Street meant.

"The trouble is that when one isn't working, everything becomes a question without an answer. Do you think it's an American weakness that we get so scared when we have five minutes' leisure?" Francis asked. "I don't think so really," he answered himself as Saul was silent, "I think it's natural to want to be useful, to be part of something. Otherwise what's it all for?" And then as if there were some connection, "this business with Solange for instance—'the expense of spirit in a waste of shame'—why?"

"You won't regret all that in the end," Saul said, glad to think of someone else's problem for a change, "you had to have it."

"I suppose so. At the expense of someone else. Oh Saul," he said angrily, filled with self-disgust, "I'm so tired of being inadequate, of always hurting people. What's wrong with me? You never do."

"I'm so much more passive. I expect so much less. I think it takes a long time to balance your fierce kind of energies. But you'll be a good teacher, Francis, I'm sure of that."

"How can you be? I'm just a mess."

"Very few teachers have your intensity; very few care as much, ask your kind of questions, admit their conflict as honestly as you do. You'll never be just an intellectual," he said with an ironic reference to himself, "you'll always be digging. We could have done with some teachers like you, Francis, you must admit." He chuckled. "God, how bored I was most of the time at school. You won't bore the kids even if you do scare them almost to death!"

Then they laughed and spent the next half hour till they drove up to the pension, remembering the horrors of school, and feeling suddenly emancipated, grown up, in the midst of life. Francis was almost sorry as the pressure of the evening began to make itself felt, the ordeal before him, what it would be like to be plunged back into the atmosphere of Solange. He felt himself with every hour dragged down into the subterranean caves of his conflict. Would it ever be over?

They pushed their way through the crowd in the lobby a good ten minutes before curtain time. Solange was sitting alone, framed by the empty seats one on each side of her. She looked unfamiliar in a new rather extreme hat.

"Hello, Solange." Francis was filled with a sudden quietness of having arrived, of having found her there, waiting, this power she had still of making the whirling kaleidoscope of his thoughts and questions stand still, of giving him peace, as tangibly as her small gloved hand pressed his politely in greeting.

"You're in good time. Fontanes will be pleased." She spoke quickly, a little nervously perhaps, pointing out to Saul various celebrities around them. She hardly turned to Francis.

"You have a new hat," he said accusingly.

"Yes, do you like it?" She smiled as she turned to show it off but it was an impersonal smile, the smile of a model in a hat.

"I suppose so. But what happened to the black hat?" He wanted her always to stay as he remembered her. This new hat with its inference of the lapse of time, disturbed him.

"Oh, that was a spring hat. It's summer now. I wore the other much too long really."

It was absurd to mind so much, and yet this new hat seemed to him ominous as if it were the symbol of an inward change, as if he would literally never see her again as he had seen her.

"You mean you'll never wear it again?" he asked, in spite of himself, in a tone of great anxiety.

And Solange laughed and turned to Saul, to say quite lightly and casually, "Francis is so intense about everything, even a hat."

The words stabbed and Francis was grateful when the lights went down and he could sit beside her in the dark and observe her face as if now that she didn't know she was seen, it might have some message for him. But the only message was his own love which came back to him as if he had never known it before, like a marvelous illness making everything extraordinarily brilliant.

They had to stand around quite a while after the theatre was emptied and all the big cars had rolled away and the knots of people and their loud voices had dispersed. They stood in the empty lobby and waited for Fontanes. Saul had valiantly borne the brunt of the conversation and he and Solange were deep in a discussion of the play, and especially of one actor's performance. "It's a shallow performance," she said bitingly. "He's one of those actors who can express everything, so there's no tension anymore. It just pours out, superficial—a monkey, in fact."

Francis did not like her in this mood. She seemed to him

suddenly French, even the timbre of her voice light and dry, French in a way he had never used the word before, in a derogatory sense. Not once in these long hours had he met her eyes.

But Fontanes was upon them now, and they were carried off on the stream of his affection. "What did you think of it, Francis, dear boy?" he said seizing Francis in his hands and facing him with a bold inquiring glance so he could not escape. "God, he is serious—was it as bad as all that?"

Finally they were seated in the back room of a little restaurant near Les Halles where Fontanes as usual had been welcomed with a mixture of affection and respect, had had to hear all about the children and the Patron's varicose veins, and now devoured an omelette while the others drank burgundy and onion soup. Francis forced himself then to say what he thought of the play. He felt that he was being judged by Solange this evening so he became in spite of himself an actor, overplaying his part, overemphasizing each point as he tore the second act to pieces and overpraised one of the actors. He knew he had made a fool of himself when at last he subsided into silence.

"Bravo!" Fontanes said, laughing with joy. "The boy can talk, eh Solange, when he once begins. Hear, hear! Unfortunately," he smiled slyly, "I think you are dead wrong, but never mind. You are five times as intelligent as the critics, so I shall be lucky if I escape with my skin," he said, suddenly moody again. "The author has gone off with Claire l'Ambre," he said bitterly (She was the leading actress in the play). "Poor boy, the claws of the tigress are in him now, and I could do nothing. It's terrible to be young," he said turning to Francis. "What hell! Thank God, I'm too old to be disturbed by your angelically disdainful air, Solange," he said, enjoying himself hugely. "You didn't like my play, did you? You thought, The old fool has allowed his enthusiasm to run away with him again, for the five thousandth time, but that is the way the good, the beautiful things come about, through the five thousand chances one takes—you wait and see! My little Belgian will write a good play someday, a play that will make his fortune—and someone else's too—because an old fool believed in the beginning," and his eyes blazed.

"My dear, my dear," said Solange, lifting her glass to him, and smiling mischievously, "as a matter of fact I thought the play very good."

"Ah," said Fontanes, equally mischievously, "luckily I didn't know or I couldn't have made my little speech." Then he laughed a rather rough harsh laugh, full of pleasure. "What actors we all are, even little Francis here. I would never have believed it."

"But Francis is a ham actor," said Solange in her mischievous mood, biting as a fox bites for she felt his eyes, the eyes of the hunter on her, asking a question she couldn't answer.

"Don't," Saul said quietly.

"There, you see, Solange," Fontanes said severely, "we have gone too far for these delicate American skins. But they are real friends. They defend each other like Roland and Oliver. I like that. And I must say that Francis is not a ham actor, not at all," he ended, gathering them together in his gigantic smile, forcing the peace, his peace and love upon them, for he sensed the undercurrent of real hostility.

As a matter of fact, Francis was in a daze. The excitement of seeing Solange again, the play itself, and now the wine and all this talk made him feel confused, half angry, half sad, wanting only to get away. When they were out on the street he heard Saul say quite firmly,

"Francis will take you home, Solange." He even found a taxi and opened the door for them. "No, I want to walk a bit and clear my head." He slammed the door shut with a sense of triumph. Now if only Francis will be calm, he thought, if only he will.

"What is this play *you* are directing?" Fontanes asked him. "Come along, I'll walk with you. I'm too excited to sleep. You really shouldn't order people around like that," he said half smiling in the dark, "they may not like it."

"I've never done such a thing before," Saul said, amazed now at his courage. "Only I think it had to be done."

"Yes, all right. Don't tell me," Fontanes said suddenly. To certain things he was so sensitive, this powerful old man who could roar like a bull, that he could not speak of them. He was too fond of Solange not to see that she had behaved strangely all evening, and not perhaps quite kindly, and he minded. They walked on in silence, a little apart, until Fontanes, as if he were forgiving them both, slipped an arm through Saul's and said quite softly and tenderly, "You see, Solange has suffered too much, too much for one person. Sometimes suffering makes people hard. She has seen too much—this second war, her husband who came back from the infernal camps like a ghost, worse, like a living man who has died and still lives. Oh Saul"—the bitterness rose up again and choked the old voice beside him in the night—"what has been done to human beings by human beings! How shall we ever be able to live, to love ever again? I brought Solange back to life. I insisted that she live, but I sometimes wonder what for—she has many masks, has Solange, but under them all, there is a frightful emptiness. Have you seen it?"

"No," Saul answered. "I hardly know her."

"Francis has seen it," Fontanes said sadly. "It's rather like the Medusa, you see," he went on walking a little faster and panting slightly as if he were making an effort, a physical effort to speak, "if you see it, it freezes your soul and here in Europe we have all seen it. Only you Americans have not—"

And then squeezing Saul's arm till it hurt, he went on, "You're both too pure for this old world, too young, too vulnerable. You will be hurt, yes even you, Saul with your wise old Jewish heart full of compassion . . ."

After that, they walked on in silence.

"I could bellow my rage and despair into the night," Fontanes said, but the voice he said it in was tired, tired and old. And Saul knew that he was near to tears.

Another sort of silence bore Francis and Solange through the empty city streets, an interminable journey to them both. Small talk was impossible, and Solange was quite determined not to say anything of importance. Once she pulled her gloved hand away from Francis' open eager one. Once she said, "Ah, the Tuileries, we're nearly there."

"It was good in Chartres," Francis said humbly, "I thought a great deal—about us. Forgive me for my letter," he said, but he knew that he was putting offerings before a goddess of stone.

"There's no forgiving or not forgiving," she said quietly. "But it was fairly devastating, that letter. You know that of course."

"Yes."

And that was all. When they came to 18 Rue de l'Université, she hurried in with hardly a good-bye, leaving Francis to pay the taxi, and to stand alone in the dark street, his heart like an empty pocket.

CHAPTER TWELVE

It was not the letter and Solange knew it wasn't. Without being able to help it, she solicited violence from him: her withdrawal was a violence. Why then? Where was the flaw? For Solange, in spite of all she said, being a woman, would never blame passion for her own failures. She blamed herself bitterly for being unable to serve this passion well, so young, so violent, so immeasurably greater than anything she had now to give it. For I am a desert, she reminded herself, as she undressed, very slowly, flinging her clothes as if they didn't belong to her wherever they might fall in this mood of self-hatred. She knew that to serve passion well, to give what must be given if it is not to become a poison, and wholly destructive, the heart itself must open to the core. This is what the implacable goddess asks, this and no less, no substitute of tenderness, none of the more subtle shades of love, but simply the Absolute. Once, when she had found Francis sitting in the café and had opened her eyes to his deep searching look, she had felt it possible to give what she had imagined she had no longer in her possession, a whole heart, without questions, a self made whole again by his love. Though even then, so long ago, she had been afraid, she had wanted to run away— No, no, she said to herself turning and turning as she tried to go to sleep and forget, love doesn't fail, it is we who fail, riddled with weakness and fear. And in her case, persistent demanding memories which would never leave her wholly free.

All this she saw clearly when she was alone, but the minute Francis was there before her, she felt herself freeze up, become implacable, say things she didn't mean, because when he was there her own conflict became unbearable. She was torn in two. His very presence had become an impossible demand, his suffering an accusation. Worse, she came back always to Persis, to the fact that she was responsible to Persis for all this. And what would Persis say now, with her clear eyes? But even she had not loved Francis well enough. Too much and too little, waking in him a hunger which she wondered now if anyone would ever be able to nourish. If so, she thought, with a flash of real insight, it would be someone with no memories or with memories which he could share, above all someone young, someone whose existence would not always be years and lives apart from his, someone with whom he could use all the rich parts of himself which he could never bring into play with her, real responsibility, fatherliness, and sharing of simple things, a woman who would have something of Saul's selfless and self-respecting quality.

In that long night in which Solange forced herself to face it all, there were hours of tears, the tears of parting, when she knew how deeply in spite of all her revolt he had entered into her, what secret fibres of her being he had taken into his possession. She buried her face in the pillow as if to shut out his dark tense face, so complex and mysterious when in repose, so simple and young when he smiled.

And when the dawn came she had passed forever one frontier. She knew that she would never love anyone again in this way; this part of her life as a woman was finished.

It is a harsh frontier for any woman to pass, and Solange's face bore the marks of the harshness when she got up the next morning. She looked at her face with a horror of growing old, of all the years to come, of the loneliness. And it was not for her to see, in spite of the fine lines round her mouth and eyes, that her face had grown beautiful in the night, as if the soul were a little closer to the surface than it had ever been, and looked out quietly from her tired eyes.

She had made her peace with herself, but to make peace with Francis, to try to help him out onto his real path without her, that would be more difficult, so difficult that she trembled and she was not prepared for Fontanes' phone call at a little after nine.

"Did you make your peace with Francis?" he asked cheerfully.

"My dear, that is really not your business," she answered, suddenly angry. It was rather like having to face an Old Testament Prophet right after breakfast. It wasn't fair.

"Of course it's my business. Pierre's son will always be my business, and you are my business too, so?"

"So, leave me alone, Fontanes. I won't be scolded so early in the morning. Good-bye," and she hung up. For once she would have liked to have the temperament which can relieve itself in a tantrum. If I were Francis now, she thought, half laughing at herself, I would throw this tray on the floor, and that would be that. Instead she called the pension. "May I speak to Monsieur Chabrier?"

"Monsieur Chabrier is out."

"Oh—" her voice must have showed its surprise, or perhaps fear, for the woman at the other end of the wire, added,

"He has gone to meet his stepfather at Le Bourget."

So Alan was arriving today. It was like an answer to a prayer. For she could never never talk to Fontanes about all this, he would simply get into a rage and say things they would both regret. But Alan, surely Alan would understand and help.

Alan would have been touched if he could have imagined that three people were waiting for him as eagerly as if he were a guardian angel flying in that warm summer morning. As it was he felt sleepy and a little sick. It had been a rough trip. But he was touched to see Francis and Saul waving at him at the other side of the Customs'.

"This is wonderful," he said and Francis realized what a change had taken place in their relations without his even having been aware of it, for he was just purely happy to see Alan's familiar rather shy bewildered look. Only, he looks old, he thought, terribly old all of a sudden.

"We have a car, you know," Saul said proudly. "This way, sir. It's not very grand, but I think we can all three fit in."

"I haven't much baggage. I can only stay three weeks."

"But you've escaped—it's marvelous." Francis slipped an arm through his while the porter arranged the bags in the back. "Did you finish the rough draft of the book?"

"More or less."

Francis plunged into the familiar land as if just having Alan here were, in a way, to be home again, and only showed some reserve when Alan said that Ann had driven him to the Boston Airport, "so I have been well taken care of at both ends." They left him at the France et Choiseul where he had stayed years ago, he said, "before I even knew your mother existed, Francis."

"It must have taken some courage for him to come here," Saul said when they were on their way back to the pension. "It won't be easy for him, meeting all your mother's old friends."

"I know. But I think he's beyond all that. He will be glad to see the people who loved my mother not as she was loved in Boston, but passionately—as Solange loved her." Francis would have liked to be somewhere alone with Alan, to have him all to himself, almost to be back in the house on Mt. Vernon Street. So many different parts of his life would be in collision when Alan met Solange. It was disturbing. And without explaining what he meant, he added, "I never foresee anything."

Saul laughed, "And I always foresee everything, that's the difference between us."

It was arranged that they all meet again at Solange's at five. Francis took care to be there fifteen minutes early.

"I'm sorry I was cross, Francis," Solange had been measuring these words all day for their exact weight, their exact honesty, "let's be friends," and she offered her hand.

"Of course," Francis looked away without taking her hand. And then, as if he had really been thinking of something else, "I hope you like Alan. I was terribly glad to see him. But he looks old. You mustn't expect too much—he's aged a lot since Mother died," he said as if he wanted to protect Alan from her gaze, to shelter him.

It was he now who was deliberately setting a distance between them. But then he broke through with his real self as he always would do, "Oh Solange, what days these are, what strange days . . ."

"Yes, my poor friend," she said gently, sitting down on the chaise longue, but without stretching out as if she too were waiting for the long-expected entrance of Alan, and with impatience.

"Is it never going to change, Solange, darling?" He sat down beside her, taking one of her hands in his with such insistent tenderness that she had to pull hers away, in spite of herself, as if it were a plant trying to root itself and she must not allow it to make roots.

"It *has* changed, dear Francis, it has changed. We go on from here," she said gently.

"Where from here? Where?" he asked, getting up and walking up and down as if the room were not large enough to contain him. But just then the doorbell rang, to Solange's infinite relief.

"Answer it, Francis. There they are."

Alan came in with his wonderful air of control and calm and kissed her hand, "How very glad I am to meet you at last, Madame."

"And I you—dear Saul, sit down," she commanded. "Francis will get us something to drink. We've talked so much of you and your coming, that I began to think it could never happen."

"I can assure you, that I thought so too. But suddenly I decided and now I know how right it was. What a Parisian room this is," Alan said, smiling with pleasure, as if he recognized everything. "It's a long way from Boston, isn't it Saul?"

"Yes," said Saul, "except for one room in Boston."

"Persis' drawing room always had the feel of Paris about it," Alan explained as Francis came back with the glasses on a tray.

There was a moment's pause as Francis poured and handed round the glasses, as if this were a slightly formal occasion.

"I think we drink to your mother, Francis," Solange said looking toward Francis with a smile that was meant for him alone. But in turning her head to find him she met Alan's glance for just a second. It was a glance which said plainly, We understand each other.

They drank in silence and set their glasses down. For a moment, each of the people in the room in his way felt at peace. It was as if in that moment Persis had passed through the room with her absent-minded air, to look for a book, or to re-arrange the flowers on the mantelpiece, not the dead Persis, but the very living one their memories recreated. None of them alone could have achieved this recreation, but it was because they were together and their feeling communicated itself, one to another, that it happened.

"She must always have felt at home here," Saul said finally breaking the rather intense silence.

"Yes," Solange said putting her head a little on one side and glancing up at the photograph on the desk, "but I think she was not one of the Americans who becomes more French than the French. She brought us something all her own; she stayed herself. That is why we loved her." Because the atmosphere was right at last, Solange felt able to say what she had never said even to Francis, and she turned to Alan to say it now, "You see, that is why we needed so much to see her—after the war. It was foolish, but for a time I felt everything depended on her coming back, life itself," she said with a shy little laugh as if she were ashamed of confessing so much.

"Yes," Alan said gently, "I know . . ."

"A great many people felt as you do about my mother," Francis said almost coldly, as if to infer that this was not a private matter between Solange and Alan.

"Oh my dear," Solange said quickly, "of course. Do you know why?" she asked them all three.

This was the atmosphere which should have been created at the luncheon after the funeral, the dear comfort of speaking of the dead, of rehearsing their virtues, of sharing one's feeling about them, Saul thought. And it was he who answered, "I think she was really attentive to other people. It sounds so little," he went on apologetically, "but it's really rather rare. We are all so busy paying attention to ourselves, but Mrs. Bradford paid attention in an extraordinary way, without becoming involved, that was what was amazing. She was all there for every one of us—and yet—"

"I suppose you are going to say she was detached," Francis said bitterly. "I am so tired of that word." He alone stood out, refused to be included in their communion, and Saul felt sad.

"Yes," Alan sighed, without self-pity, but it was a deep sigh, "she was wonderfully detached."

"At the end, perhaps," Solange said quickly, "not when she was young, like Francis here."

"Wasn't she?" Francis asked eagerly. "No one ever told me that."

"Of course not. She used to nearly kill herself playing the piano, practising for Monsieur Cortot—if you call that detached."

"But that's not people," Saul said.

"Even about people," Solange said quietly, but she did not go on. She did not want to bring Pierre Chabrier's name into this.

"I think she was never quite detached about you, Francis," she said, glad of a way out, which was also the truth.

"Surely no one can be quite detached when they love," Saul said quickly. He was afraid now. He was afraid because he sensed how many perils there were for them all around Persis' name. If one brought Persis so alive back into a room, it was to bring all the love and all the pain back too. And he was not thinking of himself now. "She was after all, very human. She wasn't a saint, thank heavens." The conviction with which he ended, broke the spell and Alan chuckled.

"I wish I had known my mother," Francis said simply. "I never knew her. She was always a mystery to me."

"Perhaps you were always a mystery to her," Solange said gently, and she would have liked to take his hand and caress it in some angelic way which would not hurt but only heal. Francis, feeling the change in her tone, looked at her shyly and then looked away. His heart turned over inside him.

Alan had been for the last half hour expanding very gently as if he had been wearing clothes a little too tight for him. It was for this he had come, to be able to talk about Persis, to get away from the harsh strait jacket of Boston.

"Francis is a mystery even to himself," he said out of this mood of quiet happiness, without malice.

"You can imagine what it meant to us all to have him come," Solange said warmly, "and Saul, too. We have all felt so much younger lately," and then as if she thought they had had enough of sentiment for one afternoon, Solange changed the subject deliberately, and began to ask Alan questions about his stay, to suggest things he must see, the exhibition at the Orangerie for instance.

"The Impressionists, yes, I must certainly wander in and see that," Alan said with his Bostonian discretion.

"So rich, so alive—in spite of all the horrors we have been through. It's rather wonderful to see that those paintings have not been touched. They just shine softly."

Francis watched as Alan and Solange talked, watched with fascination, for he sensed that they had something in common which he and Solange would never have, a whole lifetime of experience. Their edges were worn smooth, and he envied Alan his urbanity, his calm attentive air which concealed so much. Shall I ever be able to behave like that, learn to come into a room with that air of being at ease at once? That wonderful shining kindness? Shall I ever not be young? he thought desperately.

It was easier finally to go and leave them to have dinner alone, than to stay and watch. Especially as he carried away with him the remembrance of Solange's sudden kindness, of her affection as if it were a good augury for the walk they planned for the next afternoon.

For some reason when Saul and Francis had left, Solange laughed and Alan moved over to a chair near the chaise longue where she now stretched out, relaxed.

"They're terribly young."

"Well," Alan said chuckling, "you've tamed wild Francis. He has learned some manners here, I'm glad to say. Persis would be grateful," he added more seriously. And then as he saw the change in her expression, "I hope he hasn't been a nuisance—or bored you . . ."

"Francis is too dynamic to be a bore," she said quickly. "He disconcerted me at first, I must confess. He's so sudden and violent. What I like is that he believes in his own life; he has some curious belief in himself which is in the long run convincing—

in himself not selfishly but for what he can do in the world, you know. What do you think about this idea he has about teaching, Alan?—may I call you Alan? It seems that we are old friends . . ."

She is very charming, Alan was thinking, and better than that, she has feeling, but it is a pity that Francis is in love with her.

"I'm delighted that he has made a decision." And then he added, with a smile, "Heaven knows whether he will be a good teacher!"

"He won't be a bore anyway," she answered, so happy at last to be able to talk to someone about him that she could hardly stop. "And I think he has a genius for friendship. His friendship with Saul seems to me quite rare, on both sides. Fontanes— Oh, of course you don't know Fontanes but he is an old friend of mine and of the Chabriers—he talks about them as Roland and Oliver," and she laughed. "He has a heroic conception of Francis, dear Fontanes. You know he always believes his friends are geniuses."

Alan poured himself another Dubonnet. "May I?" and then spoke rather thoughtfully and slowly, "You know, I have always felt about Francis that he was perhaps a genius, but if so a genius with no talent, a sort of comet on the loose. He has tremendous power, but so far it has all been used up fighting himself . . ."

"Yes," Solange granted, "he is very good at that."

"It must be hard for you," Alan said gently, "all this—" but he didn't finish the sentence, afraid of having said too much.

"Hard for me, why?" Solange sat up and faced him almost boldly. She had wanted to talk about Francis, about everything, but now she was afraid.

"You must forgive me," Alan said quietly, "but ever since I came into this room I have had the strange sensation that I knew a great deal about you, partly because of course Persis spoke of you, partly, I don't know, a very real sympathy. But," he got up to go, "I think I have said a little too much and now I must be going."

"No, stay," Solange commanded. "I've wanted to talk to you for so long. Don't go yet. Please." And when he had sat down again she went on abruptly, "I've hurt Francis and I shall go on hurting him."

"Probably," Alan said quietly, "but someone had to hurt him to bring him alive. In the end he will be grateful to you, as I'm sure Persis would be."

"Do you think so, really?" she asked, amazed. For the first time she saw a gleam of light in the jungle in which she had been lost. "You see, that's what I thought at first, but I had not measured the years, the war—you see, Alan, I never shall quite live again. That's what I didn't know."

It was extraordinary to be sitting here talking to a perfect stranger in this way, but Solange was too relieved to stop to analyze or think what she was doing. She trusted Alan. She trusted him because of Persis, and now in the last half hour because of himself.

"I shall never quite live again . . . Yes," he repeated without wincing, "that is what Persis told me when I married her, and it was true. And yet, do you think I regret anything?" he asked almost violently for such a self-contained man.

"Ah, but you were both older, wiser—Francis is so violently self-enthralled," she said. "I sometimes think I hardly exist as a person to him. I've become a myth, a projection of all sorts of hungers and needs in him. He doesn't see *me,*" she said, "he doesn't hear what I say. He doesn't know what I am."

"He can't—not yet," Alan said quickly, "Give him time. Wait, my dear—"

"And perhaps," she said half to herself, "I haven't told him enough," thinking of André again, of all Francis didn't know, of all she couldn't tell him, perhaps ever, because he did not want to hear.

"We do what we can," Alan said gently. "But I have thought sometimes that only the wounded eye sees. Francis saw a great deal when his mother died. That was his second great wound. The first was her second marriage," he said impersonally, "but he was too young then."

"And I am the third?" she asked with a wan smile.

"It's not easy to see the young suffer—and yet," Alan said, "where would we be without our suffering? What would we know, you and I, if we know anything at all? I wouldn't worry," he said changing his tone, and becoming rather matter of fact, "Francis will be all right."

"I do care, you know," she said quietly.

"Of course," Alan got up and went over to the desk where Francis had stood so often, to pick up the photograph of Persis and look at it for some moments in silence. "And so did she," he said gravely, "and so did she."

"You have sent the furies away," Solange sighed a deep relieved sigh. "You know for days and days and nights the furies have been at the window."

"Don't be too sure they've gone," Alan said with a chuckle. "They're extraordinarily faithful females, the furies. I know."

CHAPTER THIRTEEN

FRANCIS did not know what he hoped for, except to be included, not to be excluded from Solange's inner world any more, a world which he associated so closely with Paris and all its beauties, that it seemed as if everything he had looked at with such joy was also now closed to him. It had become a huge empty city, full of strangers and where he was a stranger too. The river, the trees, the great open squares were no longer his possession and even his room at the pension was so filled with his own suffering waiting to pounce when he opened the door, that he hated to stay there longer than necessary.

He thought now sometimes of America as a sick person in a strange house thinks of home. He thought of Aunt Alison's apartment strewn with political pamphlets; he thought, in spite of himself, of Ann, who after a period of silence had begun to write him long letters which he stuffed in his pockets and forgot, and then suddenly discovered and read avidly, and he sometimes asked himself if he would not see her with wholly new eyes when he got back, now that he was himself a different, a so much more physically sensitive being. But at a certain point his imagination met a blank wall here. Then he stopped walking and ordered a brandy, and once he bought an American news magazine to see what was happening in the States, but he was so revolted by the style, the apt sneer, the slick condescension of the magazine that he found he couldn't read it. He realized that this is what he would have to fight when he began teaching, this demand for information in easy doses, this unconscious disregard of all values, these ready-made receipts for the well-informed. He was filled with a rage like happiness, a fierce joy to think that he would soon be entering a battle. He felt suddenly as if he must hurry and get to work after all the wasted years.

And yet he knew too that he would not be able to leave unless he could make his peace with Solange, unless he could feel accepted and not wholly rejected. The afternoon before when Alan had been there, he had had a moment of wild hope. She seemed kinder suddenly, almost as she had been at the beginning. This, he knew, had been made possible by Alan's presence. In a flash of a second after Saul and he had left he had seen what jealousy might be, how much worse than anything he had until now had to face in relation to her. For the first time since he and Saul were in Paris they went to a night club and got very drunk.

Now in the early afternoon after a morning of fruitless walking around in circles, seeing nothing, a little dizzy with his hangover, Francis made his way to the Rue de l'Université. What must be controlled was the irrational leap of joy whenever he was going to see her, this eagerness for her face, for her eyes, for her hands as if a glance would nourish him, a handclasp make all well. He knew now that this was not so. He knew it with his mind, knew that almost at once he would become tense with suffering, as he faced the wall she had set up between them, would be filled with rage and a desire to hurt her, to break through. And this was what he must control—the impulse to exaggerate, to underline, to try to crash through by violence, even the violence of words.

Solange too was invoking all her good angels and they met each other rather meekly, but always with the swift glance which asked, "What is he like today?" or, "What does she really think of me and will she be kind?" Nothing was safe or sure any more.

"Let's wander," she said after kissing him on both cheeks like an old friend. "Let's go out and wander about Paris, along the Seine perhaps—is it going to rain?" she asked as he helped her into a light coat. He was relieved that she did not look too beautiful, but a little tired like a pencil drawing, delicate but not dazzling.

"Yes, let's wander—" he answered.

They walked arm in arm, forcing other people off the sidewalk, resting in these moments of peace, like athletes before a contest. They talked of Alan and of Saul, while Francis saw with delight that his Paris had come back to him, and that walking like this with Solange everything had again the intensity of a dream, the vegetable store he had stopped to look at so long ago, a crucifix in an antique shop, the narrow perspective of the street itself, straight and bland against a powerful sky of dark clouds, a street full of human beings again. They stopped to play with a black kitten. They stopped to peer into a secondhand bookstore. And they felt like children escaped from school. The lapse in tension, the lapse in suffering seemed like a reprieve.

When they came out to the Seine, the wind was tearing

through the trees, turning the leaves inside out, and even the river was ruffled.

"What a sky!" Francis said as if he were eating the wind.

"I should have brought my umbrella."

"If it rains we'll go into a café and sit there for hours drinking coffee and brandy," Francis said happily.

But as they walked along, the wind fell suddenly. Until now it had blown the words out of their mouths. Until now they had been absorbed rather happily in the physical effort of walking against the powerful fluid element. Now the silence, the stillness felt strange.

"Ouf," said Solange, "that's a relief. I hate wind."

"Do you? I love it—"

"Ah, but you don't have hair that comes all undone"—she glanced up at his delightful cropped head which was like a small cap of fur, she thought, and which she always wanted to touch—and then rearranged hers and put on her soft felt beret again. They had stopped for this operation. Francis took her elbow very gently and forced her to look at him. For now the time had come when he must be reassured, when he could not wait another minute.

"My love—"

"Your sad love," she said ironically.

But it was enough. A crumb of love is enough, now, he thought without shame. If she only knew. And they walked on, without talking, glad not to talk. Every step they took together was healing, every moment of silence brought them closer one to another.

As they approached Notre Dame the sun broke through and lit up the spire like a spotlight and they stopped to lean on the parapet of a bridge and watch the great clouds moving over, remembering the day when they had come here, when there was so much love that it overflowed—when it was not a matter of crumbs, but oceans.

"It has been a long journey, Solange," Francis said gravely. But though it was a statement and not a question, she was sorry that he had spoken. Sensing his eyes as she had felt them once before like hands on her cheekbones, on her eyelids, Solange drew away from him. The wall was there again. She could have cried out, "I can't help it, don't you see? I can't help it." But the reserved closed mouth, the withdrawn eyes told him nothing. The brilliant sunlight splashing down on the cathedral, turning the river blue for a moment, seemed a mockery.

A little further ahead there was a small crowd gathered on the bridge looking down at something below, and they walked on fast, glad of something to look at now, outside themselves. It was not possible any more to walk arm in arm.

"Perhaps someone has caught a fish," Solange said and giggled, "that would draw a crowd all right."

Now they were at the bridge, they turned in eagerly to see what was happening. Just below them in the underworld where Francis had walked with his joy in his hands, where he had left a package of cigarettes—how long ago?—there on the stone pavement by the river two women were locked in a frightful embrace, the embrace of rage like two beasts. A circle of men, cigarettes hanging out of their mouths like the audience at a cockfight, hands in pockets, stood and watched, some of them smiling, and even here high up on the bridge they could hear the curses. The woman on top picked up the other woman's head by the hair and banged it down on the stone, not once, but five or six times as if she were going to kill her antagonist there and then while the men smoked and stood at ease, their hands in their pockets.

Francis froze to the marrow. It was a violence so complete and disgusting, two human beings stripped down to nothing but bestial need to destroy and punish, that it was fascinating. He did not look at Solange. He dragged her away without a word. They ran across the bridge as if they were running away from some terrible danger, as if they were pursued, but they could not run away from that devastating image.

"I feel quite sick." Solange sank down on a bench behind the cathedral. "Give me a cigarette."

"I should have done something," Francis said, with bitter shame. All the images of the camps, of the atrocities human beings have perpetrated on each other in our time were with them now. And just like this, Francis thought, Germans must have run away when violence was done, because they could not face it. It seemed as if something had been done to his own body. He felt violated, because this image of passionate hatred came dangerously close to being an image of passionate love.

Solange sat very upright, smoking and trying to conceal how upset she was, to conceal it even from herself. But she would have liked to get away from Francis, from everyone, to hide, not to be seen like this—above all not to *see*.

"Francis, go and find a taxi—we'll go home and have some tea," she said calmly. "That was rather a shock, I must say."

The furies are never very far away, that was what Alan had said. She looked up at the flying buttresses and the lovely spire, the beauty no human ugliness could touch, the image of consolation and purity, but it all seemed false, a façade built to hide the horrible truth, which is that the beast is always there just under the surface, however we may sublimate or romanticize. We are all guilty, she thought, all of us. And perhaps it is better to be reminded of it.

Why did this have to happen today, Francis thought, bitterly, why did it have to happen when I was with Solange? he asked himself, not even disturbed by the distance between him and the woman who sat thinking her own thoughts in the other corner of the taxi, because the distance was so absolute. It was as tangible as if a sword had come down out of the sky and cut them apart.

"My poor Francis," she said when they were finally sitting in the familiar room, drinking tea, "you look shaken."

"Not exactly," he said, "I feel guilty and dirty, I don't understand why."

Solange sighed and lifted her chin in the gesture he remembered always with tenderness, and looked off out of the window at the piece of cloudy sky. "None of us can stand very much reality," she said lightly, "we have weak stomachs, Francis, we who pretend to be sensitive."

"It doesn't seem real," he said frowning, "it seems like a nightmare. And yet one was involved—in spite of oneself. It was fascinating really, that is what is so horrible. I saw myself there"—he put down his cup and sat with his hands on his knees—"yes, that was it," he said, clasping his hands and looking at them as if he had never seen them before.

"We are not angels, my poor Francis," she said, and then with an unconscious glance at the photograph of Persis on the desk, "most of us."

"We are monsters," he said filled with self-loathing, above all loathing of his body which at one time he had brought as if it were an offering, with all its powers and glories, to Notre Dame. And then, putting his head in his hands, he said, "Oh, Solange, if we could only be more human, if we only could—"

It's easier perhaps to be an angel," she said gently. "What is difficult is to be this curious mixture of fire and earth and air and water."

"You are so wise," he said looking at her with a look so humble that she lowered her eyes before it, "but I can't be. I'm just torn in pieces," he said getting up quickly because he felt he would begin to cry if he stayed there a moment longer and that was impossible.

Suddenly the door which had been locked inside her opened.

She got up and went to him, took his two hands in hers and said simply, "I'm with you, Francis. You're not alone in this. I'm torn in pieces, too—every day . . ."

For a moment they stood, resting in each other's arms, holding each other's solid human weight as if it were the lightest burden in the world and not the heaviest. And then it was finished.

"You'll be all right, Francis. We both shall. Only it will take time. It's true that it has been a long journey."

CHAPTER FOURTEEN

ALL THROUGH this extraordinary summer Francis had been aware that he reached understanding, a vision of reality one might call it, which he was quite incapable as yet of living. So what was bearable when he had stood close to Solange in those few seconds of real communion become quite unbearable when he got back to his room alone and faced the fact that that moment of arrival had also been the moment of final parting as far as their love was concerned. There would be no going back ever again. The flash of misery burned through him and it was a welcome interruption to be called to the phone by Fontanes.

"It's such a fine day, let's get out of Paris into the country." He had been to Brussels to give a lecture and was just back, it seemed.

When Francis walked into the tiny crowded office, where he had never been, Fontanes was talking on the phone, so he had a chance to look around. It was an amazing little cubbyhole up a steep flight of steps at the back of a small courtyard and it was filled to bursting with the signs of Fontanes' inexhaustible interests and energies. On one desk, letters and telegrams were all mixed up with drawings and lithographs; on another, piles of plays, with notes sticking out of them, autographed books, and everywhere cracked boxes of notes and files, often hanging open with all their orderly confusion visible—orderly because Fontanes always seemed to be able to lay his hand on anything he had to find.

"But, old man, it's simply not possible. You must believe me—no . . . no . . ." Francis felt Fontanes weakening in his decision, for it was obviously more impossible for him to say no than to do the impossible thing he was being asked. "Oh, very well. You can count on me, but it's a terrible bore and I'm furious, goodbye," he said angrily. "There, I'm ready." But before they actually left, Fontanes had called a hospital to see how an old friend was getting on who had been operated on that morning; he had sent three wires to friends in Buenos Aires, Boston and London, and scribbled a note to someone in Paris, and stuffed a batch of mail into his pockets to read later.

"It's time we got away," he said when they were safely in the car, "I could see that I was going to get caught, cornered and then I should have been in for it. Oh my dear, forgive me, there is one thing I must still do. Stop at a florist. No, not that one, he collaborated—further on—there—" and Fontanes extricated his huge body from the little car with a groan, and disappeared into the florist where Francis watched him choosing flowers with the absolute concentration he gave to everything, shaking his head at the carnations, sniffing the roses with his enormous nose, and finally pointing in triumph to a bunch of pale blue larkspur, all the time keeping up a running commentary so the girl in the shop was convulsed with laughter when he left.

"There, now we are off. I had to do that. It's the wife of one of my actors—she's terribly depressed. Of course her husband is a cad, but that is not my fault," he said angrily.

"Your mornings must be rather like God's," Francis teased. "Can you really afford to go away even for an hour? Won't the whole world collapse?"

Fontanes laughed and then looked suddenly mournful as he took out a cigar and puffed at it for a moment in silence. "There is too much suffering in the world, Francis. At times it becomes a shade unbearable. Then one must send flowers and telegrams and letters—I really send them all to myself, you know, to encourage myself. That's the truth," he said as if he were rather surprised and had just discovered it.

"I don't doubt it."

"Listen, old man, you don't have to drive like a lunatic just because everyone else in Paris does." Francis was swerving in and out of the traffic as they crossed the Place de la Concorde, but now he slowed down with a grin.

"That's better. Remember you have a very old frail passenger with you this morning, who may die at any moment, of fright. That would be embarrassing to say the least. And now," said Fontanes with his usual absence of transition from the light to the serious, "what is all this with Solange? You look like a ghost. She is cross and impossible on the phone. Nobody tells me anything and I am enormously curious," he said settling back to puff his cigar as if he expected the truth and nothing less than the truth to be laid before him like a pack of cards.

"Nobody tells you anything because it's none of your business," Francis said shortly.

"Ah! I see—" Fontanes was silent for some minutes. "By the way, where are we going?"

"I thought to Rambouillet—maybe to walk in the forest—have lunch—" Francis said, delighted to change the subject. "What a lovely day!"

"I am not devoting my morning to weather reports," Fontanes said firmly. "How long has this been going on?"

"Well, we've had three good days, I think," Francis answered wickedly. "How was the weather in Brussels?"

"Listen, my dear boy. I am seventy-three years old. My faculties are unimpaired and even if I were blind and deaf I could have seen that you and Solange were having a love affair. So don't be a fool and tell me why in heaven's name you chose her out of all the women in the world? You were bound to make each other unhappy. It was a frightful mistake and I am very cross with you both. At least Solange should have had more sense." This was not the fake anger which Fontanes put on like a clown's dress when he was feeling happy. Francis sensed that he was really concerned.

"If you are really seventy-three years old, which I doubt, you should know better than to ask such questions," Francis said unwilling to be serious as long as possible. He was afraid of Fontanes.

"I don't like it," Fontanes said brusquely.

"Why not?" Francis challenged.

"I expect you'll learn a lot," Fontanes granted a little grimly. "But all this romantic rubbish about suffering helping people, that's what I dislike. Suffering withers and diminishes and destroys. Solange has had enough of it, too much. As for you—

what you need is a little simple pleasure and joy. No, it's all wrong," Fontanes said as if he were giving a judgment in court. "We're becoming a race of masochists and sadists—where is the joy gone?"

"It's gone all right," Francis conceded. "But as for Solange, don't worry about that any more. It's finished between me and Solange."

"All except the suffering, eh?" Fontanes said almost gently, putting a hand on Francis's knee. "You see, Solange needs friends, we all need friends," he said soberly.

"Yes," Francis said drily, "I suppose so."

"If you'd seen her husband when he came back from the camps, you'd know. She's been through too much. That's what I mean about suffering. It kills. You never saw the real Solange, she hides it so carefully. You saw someone you half invented, some marvelous creature of the imagination. She is very good at playing that game. But *she* knows, and that is why I don't understand."

"You see I love her," Francis said, "I love her too much."

"You don't know what the word means," Fontanes answered savagely. "You love yourself, because you are young. You love what you want for yourself. If you loved Solange you would have become her friend, not her lover," he said with fierce honesty. "It's better that I tell you the truth, Francis. And that is the truth."

"I know it is," Francis said, frozen inside his face.

"Very well," said Fontanes inexorably, "then you must go away. You must find your joy, Francis— No, don't be furious—I know that sounds cruel. Take all this with you and learn from it and use it. As long as you stay here, you will just worry it, worry yourself and Solange and make things worse."

"Have you talked to Solange?" Francis said accusingly.

"Of course not. Solange would never speak of such a thing to me. But I was there, you remember, the night when you first spoke of teaching, when you found your joy. And then I saw it go— Oh, that New England face of yours that thinks it can conceal everything and conceals nothing!"

"It was all too short," Francis said bitterly, after a moment. "We never arrived anywhere . . ." he said helplessly.

"Because there was nowhere for you to arrive, as you know very well, Francis. Did it ever occur to you that if Solange had really loved you, you would have broken her heart? You're at the beginning of your life, Francis—don't you see?" His tone now was all impatience, irritation, as if he were unaware of the implications in what he said, that "if Solange had ever loved you" that rang on in Francis's mind.

"You don't know," he said sharply, "you only guess."

"No, I don't know," Fontanes answered equally sharply, "but when I see two exceptional people, suffering uselessly, stupidly and making each other suffer, it enrages me." He puffed violently at his cigar and threw it out of the window.

"Evidently."

"There's too much *real* suffering, Francis," he said more quietly.

"And this isn't real?" Francis accelerated up to 70 out of sheer rage.

"Real the way poetry is, the way music is, perhaps, on that level of your imagination, yes, I'm sure it is real enough. But it isn't your real *life,* Francis, that's what I mean. Any more than it is Solange's—you must admit that . . ." he almost implored.

"You talk as if all this were something one decided rationally, as if one could make a choice, as if one could turn love on and off like a faucet. How can I stop one day, just like that, say to myself, 'Today I shall stop loving Solange,' and go away? I don't understand," Francis said more humbly. With his whole being he resisted Fontanes, resisted the truth. For in his heart he knew that it was the truth, but how could he accept it—yet?

"Oh, I expect you'll be feeding on this for years, my dear Francis," Fontanes said ironically, but with a shade of compassion, "but also you will be living all the time, living your own life. Little by little you will find that it is quite possible to go along, you know. Work, too, can become a passion. And if you are a teacher, a real one, you'll spend your life renouncing, so you may as well learn how it is done," he ended giving Francis a mocking sidelong glance. But Francis looked moodily ahead, seeing nothing except the road, hardly thinking. He felt numb.

"What a narrow range a love affair has, at best," Fontanes went on, for he had not finished what he must say once and for all. "It's an essence. You can't live on an essence."

"It opens the world," Francis said out of his dream.

And Fontanes laughed not his roar of laughter, but a gentle laugh, "My dear, it doesn't open the world. It opens you—and you may imagine in your madness that you are the world, but you soon find out that you're not. Of course," he conceded, "I expect this was just what you needed, you were such a little Puritan when you arrived— But I still don't like it."

"I suppose," Francis said, frowning, "that it is a madness, really."

"And we've had enough suffering, enough madness, all of us, in these last years—slow down," he commanded, "look at those people fishing, there by the poplars, with their picnic basket ready—what peace! That's what we all need, peace, sanity, every-day things—" he said with the conviction of one who obviously has never fished and never had any peace.

"I'll never have any of that," Francis said bitterly.

"Nonsense! You'll marry and have five children. You'll become fearfully domestic and drive around Europe in a huge open car forcing your children to absorb culture. Your passion will be your vegetable garden," and Fontanes leaned back his head and laughed his great clown laugh, of joy and defiance.

"All right," Francis laughed too, it was so incongruous, and yet somewhere inside him he recognized that scene. He knew that he wanted a home, children, a wife, long peaceful years. He knew but he wouldn't admit it. "It's all very well for you to talk, but what about you? That isn't the way you've lived, is it?"

Suddenly Fontanes was serious. He laid a hand gently on Francis' knee. "You see, I couldn't, my dear. My wife died when we had been married just five years. When I was your age it was all finished for me. There couldn't be anyone else."

And then his abnormal sensitivity told him that in some way this purity seemed to Francis like an attack and Fontanes went on, "So I had to make a passion of friendship, had to become a great meddler in other people's affairs, a clown, an actor, what you will. That is why I want it to be different for you, Francis. It's all very well, this sort of life—and mind you, the theatre is a wife for me, in a way—but one gets lonely," he admitted. "It's better not to grow old alone."

"Solange," Francis murmured, his eyes suddenly full of tears.

"No, it's not going to be easy for her either. And later, much later, she'll need you Francis. She'll need you as a friend. Don't forget that in these difficult days, maybe years. In the end, if you really care, if you really love, it won't be wasted, believe me."

They had reached the forest and Francis turned in to a dirt road, glad to go more slowly, to breathe in the green fragrance, to be among the healing old trees again. He was silent, having much to think about. Much later he said humbly, "I'm only just beginning to realize what love might be."

But now they were all enclosed in the green perspectives, they did not talk any more. Fontanes walked ahead, pointing out things that interested him with his stick, a fungus on the end of a fallen trunk, the brilliant green of the moss, and in a small glade a host of foxglove. And Francis followed, listening and accepting it all like a child. If he had come to Europe partly in search of his father, it seemed now that he had found him, the father a real father is too shy ever to be.

CHAPTER FIFTEEN

NOTHING WAS FINISHED; nothing was easier than it had been. The hot summer days opened one after another like heavy-headed roses too heavy for their stems, but Alan out of the wisdom of his heart arranged the days as a prince ruling a small country might arrange them, hired a big car, carried them off to Amiens to see the cathedral, took them to the ballet and the few plays still on, and himself enjoyed Paris like a boy on holiday so that his appreciation, always delicate and subtle, infected them all. And in this atmosphere of summer pleasure, of friendship, of laughter and picnics and late evening suppers, Solange and Francis saw each other more peacefully, as if some sharpness of anguish and anxiety were smoothed down. For Alan's sake they were gay and they discovered that a gaiety which at first had been put on like a mask became a real gaiety. To Francis it seemed like a difficult but entrancing dance and that if he ever stopped dancing his heart would break, but as long as he could follow the intricate steps, he was curiously happy, catching Solange's eye now and then, exchanging a smile, lying awake at night remembering, remembering—nothing was finished. But the great lines were drawn. There was no going back now. And he knew that in these short months he had really come into his own and this was a last coming of age party, after which he would put away his dancing slippers and begin his real life at last.

But the days were flowing by so fast, it was frightening.

He had been offered a temporary job in a small college in Iowa and had accepted it. He would go back with Alan and spend a month getting ready. All this was decided. There was nothing more to do now but make his farewells to every tree and every bridge, to the river and to Notre Dame, to the cafés where he had sat alone or with Solange or with Saul, to the beautiful soft light in the late evenings when the whole city seemed bathed in radiance, to the moon and the stars which would never look the same again, to Solange, to Solange, to Solange.

Francis was enclosed in a brilliant solitariness, wearing a golden armor of resolution. Long before the last day, the last night came, he had gone. The actual parting was strangely formal, the final step in the dance when the partners curtsey and bow and the lights are turned off.

It was Solange, left alone in her salon, in the perfect stillness after all the noise of departure (Fontanes had insisted on going to the airport with Saul to see them off), who sat with her hands abandoned in her lap and wept while the petals of the roses Francis had brought the day before fell one by one, each with a soft heavy plop, as if they too knew that summer was gone forever. But by the time Fontanes came back, she was hard at work.

"My poor friend, you look exhausted. Eugénie will make us a cup of coffee," she said briskly, hoping that by now her face showed no sign of those tears she had wept so selfishly for herself.

"I'm too old," he said with a grimace, sitting down heavily. "It's hard to say good-bye when one is old." And then, as he took out a cigar and cut off the end with a brusque gesture, "I love that boy. He's human, more human than we are with our hard old hearts."

Solange laughed gently, "Is yours hard, Fontanes, really?"

"I embarrassed him by weeping at the airport," Fontanes chuckled. "To a New Englander, you know, it must have seemed quite mad. Oh dear," and he chuckled again, "silly old fool."

"They'll come back, Fontanes. The new world will come back to the old—the old nurse—" she said ironically.

"I wish I could live to be a hundred," Fontanes said dreamily, "to see—"

"The Americans grow up?"

But Fontanes was hardly listening to what she said. "What a dear kind man that Alan Bradford is," he said puffing at his cigar.

But Solange didn't answer. At the moment it seemed to her quite unbearable that life must so often take so much away from those with the greatest gifts, Alan whom Persis had never loved as he needed to be loved, Francis—how little we are able to give each other for all we feel and know. That is what she thought, even as she got up and went out to tell Eugénie to bring coffee in at once.

PART THREE

"Agir librement c'est reprendre possession de soi, c'est se replacer dans la pure durée."

HENRI BERGSON

CHAPTER ONE

FRANCIS SANK almost at once into an apathy of waiting. His head ached. The roar of the motors made conversation impossible and the plane journey, instead of seeming shorter than the way over on the boat, became with every hour interminably long. He slept fitfully, dreaming crowded tiring dreams in which all the images of the last months got mixed up and couldn't be sorted out. Once he turned to Alan, reading a French novel beside him, and shouted, "Department of utter confusion."

At dawn they saw the sunrise over a thick bank of clouds and had breakfast somewhere or other on the ground; places approached by plane have no reality. They are just suddenly there, and as suddenly not there.

It appeared that in two hours they would be landing. Alan treated him kindly as one treats an invalid and didn't try to talk. And Francis was grateful not to be alone just yet; eventually, he supposed, he would come to a great stillness, lie down on the bed in his room and begin to feel. Begin to suffer. For the time being he was grateful to do neither, just to be a body transported with unnatural speed from one world to another. And in the air, in the huge throbbing monster, no world was tangible. He did not have to think or try to make an adjustment. He would just be planted down in two hours in the middle of—what? What would it be—America? Boston? His job? Himself? Ann? He turned away from her name as if it made him feel rather ill even to imagine Ann just now.

The last few moments were taken up with fastening the landing belt and swallowing to keep his ears from hurting. Suddenly a great round piece of earth swung dizzily into view, houses and a flash of river tilted up at them dangerously, then flowed away, as the plane straightened out to circle the field and come in. Francis resisted this landing with his whole being. It seemed quite monstrously inappropriate to be thrown down like this into the middle of life again, unprepared, slightly sick-feeling, his bones tired, his head muzzy. I can't do it, he thought, as if his will had any power here. It's quite impossible.

But just then they hit the land with a terrific hard bump. The hideous low lands around the airport flowed past and they taxied in. Before there was time to appreciate the stillness and relief from vibration, they had to struggle to their feet and get out.

"Of course," Francis said, pushing into a wall of solid heat as he reached the door, "it's August."

"August with a vengeance." Alan was panting slightly when they were finally through the Customs and sitting in the taxi.

Now the hot damp air, filled with dust, blew in but did not dry the film of sweat on their faces. Francis looked out and couldn't believe that there could be such ugliness, the dirty red brick slums, newspapers blowing in the gutters, filth everywhere and the smell of train smoke. Had it always been like this?

"Has this been going on long?" Alan asked the driver and

Francis smiled at the double meaning that question had for him.

"Ain't you seen the papers? We've beat the record. Two straight weeks never below ninety. It's crazy . . ."

They gulped down the hot stale wind in the tunnel and then began to thread their way through the narrow streets of downtown Boston. No sky now. Just buildings, heavy hot stone walls holding the heat in like the walls of an oven. The driver's shirt clung to his back.

Even the elms on Beacon Hill looked wilted, shriveled brown here and there, and more like feather dusters than ever. The house stood in full sun, hurting their eyes as they looked up at the blind windows. Heat bounced off the façade and hit them like a blow.

Inside it smelled stale. Alan and Francis separated to get out of their crumpled clothes and take showers; Francis thought, Eventually I shall be here. I'm not yet, so I don't know what it will be like.

Later they sat in Alan's study, having torn dust-covers off the chairs and made a human island here, bringing up ice from the kitchen to drink tall glasses of iced water. It was too hot for a real drink. Francis had on some dungarees and no shirt or shoes. There was a smell of old tobacco and dust everywhere. It was clearly a house in which no woman had lived for a long time, stale and desolate.

"We'll have to get out of here," Alan said. "The maids won't be back for another week. Mother expects me at Mt. Desert as a matter of fact. What are you thinking of doing?"

"I'll be all right," Francis said without conviction. "I'll go to the movies," he added bitterly, "read *Life* and *Time,* eat in a cafeteria, get the car out of storage . . ." Yes, the car. That meant one sort of escape, escape from the house. He could drive off, find a beach and go for a swim. Some one of the people battling inside him could do this. Another might write a letter.

"There's the job," Alan said, "I expect you'll have to do some work at Widener—that should be cool anyway."

"Yes," Francis said, "do you suppose there's a map around? I'd like to find out where I'm going." But neither of them moved. They felt stranded. The house might have been a desert island.

"I don't suppose anyone's in town," Alan said meditatively; he meant Ann.

"Nope, guess not."

"Maybe that's just as well. It'll take you a while, you know, to get adjusted. I've only been away three weeks but I feel like Rip Van Winkle. Did you remember, Francis, that America was quite so ugly? I think I had forgotten."

"I think I'll go down and play some music," Francis said. If there was a refuge here at all, it would be in the drawing room. "Come down when you feel like eating, Alan. We'll go someplace cool." The American language fitted him again like the dungarees. He tasted the words as if they were food and suddenly liked the taste.

He stripped the dust-cover off his mother's chair and sat down, reached mechanically to the box on the table beside him and by a miracle found an old package of Luckies there. Then he got up and put on a Mozart concerto, lay down on the cool floor and listened. He didn't listen well because his head was still whirling, but at least the music opened a door into a more constructive kind of thinking or feeling. This room of his mother's was restful just because it did not suggest France or America, but only one person and her way of looking at life, a way of life that included the two warring parts of Francis and made a synthesis. His eyes rested absent-mindedly on the shelves of paper-backed books. Montaigne, they read; Pascal; Bergson—this last brought him to his feet. But he sat down again, compelled by the music to be still and to listen. Later he could explore this library. Just because he was very tired and in a state of shock, he was extremely wide awake and aware, listening to more than Mozart, listening in the way a poet listens just before the poem begins to arrive, a lucid passivity that at any moment will turn into an intense kind of inward action.

So now, carried along on the suave poignant music, Francis felt pieces of his life come into focus like the lines of a poem. He measured for the first time consciously the distance he had come since the day of his mother's funeral, compared his revolt, his cold lost self of that time with the sudden warmth about his heart now when he remembered Solange and the sense not of parting but of arrival that had carried him through their good-byes. Work, for Francis, had been outside his real life, and now suddenly he realized that it would be the root of everything. His head was full of ideas—could he start his classes out with Montaigne? Find some way of building up a course that would be an inward experience as well as the exploration of a language? What a lot he would have to do before the middle of September! The rage of learning which often possesses teachers, but rarely students, took hold of him. But still he lay on the floor and waited and listened while the intricate pattern wove itself in and out, that thread that time cannot break. And Francis knew and was grateful that all this was happening to him here in this room not because of any strength in himself, but because at last, being free, he could accept all the human gifts.

What was held in this room was his to take out and put to use in his own life, was his both to receive and to give. He felt a wild excitement when he thought of standing up before those twenty or thirty human faces, those boys and girls to whom, he now knew, he had everything to say, and from whom he also imagined he would have much to learn.

While the last record played, Alan came in and sat down in Persis' chair, very quietly. And when it was over, they stayed in the silence for some minutes until Francis, unable to contain himself any longer, sprang to his feet and said,

"Alan, it's wildly exciting to be alive!"

"Well, well," Alan said, looking with admiration at the glistening expression of Francis' whole body as he stood and stretched and yawned. "You seem to have been rather busy down here."

"I don't know," Francis said. "It's strange being back of course, but here in this room everything seems to be all right. Mozart, all these books, Mother and what she was—what I've been thinking is these things have nothing to do with times or places, with countries, but they have to do with people. One can be a person anywhere, Alan, don't you think?"

"It would seem fairly obvious," Alan grinned.

"Don't laugh at me. I know I'm just finding out what you've always known. It's true Boston looks terribly ugly and there's enough to hate all around us to keep us in a fighting frame of mind, but the thing I've been seeing, Alan, is that we can change it. You see, it's ours—mine, perhaps I should say. I love this country the way you can only love something imperfect—well, I suppose the way people love their children. One is involved. In

Europe I was at home, as I'll never be here, but I was not involved."

"Not involved?" Alan teased.

Francis frowned and rubbed his forehead, "Well—I suppose I was—but I was not responsible, that was it, wasn't it, Alan?"

"Perhaps . . ."

"They all felt responsible for me, I think. But I couldn't be responsible for them. I just took and took from them and had nothing to give. Here I have something to give. I have something to be which is all my own, which no one can take from me. The relief of it, Alan!" And then, as if he were already responsible for Alan, Francis' tone changed and he said, "Come on, I'm inviting you to lunch at the Ritz. Boy, won't a glass of milk taste good!"

"A glass of milk at the Ritz?" And they both laughed.

But as they were going down the stairs, when Francis had changed, he said, "By God, Aunt Susan is not going to have this house. I want it and you in it, Alan. I want to be able to come back here."

He had not even thought of Ann, yet.

CHAPTER TWO

BUT WHEN ALAN had left the next day to go to Mt. Desert and Francis was alone in the house, and knew that he must begin to work in earnest and not just have grand ideas about work, as the long hot day began, and he felt the reaction to the journey and his sleepless night, he did think of Ann. She was at Bar Harbor just a few miles from Alan and Alan would surely be seeing her.

In her last letter she had said, "Come back, Francis. We are just the same, even if you are not. You must come up and have a swim before you leave for the job. I want to hear everything." And much as he wanted to see her and to tell her, he knew she was the one person he could not tell. Only when he thought of Ann did some of his old atmosphere of conflict come back, like an illness. To push it away he wrote to Saul, a long letter all about himself, full of the future, hardly mentioning the past. He brought in bottles of milk and cereal and settled in to work for the day. But work did not come easily, after all. There were so many questions—he knew so little what it would be like in the little college which he had found on the map. What if they had a textbook he would have to follow? He thought he had better write a letter to the head of the department and find out just where he stood. And to do this he must first draw up a plan of what he would like to teach. He lay around most of the morning, making notes on a small pad, taking books out of the library and not putting them back so he was soon sitting in a disorder of records and books and empty milk glasses and cigarette stubs, and his mother's room had ceased to be hers and become his own. After four or five hours of this he went up to his bedroom and lay down.

The house, now he had stopped moving about in it, was very still. And the air weighed heavy in the heat. The heaviness and the stillness kept him on the qui-vive as if they were slightly unnatural and would be broken by some ominous sound, a thunderclap or a large rat scuttling across the floor. The house no longer seemed aware of his presence, and his sense of his own reality, so acute the day before, began to ebb. With the ebbing, the pain he had feared came back. The emptiness. Would he ever see Solange again? But if so, never never again as he had seen her, lost in sleep by his side. How can I go on being what she made me, alone, he asked himself? And then, how long does it take to forget some things? In seven years one has a new skin, they say. In that time does the blood forget? What do people do, he thought? How does one live?

It had been too quick, too sudden, this flowering of all of himself and then the cutting off. And the spirit could move at this speed, but not the body. Memory which comes so much from the senses would have its revenge now, would come back again and again to tear his peace to pieces, whatever his mind knew and had accepted. He lay and tossed through the long hot afternoon and got up at four, thoroughly demoralized. He couldn't face the mess in the drawing room. Where would he go? And then he suddenly remembered Aunt Alison. It was just possible that she was here. The telephone was cut off. The easiest thing to do would be to walk over there. Francis went out in his shirt-sleeves, dungarees and sneakers and wondered, hearing the door snap shut behind him, if he would ever have the courage to go back.

"Why, Francis! I thought you were in Paris!" Aunt Alison opened the door wide. "Too hot to kiss anyone," she said smiling and Francis loved her for being so pleased to see him, "but welcome home. I'm just making some iced tea."

Francis sat down on the old sofa and looked around him enjoying all the familiar things, the piles of political journals, the open checkbook on the mantelpiece, Aunt Alison herself, but she looks tired, he thought.

"The last time you wrote you were all set to study all winter —what brings you back into this inferno?"

"This apartment must be hell. You should have moved over into the big house," and then, delighted with his inspiration, Francis got up and followed her into the tiny kitchen to say, "Why not come over now? You could have the guest room. It's the coolest room in the house."

"Well," she turned to pat his arm gently, "we'll talk about that, Francis. First I want to hear all about you. What on earth happened to bring you home? I don't suppose you gambled away all your money?" she teased.

"No, I got a job, teaching French to advanced students at a little college in Iowa."

"Teaching?" Aunt Alison asked, unable to hide her amazement.

"Yes, anything queer about it?" Francis asked.

"Sit down, dear, and drink some tea. I'm quite exhausted by so many surprises in five minutes—" and she pushed her hair back with a tired gesture—"this heat."

"You should be in Maine," Francis said.

"Well, there's a lot to do getting ready for our winter battles in the legislature—and with everyone else away I thought I'd better stick around and do a little work." It was so like Aunt Alison that Francis smiled.

"I wish you'd surprise *me* sometime by doing something outrageously selfish and luxurious. Do come and stay at the house," Francis said, "I might even learn to cook if you did, or at least empty the ashtrays—it's amazing how messy one lonely man can make a house in twenty-four hours."

"Are you sure it wouldn't be me who emptied the ashtrays?"

"Quite sure," Francis said with his new masterful air, "I want you to come. For my sake," he added cleverly, "if not for your own. It's damned lonely."

And he caught her expression, looking at him, half amazed, half amused. He would have liked to hug her but it was too hot.

"It's wonderful of you to be here," he said, stretching out his legs comfortably and sipping the cool drink. "Alan had to go to his mother's, of course."

"Does it feel very strange—being back?" Aunt Alison asked out of her contemplation of him.

"Yes—no . . ." Francis hesitated, "I don't know yet. Luckily, I have to work like a beaver to get this course ready in a month."

"And it's what you want?" she asked, "what you really want—this job? Coming home?"

"Yes," Francis said, without comment.

"You've grown up Francis." She had reached her conclusion now. "In just two months or a little more. I never will understand about people," she said humbly, "but I can see that that's what has happened and I'm awfully glad about the job. I think you'll be a wonderful teacher?"

"Why?" Francis asked to tease her.

"Well," Aunt Alison's honest face looked troubled, "maybe because you don't seem like one or a person who would wish to teach. You're not the type," she ended, smiling, "and that's a good thing." And then she added, "They'll tease you about your Boston accent, you know—out there."

"I expect so. That won't matter if I can get them interested in the subject, get them mad and thinking—even if they hate me, it won't matter," he said thoughtfully. "The trouble with my education," he went on, "is that I never got really bitten by anything. It was all on the surface. And the trouble in Paris was, you see, that I got so filled up with things, all sorts of things, and there was no way to use it all. I suppose I'll have to go back now and then just to get filled up again, but I know now that it's here I have to live and work. I used to be awfully pretentious, don't you think, Aunt Alison? About being half-French, I mean." It was all pouring out in a jumble.

"Perhaps, a little."

"Go ahead, I can take it." But before she could go on, he said, "I'm glad I am, though. Unadulterated Boston—forgive me, Aunt Alison—might be too much of a good thing."

Then they both laughed.

"And yet," Francis said thoughtfully, "I suppose one is never really at home except where one's anger lies. I never got angry in France, with the French, the way I get angry here—the way they get angry." He was thinking of Fontanes.

"What about Saul?" Aunt Alison asked.

"Oh Saul's staying over. He can do his work there—he's burrowed his way into the Bibliothèque Nationale and I expect he'll be there for years and years. Saul's a real student. It doesn't matter where he is—though I think he'll always be happier over there. You see, Saul can't go home, the way I can. He had to break away so completely from his family, from his background. He can make his roots anywhere now."

"I thought that's what you wanted to do . . ." She couldn't get used to this new Francis. He surprised her every minute.

"I?" Francis laughed, "I was really looking for my family. I was just the opposite."

"And did you find it?"

"I found a father," Francis said quietly, "I guess that's what I needed most."

"Ann will be awfully glad to hear all this," Aunt Alison said without thinking.

"What has Ann got to do with it?" Suddenly Francis was on edge again. His sense of mastery quite gone. Why did everyone always bring Ann up? But of course he knew very well why. "Oh, never mind," he said getting up. "I suppose I'll have to go up to Mt. Desert before I leave, make my fond farewells to Mrs. Bradford and all the tribe."

"It might be a good idea," Aunt Alison said quietly.

"Damn it," Francis said, "nothing's ever all settled, is it? You get one thing settled and then another pops up before you catch your breath. I ran away from Paris," he said half defiantly. "I had to."

"Yes, so I gathered. You know, I didn't really think you'd grown up in two months just by going to the Louvre."

"Is it written all over me?" Francis asked half laughing, "as if I had had the smallpox?"

"It must have been hard to leave," she said gently.

"It would have been harder to stay."

"Yes, I suppose so," said Aunt Alison as if she knew all about it. It was faintly disconcerting to be so well understood having explained nothing. "I wouldn't worry too much about Ann, though. She told me she hoped to God you were having a love affair in Paris." There was some malice in the statement which Alison didn't bother to conceal.

"She did?" Francis sat down again. "Whatever made her say that?"

Alison was suddenly impatient. "You've grown up, Francis, but you still have a lot to learn."

"Yes, Aunt Alison," Francis said like a small boy who answers what is expected of him, but understands not at all. And with that they began to make plans about moving Aunt Alison over to the house. She would go back to her apartment and work every morning, she said. It was impossible for Alison to say how sweet, how unexpected this fellowship with her nephew was. And Francis, with a surplus of love and energy, enjoyed himself taking care of her, even brought her breakfast up one morning, but Aunt Alison couldn't change her habits of austerity in a night and she insisted on getting up. They spent long hours in the kitchen, messing about with the cooking and laughing at how often the steak burned or the water boiled over because neither of them could manage to pay attention at the right time. Francis got the car out and once they took a picnic to the Ipswich beach and lay on the sand all afternoon.

Fontanes' letters began to come, every three or four days, short notes in which exclamation points and dashes conveyed his concern. He was sending over piles of books, he said. He said that Solange had gone away to Brittany for a month; that he had dinner with Saul who looked tired and was working much too hard ("Oh, you Americans! Why are you so pursued by time? You have time and don't even know it.") And always these letters ended, half-laughing, half-serious with references to the job Francis had on his hands. "Don't forget to civilize the barbarians, young barbarian." After a week or so they were answers to Francis' own letters, brushing his doubts away with a snort, needling him, pouring faith into him, asking the best of him. And Francis worked as he had never worked before, found himself sweating with excitement, was amazed at how many ideas he had about education, just from having been more or less educated himself. He was determined to plant the class down in front of something and make them dig to get it. He was never never going to deliver a lecture. And often in the middle of a sentence he would pause and lift his head, wondering what "they" would be like, his first class.

"You're going to expect too much," Aunt Alison said when he talked about his plans, "but there's no harm in that, as long as you don't give in."

Francis looked up then with a vivid smile, "I shall enjoy the fight," he said, "that's why I came home."

It was above all a time of beginnings, of hope, in the middle of the dead waste of August when usually life is as still as a still pond, a time when both Francis and his aunt were preparing themselves for battle. But there was a faint suspense in the air, too, because they both knew that eventually he would have to go to Maine and face the family and Ann. Aunt Alison tactfully refrained from mentioning Ann. Instead she got Francis to talk about Solange, to tell her all he could. Perhaps there was a judgment in the clear gray eyes that listened so well but if so, Aunt Alison never spoke it aloud. When one loves people wholly as she loved Francis it is hard to accept that they must be hurt to grow. And without even being aware of it, he pleaded his side of the affair. She could not guess how violent and difficult, how demanding he had become in those few short weeks of his passion. But in his heart, Francis knew it, and constantly pushed to the back of his consciousness the sense of failure. It was not easy to accept Solange's silence, but he respected it, though he wrote a dozen letters a week and tore them up. In the end he knew there was nothing to say to her yet. He would only be able to write to her when he was free, when he could accept the summer as past. Meanwhile the very continuity of his feeling pushed him on into his work, kept him going at an accelerated pace. He slept badly on those hot nights.

Sometimes Alison heard him creep down the stairs after midnight and go out to walk along the river, so she guessed. He always came back within an hour, though at first she had been anxious. And the next morning he was wide awake at seven and ready to make the breakfast while she was still trying to pull herself up into another of the heavy still days.

"I'm about ready to stop," he said after two weeks. "I think I'll make a break and go to Maine tomorrow."

"Would you like me to come, Francis?" she said with her perfect directness of approach.

"No," Francis grinned, "you see too damn much, Aunt Alison. I'm afraid I'll be self-conscious enough as it is."

To celebrate the last night, he took her to the movies. Now it seemed to them both that these two weeks of peaceful companionship had gone by too fast. It was the end of something. And Francis, as he waved good-bye, thought that Aunt Alison looked very frail and old suddenly. He hated to leave her. But when he was out of the Boston traffic and on the post road, he felt elated at being alone in the car, able to drive fast. Everything on the familiar road looked new and splendid—the roadstands piled with squashes and pumpkins and bottles of cider, the red of the scrubby sumac trees, and the occasional flash of crimson or gold in the maples, even the salt marshes looked like a strange country which he had never seen before, and of which he was taking possession. It's funny how one can love this country, he thought, as a white farm with two elms in front of it came into view and then vanished. It's nothing much really.

CHAPTER THREE

AS HE WENT NORTH the temperature dropped. Next morning after spending a night in a tourist camp, Francis put on a sweater. The change in temperature was such a relief that he felt like a released balloon, ate an enormous breakfast and breathed in the smell of salt air and pine with extravagant pleasure. Forever and ever summer had meant rocks and icy dark blue ocean, pine trees, blueberry bushes hot in the sun, the feel of heavy oars in the palm of his hands, or a tennis racquet. And Ann. Here whatever the winter had been, they always met, invented their own games, were tree-people or Indians, later were kept busy making plans to "escape" the others, to go off with a Shaw play to read and discuss, and some hard-boiled eggs and bread and butter in a paper bag. They had various secret places. But Francis smiled as he remembered that it usually took them so long to find the place that they never seemed to have much time when they got there. They were bitten by mosquitos, or there was a cold fog and they shivered. Why then were these all happy memories, the only really happy ones of his childhood?

On the wave of all this, without stopping to think, Francis

drove up the winding hill road through scrubby trees to Ann's house, an old-fashioned white house surrounded by screened-in porches, where the work of "cutting a view" was never ending—and this was one of the tasks Ann and Francis ran away to escape. When the car stopped with a screech on the gravel, Francis could hear the familiar sound of someone chopping just below him. In a second he was crashing down through the leaves, calling,

"Ann!"

"Francis! Listen darling, for heaven's sake help me get this horrible tree down. Then we can talk. But father insists that it's this one that gets in the way at the dining-room table—do you mind?"

She was so absorbed in the work that she had hardly stopped to look at him. Tall, brown, her fair hair cut short for the summer, she looked wonderfully well, Francis thought, as he silently took the ax from her.

"It's rather mean, poor Francis, when you're just back," she said standing off, a little breathless, while Francis went to work.

"I forgot about ax-handles," he said. "Just now I was remembering the feel of oars and a tennis racquet. But I'd forgotten ax-handles." For some reason it amused him very much. He laughed aloud, swinging the ax too far and almost dropping it.

"Hey, look out!"

"All right, I'll concentrate." How well she remembered that fierce look he had when he was trying to do something he found difficult. Francis always went at everything with too much energy and too little skill. But after a few swings he began to get the rhythm. It wasn't a very big tree and after ten minutes of whacking at it, it suddenly toppled over, so much lighter than one expected, and crashed through the trees.

Francis sat down rubbing the palm of his hand. Ann, leaning against a tree, lit a cigarette.

"It smells good here," he said, leaning back on his elbows. "I'd forgotten how good it smells."

Now that he was here, so simply here, they both took the fact for granted. They were enclosed in the familiar green world, the smell of dead leaves and mushrooms, the damp woodsy smell. The past flowed through the present like a peaceable river.

Ann slipped down beside him. "I never thought you'd come back," she said quietly. "I thought France would be it."

"What?" Francis turned to face her clear wide-open eyes, blue as the sea hidden by the trees, unwavering before his quick shy glance. For now it was he who felt shy. She seemed perfectly at ease.

"Whatever it is you've always been looking for. I suppose, a person," she said matter-of-factly. "It was too queer going on and on never falling in love, you know."

"It was stupid of me," he said. He felt ruffled and disarmed, a little on the defensive. He was annoyed with Ann for being so calm.

At the same time he realized that it was a great relief to be talking to someone who looked on him as an equal, not from some great height, or across an abyss of time and experience, but straight from where she stood and he stood in life. The absence of tension was so vivid that he felt almost shaken by it. And after a moment, he lay down flat on his back, his arms under his head, looking at the sky through the irregular patterns of the leaves. He looked at them very differently from the way he had looked at the leaves in Paris, for here the leaves did not speak, the rocks did not burst open and speak, but everything was just itself, as he remembered it, in the fullness of time. On a fallen log not very far from his head a large frilled orange fungus stood out.

"I learned a lot in Paris, about myself, I mean," he said out of the silence which had been neither long nor short, but like the rocks and leaves, its necessary self. "So much happened in such a short time, Ann, I was almost too alive to live. It became nothing but pain, failure . . ." he hesitated.

"And revelation?" she asked gravely.

"In a way, yes. Yes, it surely was that. How did you know?" He sat up to face her again, to try to read her face, herself, she who seemed to him now to have become so transparent that she was hardly there, so honest that she was a little more than human.

Ann laughed. "By all your letters didn't say—and by what Alan has told me."

"You can believe anything Alan says," Francis said, without a shade of irritation.

"How you've changed!"

"Have I?"

"A year ago you would have been furious at anyone saying anything about you. You would have made a scene." She laughed. "I rather enjoyed your scenes, did you?"

"I expect I did," Francis laughed too, and then winced, remembering how he had battered against Solange's walls in vain.

"I'm sorry it was such hell, Francis. It should have been happy—perhaps not happy, exactly, but gay and delicate and warm like Mozart." She stopped as if she had gone too far.

"No, it was not like that. Solange—" he stopped, unable to go on. Here was the abyss. Here was the moment he had dreaded all the last weeks, the real crisis. He couldn't go on. "I threw it all away by wanting too much," he forced himself to say, as if he were by some immense effort pulling himself up out of a whirlpool.

"You used always to blame other people for things that went wrong, do you remember, Francis?" Ann said gently.

"Did I?" he was startled.

"You were never quite honest."

"I'm not honest now," he said harshly. "I've never known anyone who was except you."

"It's a dangerous trait. It scares most people." He was surprised by the sadness in her voice.

"Let's go down to the sea," Francis said. "I haven't really seen it yet." He got up, restlessly, and lit a cigarette. Things were happening to him which he had not foreseen, which he was in no sense ready for, which horrified him. He felt as if he had no shell at all. Everything here touched him too closely. He was slipping back into the peaceful river of the past, but he realized now that it was a different part of the river, or that in some curious way the past itself had changed because of what had happened to him in France. The emphasis had shifted. It was true that there was peace in it, but peace meant something different now. What he had taken for granted had suddenly become infinitely desirable, and at the same time impossible. Solange who had opened the door for him into his real life, now stood between him and it. The fact of his feeling for her, of her existence, of Ann's knowledge of both, was there, would be there always. He led the way, running down through the wood, as if he were running away from Ann. They were both breathless when they came out onto the road. Here they could walk side by side.

"Alan was afraid that America would seem ugly, too ugly to bear—I must say the drive in from the airport was pretty grim, and Boston looks rather cramped and dusty," Francis said, groping for a transition from the private world where they had been, to this public road where they walked side by side, "but all the way down here I kept looking and looking at everything. It's not beautiful exactly, but it's home, Ann. You don't know what a relief it is to have finally proved that to myself. It makes all the difference. I think it's because I know what I can do here, now. Always before I've been outside looking on and I think I pretended to be French just to evade the real issue."

"But you are partly French. It's true that you are," Ann protested. "That's not an evasion."

"Everyone American is something else too. That's part of being American. The difference is that most people bury that other part and I want to keep it alive, but keep it alive by using it over here. Oh Ann, how beautifully right it all seems now!" Something of the exuberance he had felt in his hour of elation in Boston had come back to him.

"All right, but don't run. I can't keep up with you," Ann said cheerfully. "Of course everyone imagined you would do something brilliant and extraordinary, you know Francis—I think they're a bit miffed that you've turned out to be so normal." She was smiling mischievously at him.

"And unimportant?" he asked with a shade of contempt in his voice.

"Maybe."

"They're another generation, Ann. I've been thinking a great deal about all this. They went out for being stars, you know. One had to do something big in the world. And then it was still possible. We want something different, something simpler. I think that's a good thing. Maybe it's the beginning of being civilized,

Lots of bright boys are leaving New York to go and live in the country and bring up families. The values have changed. In that, my mother was way ahead, you know. She knew that living was the important thing, living and being useful. She wanted people to be themselves."

"And Solange?" Ann asked, deliberately taking the leap and this time for her own sake, not for his.

"Solange wanted that too, Ann," Francis said gravely. "She made it possible for all this to happen, for me to come out into what I can be, but she always knew that she was doing it not for herself, and I didn't know it. I had to try to keep breaking her down, because I was so in love, because I was so much younger, because . . ." he hesitated, and then went on in a low voice, "passion like that shuts everything but itself out. It has to end badly, painfully. She knew that. She said at the very end, 'It's been a long journey,' and she meant—I see it now—so completely and irrevocably meant, that that journey was over, for both of us."

Ann was silent. "It leaves you kind of out on a limb," she said just as they turned off to the rocks, to the sea.

"Yes," Francis said honestly, "it does."

Ann climbed down to the rocks, swiftly on her sure dancing feet and stood very close to the water, her back to him. The wind blew her dress back. Francis did not look at the sea. He looked at her, until he could not see her any more through the inexplicable savage tears.

CHAPTER FOUR

THAT EVENING the whole family gathered on Mrs. Bradford's porch for cocktails to welcome Francis home. He was glad to see them all together, to get it all over, so to speak, at one go. This was very different from Ann's casual, simple taking him for granted, putting him to work chopping down a tree. This was running the gauntlet of all their conjectures about him, having to meet their curious amused glances, for here was the young man who might have been going off forever, back again before the summer was even over. He might, indeed, never have been away. Francis, conscious of what he had to meet, had dressed for the occasion, had put on as much protective coloring as possible. He had on immaculate white flannels, a shirt and tie, and a blazer he unearthed over at Aunt Sukey's. The cupboard in his bedroom was full of old sneakers, dungarees—and, by good luck, this dark blue blazer left over from the summer before, as well as his tennis racquet which he was very glad to find. He had hardly seen the Thorndikes who came in from a sail while he was dressing, and he slipped out to walk over to Mrs. Bradford's, calling out to the house in general, "See you later." So now at a little after six he walked up the path alone so silently on his rubber-soled shoes that they did not see him until he was at the steps.

But he had seen them, had taken them in as completely as the eye of a camera taking a snapshot in the few seconds of his approach. Aunt Sukey was sitting on the porch steps in a low-cut white cotton dress that exhibited her bronzed arms and shoulders to great effect. Her head was thrown back and she was laughing at something her husband had just said as he leaned over with the big silver shaker to pour her cocktail. John Thorndike was standing against the pillar opposite her and Alan and his mother sat in two wicker armchairs near the edge of the porch. For some reason the group made Francis think of family portraits he had seen of the early days of photography. They were carefully posed to look casual, a summer picture.

"You look very charming, all of you," Francis said, amused at their not having noticed him, amused at their startled and self-conscious breaking up of the picture, as if they almost resented his taking them like this, by surprise.

"Heavens, Francis, you walk like a cat!" Aunt Sukey said.

"I saw him," said Mrs. Bradford, "but I didn't wish to spoil the picture. You were taking our picture, weren't you, Francis?"

"Yes, I was, how did you guess?"

"Because you had the photographer's expression, as if people were objects. I'm glad you find us charming," she said lifting her chin with a slightly defiant air.

"It was a family portrait, only I miss Aunt Alison," Francis said and then shook hands with his Uncle Samuel, with John and Alan, reaching Mrs. Bradford last. He kissed her on one cheek and then, forgetting where he was, stooped to kiss the other and bumped into her head.

"I was giving you a French kiss, by mistake," he said and laughed with genuine amusement. "Please forgive me."

"How charmingly effusive of you, Francis," Mrs. Bradford said rubbing her forehead where he had bumped into it.

"It was rather clumsy," but he was still amused and did not hide it. Then, as he accepted a cocktail gratefully from his uncle, Francis turned to Sukey, sat down one step below her and said,

"Aunt Sukey has more chic than any woman I saw in Paris."

"Goodness," Aunt Sukey said, but she was awfully pleased, "how Paris must have deteriorated since the war."

"That was one thing the photographer thought," he said.

"What else did he think?" John asked, rather glumly. "We're a dull lot, as a matter of fact."

"Good photographers keep their thoughts to themselves," Alan said quietly. Francis, feeling the alliance strong between him and Alan, glanced up and almost winked.

"You held the pose beautifully, but what I was really thinking," Francis said, amazed that it could be the truth, "was that I am awfully glad to be home."

"Hear, hear!" Uncle Samuel said heartily.

"Now tell us about Paris," Aunt Sukey commanded, "and stop being polite. Was it all you thought it would be?"

"Yes," Francis said, without comment, "it was."

"And yet you're glad to be home—well, that's very nice of you, Francis," Mrs. Bradford conceded. "I can't say as much for Alan. He's pining already to get away, aren't you, Alan?" She turned her icy blue gaze on her son and waited for the arrow to land.

"It takes a while to settle down again," he said amiably and evasively. "But I expect I shall."

"Francis seems very settled," Mrs. Bradford said.

"He's only passing through on his way to the West, after all," John said. "He knows he can get away."

"It's only for a year, you know," Francis said, "I expect I'll be back eventually. There's the house . . ." he said vaguely.

"Yes," Sukey broke in eagerly, "there's the house. What about the house, Francis? Something will have to be decided. I don't expect Alan wants to keep it on alone."

"I want him to stay if he wants to. I think I shall be living there myself. The continuity seems a good idea," he explained a little stiffly, "I mean, if I can, I'd like to carry on where my mother left off."

"You have changed," Aunt Sukey said, lifting her eyebrows. "I thought you couldn't wait to shake the dust of Boston from your feet. You're not going to turn into a proper Bostonian, after all, Francis—what a disillusion!"

Francis laughed. "I might try to be one. I fear I shouldn't succeed."

"I want to know about Paris," Uncle Samuel said. He was bewildered by Francis and all he had said in the last few minutes. "Did you go to any night clubs? Is it still gay Paree?"

"I guess so," Francis answered kindly, "I didn't see much of that Paris. I spent an awful lot of time just reading and wandering around looking at things. It seemed enough just to be there, really." He wanted to tell them, but he wasn't sure they were interested. Samuel poured more drinks and for a while the conversation drifted and they relaxed. Francis looked out at the sea, dark blue now as the light went, with a clear light band at the horizon. He felt detached and at the same time part of everything. He took them all for granted now. He did not have to fight them any longer. It gave him a feeling of peaceful power. John and he planned a game of tennis for the next morning. There would be a picnic on the rocks over at Aunt Sukey's. The murmur of voices rose and fell around him and he did not have to pay too much attention. There were so many summer evenings held in this one evening; it seemed a distillation of them all.

Of course Mrs. Bradford eventually broke the peace by asking, "You've seen Ann, I suppose?"

"Yes, I spent the morning chopping trees over there," Francis said as casually as possible. But his heart gave a queer leap like a fish who feels the line.

"Ann was convinced that you would never come back," Aunt Sukey said, looking at Francis with a special attentiveness. But it was not an unkind look. It seemed that for this evening they too had laid down their arms and were glad to have him home, to be together in this place of good memories.

"Well," Francis rubbed his forehead, "I didn't know myself. I had to find out a lot of things. But I didn't see how I could be useful in France, really live there. I would always have been an American to whom the French say kindly 'But you are really a European, you know.' " He smiled a slightly disdainful smile. "I didn't have anything to offer them, you see."

"And you feel then that you have a lot to offer us?" Mrs. Bradford asked sweetly.

Francis flushed and felt something of the old anger rise in him for the first time. "You know what I mean," he turned to Alan. "It sounds arrogant, Mrs. Bradford, but I think what I have here is being still close to France. Civilization—or what I mean by civilization—still flows that way, from Europe to us. Oh dear," Francis said, bogging down. Now he had begun he found that he didn't know exactly what he meant. He felt baffled by their polite attention, their sceptical kind glances.

"Just what do you mean by civilization, Francis?" Alan asked. He was afraid now for Francis, afraid the bloom of his new faith and certainty would be brushed off him by these rough hands. He didn't want it to happen yet.

"I knew you'd ask that," Francis flashed a smile at him. "You make me feel as if I were passing an exam. But I'll try to answer," he said thoughtfully, "because I want to know, myself. I suppose it's something about certain human values being more important than knowledge or success or money or social position or any of the things we still believe in like fetishes, that it's day-to-day living, what goes into each moment that counts, and how rich one's capacity for experience is. Most of us Americans seem flat as if there were one dimension missing like primitive painting. It shows in our faces, flat faces," he said bitterly. "I think we're all scared to death of living, really. We're always making up games so we won't have to do it."

It was amazing to be talking like this in the presence of Mrs. Bradford, Uncle Samuel, John, Aunt Sukey. And for a second, Francis regretted bitterly having given so much of himself away, so clumsily. It was nearly dark now and suddenly quite cold.

"I expect you lived in Paris, all right," John said with unexpected envy.

It broke the spell and they all laughed.

"We'll have to go in," Mrs. Bradford said getting up, "or I'll have rheumatism tomorrow. You're young, Francis. And you know a lot but you don't know about rheumatism yet," and to his surprise beckoned Francis to help her up. "There," she said, leaning a hand rather heavily on his arm, "I think we're rather proud of Francis, aren't we, Alan?"

"I think we are," Alan said quietly. It was the first time in many months that he was able to feel fond of his mother.

"So now let's go in to dinner and drink his health. We're having champagne, Francis. You won't see much champagne in the Middle West."

"I bet it's a dry town," Uncle Samuel said. "That would be a joke."

CHAPTER FIVE

IT WAS not quite like anything else in the world, Francis thought, this gathering of Sears and lobsters, of Thorndikes and clams, of Cabots and seaweed, of Endicotts and corn in the ear for the big yearly clambake on the rocks near the Thorndikes'. The preparations were heroic and began early in the morning when he and John went down to a pebbly beach and struggled for hours in icy water to drag up bushels of slippery shining seaweed that tangled round their rubber boots, slid out of their arms and behaved as perversely as only inanimate objects can. Francis slipped and fell twice and was soaked to the skin, but he was enjoying himself hugely. John and he communicated by grunts and groans and occasional laughs and felt a great sense of triumph when they had loaded their plunder into the back of the station wagon. It was a perfect day, just windy enough to be exhilarating and to make the fire welcome, just windy enough to dot the dark blue of the ocean with white frills of foam, but the sun was warm and there would be sheltered places on the rocks, where the frailer members of the party could sit. Uncle Sam meanwhile had been working away at the fire with the hired man for help; Aunt

Susan was making the ice cream herself. They were all having fun in their particular tribal way and Francis was glad to be part of the tribe, for once. It had occurred to him before that his family were at their best down here in Maine.

"Isn't this fun?" Francis bubbled over in his enthusiasm.

"I wonder why," John said cautiously, "we all nearly kill ourselves getting ready for it. Rather childish really—"

"Nonsense," Francis rebuked him, "you know very well that all this mucking about leads in the end, when the last clam is consumed, to a discussion on Honesty or The Atomic Bomb," and he laughed—"what funny people we are!"

John noted the "we" but made no comment.

As a matter of fact Francis had been excited all day. He hadn't seen Ann since that first good talk—she was always out sailing, it seemed. But in his mind's eye he held the image of her standing on the rocks, straight and gold. For the first time he had felt the wildness in her, which was partly the child wildness he knew when they ran off together by themselves to the woods, and partly a grown-up wildness, something free and open, and rather grand, something that spent itself without calculating, that moved about in life with a beautiful unself-conscious thrust. He no longer took Ann for granted. He speculated about her. What had her summer been like?

John and he changed and hurried down to the rocks to help Uncle Sam with the fire, to bring stuff down from the house. By noon the guests had begun to arrive while the heaps of seaweed steamed, concealing their wonderful mess of lobsters and clams and corn; the air was full of sea fragrance. Everyone was dressed in his most cherished old clothes, carrying rugs and, in some cases, folding chairs, and everyone had to say what a perfect day they had, and to breathe in the mixture of pine and salt and clam and seaweed as if it were an intoxicant. This was the last big shindig of the summer, an immemorial tradition, filled with nostalgia and parting; soon these people in their old sweaters and dungarees would be scattered in banks and colleges, so the light did seem particularly beautiful, the sun already stained from gold to a deep rose. It was already autumn light and the sea already an autumn sea, dark blue with an air of containing whales—soon the people would not be here any more.

Francis sat down unobtrusively and watched the gathering of the clan, setting them in perspective against the immensity around and above them. He was waiting for Ann. But as he waited, lifted up by the familiar beauty of it all, he thought also how precarious this ragged human gathering looked close to those cruel immensities, how frail and gay. Voices out here sounded brilliant and a little lonely like the voices of the gulls. Only Mrs. Bradford looked indestructible, firmly planted in her canvas chair and not willing to be done for in any way.

He was sorry to have to get up and help pass out plates, as he had wanted to be able to watch Ann arrive, to have the whole picture of her coming, to run to meet her and to tell her—what? How glad he was that she was there, alive and glowing? To thank her for being herself just now, just today, now he was a stranger come home? The waves poured in and broke on the rocks one after another, but still Ann did not come. Now Uncle Sam was standing like Old Triton with a pitchfork and the great, the crucial moment had arrived. Everyone watched him at this rite and he performed it with due solemnity until Aunt Sukey called out, "We're starving, Sam! Do hurry—"

But Oh, wait for Ann, Francis wanted to say, as the snaky

piles of seaweed were tossed off the fork and the glorious pink lobsters revealed, and everyone sighed with anticipation.

"Has everyone got nutcrackers or rocks or some proper instrument?" Uncle Sam asked like the starter of a race.

And at last Ann, her father and mother and two young men poured down from the clifflike rocks and hallooed.

"Come on down. There may be a few scraps left!" Uncle Sam called cheerily.

"Are we late?" Ann leaped, ahead of the others, as light and sure as an Indian, and almost fell into Francis' arms. She was out of breath, a little startled perhaps to see him there, thrusting a plate into her hands, impatient and commanding.

"I thought you'd never come. Who are those horrible young men you have in tow?"

"Oh you remember Bob—I go sailing with him. He's quite nice. The other one is Andrew, a physicist, terribly learned. He scares me," she confided, and then with a mischievous glance at Francis who was frowning at them, "but he's a wonderful dancer."

Francis thought Andrew was helping Ann's mother down the rocks in a rather filial way. He looked suspiciously at Ann, but didn't have a chance to say anything more as Mrs. Bradford said,

"Come over here, Ann. I want to talk to you." She never raised her voice, but it carried, Francis sometimes thought, to the remotest corners of the earth.

Ann gave Mrs. Bradford her plate while Francis went to fetch another, feeling extremely disgruntled.

"Francis looks depressed," Mrs. Bradford said wickedly.

"Does he?" Ann said in an offhand way, "I thought he

seemed very cheerful." But when she glanced up to find Francis, he was standing with the full plate in his hand as if he had forgotten where he was.

"Over here, absent-minded professor!" she called and met his startled glance. "You'd make a very poor waiter, Francis."

"What have I forgotten?" he asked nervously, "Oh yes—the corn," and he disappeared again, looking flustered.

When he came back he found that Ann had moved over to where Bob, Andrew and John were sitting some distance away on a round flat rock. It was always like this at first, everyone doing as he pleased, and that was what was nice. A gang of the men, Francis noticed, had gone off by themselves; their harsh happy laughter cut across the discreet murmur from Mrs. Bradford's corner, and Francis remembered how annoyed his mother had been by this New England habit of dividing the sexes. "Barbarous," she called it. Almost imperceptibly in the last half hour Francis had become an observer and not a participant; his old critical isolated self was back again. He sat down alone, to eat ravenously and to look rather ostentatiously out to sea. But he was haunted by the voices from Ann's rock, her own so clear and cool sounding like a flute among the boys' voices. Finally he got up, collecting some cans of beer as an excuse to crash in,

"Hey! What about some beer!" But he felt as if the perfectly free gaiety of their group changed with his arrival. After all, they had all the summer pleasures they had shared in common, and all the summer jokes. He made himself busy opening cans, trying to assume the protective coloring of the place. But he knew very well that he was supercharged by his morning excitement and now all the confusion of his feelings. He was not one of them, careless and happy as gods.

He felt that Ann was making an effort to include him when she asked, "What were you thinking about all by yourself, Christopher Columbus?"

Francis colored, "I don't know—nothing, I guess . . ."

"No long, long thoughts?" Andrew teased. "We decided you must be looking across to France—"

"Hell no," Francis said abruptly. Above all he did not want to be reminded now of France. "Tell me about the summer," he said turning to Bob. "That's what I want to know."

"Ann and I got second place in the races, a pure fluke, I must say. The Peabodys upset halfway through the course and held up two other craft. Boy, that was a lucky day! As a matter of fact, Ann's quite a sailor," he said possessively.

"Nonsense, I obey orders, that's all."

"A rare trait in a woman," Bob chuckled.

"I wish she'd obey *my* orders," Andrew said significantly.

"Get me some more of this delicious mess, Andrew, and don't be silly," Ann said. What struck Francis was her atmosphere of ease and—he hesitated, but decided it was the truth—happiness. It was as if she had shed a skin while he was away, had emerged, all whole and shining. The contrast with his own confused state of mind about her was almost too vivid. Francis felt more and more depressed. Happiness, he thought, is the great barrier, like riches, of any sort. The poor can't talk to the rich.

"When do you go back to work?" he asked, wanting to know all about her, wanting, painful as it was, to hold time back, not to have the summer, the week, even the day slip through his fingers.

"I'm thinking of taking a year off, of going to England

maybe, to find out what's going on there. I have an idea that the whole approach to social work must be different in a socialist state," she said turning her whole attention to Francis for the first time, as if she were glad for this chance to talk. "The danger in my profession is that one gets too involved. I really think I was beginning to live out all my peoples' problems instead of my own," she said looking out to sea now, and half smiling. "When you get to that point, you cease to be any good."

"How long have you been working, Ann?" Andrew asked. Francis could see how he admired her and for the first time, it pleased him instead of annoying him. That was because he had divined in the last half hour that she was not the least bit interested in Andrew.

"Four years." She gave a great "Ouf!" and then sighed, "it seems like a lifetime."

"One gets to be as old as the hills," Bob said humorously. "Look at Ann. She talks as if she were a hundred."

"You know why?" Francis sat up, suddenly involved, part of the group at last because he was interested and he saw that their problems were his problems. And these were his people—not thousands of years older, but his own age. It felt good. "I think we work too hard, we Americans. There aren't enough spaces—how many people ever get a chance or take the time to sit around for a couple of months?"

"We manage pretty well here," Bob grinned. "I haven't cracked a book since June."

It was not quite what Francis meant. He caught Ann's eye and they both laughed. Their laugh included Bob, but it said, "Good old Bob." It said, We know. Francis felt the happiness come back as swiftly and completely as if the sun had come out from behind a cloud.

"I want to talk to you," he said, "we haven't even begun."

"Any time," Ann smiled her clear smile, "Bob just told you I'm very obedient."

It was time for Francis to make himself useful but this time he got up gladly because he carried Ann's smile with him as he passed plates of ice cream and cups of coffee around. The rocks were littered now with lobster shells. The time for general conversation had begun and Aunt Sukey was marshalling the scattered groups round the fire. All this was traditional, easy, because it had all been done for many many summers and before they parted they really wanted to know all the things that had not been said more casually.

"Tell us a little bit about your work, Andrew," Aunt Sukey started the ball rolling. It would go from one to another, as the group emerged into amazingly different individuals and individual lives. Andrew gave a modest and charming little speech about atomic physics and this led to an all-out discussion of the bomb in which Mr. Endicott grew perfectly furious and Mrs. Bradford provided the ice of peace finally when things almost got out of hand. Francis, looking around at the group, centered now round the warmth of the fire, wondered if ever before personal lives had been set against such a huge dark background of fear and conflict. They could still talk, they could still communicate, old Mr. Endicott, savage individualist, and Carradine, the mathematician, who was if not a communist, certainly a fellow traveler. Here on the safe American rocks, they could still turn over these matters as matters for speculation.

But for how long? When would the personal world split open and terrible decisions face them and divide them? Francis, more than usually alive to all that was going on around him, looked over at Ann with a constricted heart. It seemed amazing that for three months he had lived entirely on his own sensations and emotions, as if they were important. Now he wanted to plunge into the work ahead. He had not noticed that Ann's turn had come, but now he turned to her eagerly. How often he had changed the subject when she talked about her work! Now he listened as if he had to learn everything all at once, to make up for years of selfish indifference, years when he had been too involved in his own problems even to see Ann for what she was.

She was talking about one of the temporary homes for children brought in by the S.P.C.C. A baby three years old black and blue all over, the last of seven children, the one his mother just couldn't take, talked about it quietly as if these things could be taken almost for granted in the world of poverty, of suffering which had become her everyday world. But under the plain direct sentences, the full charge of her compassion and anger came through. It was almost as if she were accusing the intelligent aware faces around her who knew so much about atomic warfare and its dangers and so little about the starvation and cruelty only a few doors away. And when she had finished, she was suddenly shy. Their attention troubled her. She turned to Francis putting a hand to her heart with a queer little gesture as if she were hurt. "It's hard to stay dispassionate," she said quietly, "I didn't mean to make such a revivalist speech."

"Gee," said Bob, looking at her with a puzzled troubled face as if he were just waking up, "the things we don't know."

Francis said nothing. He was thinking too many things. He was thinking how Ann should have children, children she could bring up herself, not other people's children. He was thinking too, and it stirred him deeply, that this concern, this sense of responsibility, this willingness of the privileged to work for the underprivileged was something peculiarly American. Slowly while John talked about the anti-communist bills that were to come up in the Massachussetts Legislature and why they must be fought, Francis looked at one face after another in the group. There was old Mr. Peabody who had spent his life trying to get the standards of teacher training raised in the public schools. There was Mr. Endicott who gave a dozen scholarships a year to Harvard for boys on the wrong side of the Hill. There were the Cabot twins who had spent this summer and the last in Mexico with a Quaker group building schools. Education and all that it could mean obsessed these people, the American dream obsessed them. They believed in the continual emergence of the uncommon man from every group and perhaps especially from the underprivileged groups. Suddenly Francis felt humble before them, felt how much he had to do to be worthy of them, even a fussy old eccentric like Mr. Endicott. "They're all so terribly good," he had said to Solange, but now he felt it in a different way. And most of all, he felt it about Ann.

He was haunted by that unconscious gesture she had made of putting her hand to her heart, by the way she had turned to him apologetically, by the slightly bitter self-deprecatory twist of her mouth. He knew now clearly why he had come back. But at the same time, knowing it, he thought he knew that it had become impossible. Solange and all that had happened in Paris made it impossible. One doesn't love two people in the same way. Only a heel could do that, could move so fast from one such personal relationship to another.

When Aunt Susan turned to him, Francis looked up, winced, and said quietly, "I'm sorry, Aunt Susan. I don't think I have anything to say, not after all we've been hearing. Maybe next year—then I might have something to bring and not just everything to learn from this group."

"Mercy, Francis, such humility doesn't suit you at all," Mrs. Bradford said sharply. At this moment of honesty, Francis felt cut off. He should have known better, and he looked despairingly at Ann but she had turned away and was looking out to sea, the slight flush of excitement from her speech still in her cheeks.

When the party broke up, though Ann looked for him, Francis seemed to be avoiding her. He made himself very busy picking up litter, though he caught the quick hurt look in her eyes, the elaborate casualness with which she called, "Goodbye then, Francis. Come over before you go."

Intolerable bungler that I am, he told himself bitterly.

CHAPTER SIX

FRANCIS FOUND in the next few days that he could spend an amazing amount of time doing nothing. A little like a sleepwalker, he went down to the grocer and drank Cokes and got the morning papers; he played tennis with John; he lay on the rocks for hours in a half-waking, half-dreaming state of consciousness in which he carried on long dialogues with himself and got nowhere. But the day came when, half asleep on a rock he stood up suddenly and realized that he had only one more week here. He was shaken with loneliness at the very idea. And he walked over to Alan's house as if he were in some great trouble.

Alan was sitting on the front porch reading a French novel. The house was blessedly empty of Mrs. Bradford who had gone out to lunch.

"I hoped you'd come around," Alan said. "I've hardly seen you and I've been thinking that the winter will be strange without you, Francis."

"I know. In some ways I wish I weren't going so far." Francis rubbed his forehead as if he were rubbing out an image behind his eyes. "I feel rather peculiar about leaving, as a matter of fact. It's quite a wrench. I hadn't expected that."

"Well, you've conquered the last bastion—my mother," Alan said smiling his Buddha smile. "That is quite a triumph."

"You're not going to let her persuade you to live in Chestnut Hill, are you, Alan?" Francis asked anxiously. "I'm afraid my walking out on you like this will have made it a bit harder than it might have been."

"What would you think of my trying to get Alison to come over and keep house while you're away? I'm sure she never has proper meals. It might be good for her and it would be a help . . ." Alan said tentatively.

"I was going to suggest it myself, only I didn't quite dare. It's a wonderful idea," Francis said warmly. He was suddenly happy and less lonely than in his moment of panic on the rock. It would be good to know that the two people he was fondest of in the family would be together in the house. For the house had assumed great importance in his mind since he had come back. He felt that it was his house now, and not merely his mother's house. He felt responsible for the kind of life that would be lived there.

"We'll only be holding the fort till you come back with a wife," Alan said, looking out to sea and not at Francis, deliberately.

"Oh, I shall never marry," Francis said quickly.

"Why not?" Alan sat up, startled. It was not the answer he had expected.

"It's become impossible. I can't tell you why." Francis closed up like a clam. He felt very much confused.

They sat, Alan in the wicker armchair, Francis on the steps, and looked out at the sea. The wind in the pines sounded like waves. The air had a tang in it and all around them the stillness, the sun-soaked peace flowed, punctuated by a large bee who flew into a snapdragon by the steps, pushed down the lip of the flower with firm legs, and disappeared. Francis watched it attentively. His mind was a complete blank.

"I know you've been hurt, Francis," Alan said after waiting for Francis to change the subject if he wished, "but I imagined, perhaps wrongly, that you and Solange had come to some sort of understanding before you left. I mean, a good understanding."

"Yes," Francis said slowly, "I think we did."

"And yet you feel so bitter?" Alan probed gently.

"Oh, it's not that, not that at all," Francis said quickly.

"No, I know," Alan said with a flash of intuition. He had observed Francis and Ann at the picnic. "It's Ann. I think you love Ann more than you're able yet to admit, Francis. But sooner or later you'll have to take a leap and recognize it."

"I've been a beast to Ann since we were grown up—and this is the final beastliness," Francis said miserably. He felt literally torn in two.

"What?"

"Feeling like this about her now—just *now*—after all those years, just now, when she knows about Solange and everything. I feel like a monster."

"I see." Alan lit a cigarette and offered Francis one.

"It's everything I ever dreamed of," Francis said quietly, "and I've made it impossible."

"What makes you think that? Perhaps on the contrary you have made it possible—"

"Possible for me, yes. Not for her. She'd always imagine she was a substitute."

"She would if it were true. Ann is a very honest person. Do you think it's true?" Alan asked.

Francis got up and clenched his fist on the porch railing. "I don't know. How can I know?"

"Perhaps I shouldn't say this, Francis, but I think it may help. Solange talked to me about you, you probably guessed that. One of the things she found difficult was the terrific tension you created—she said there was never any peace."

"I was trying to gather the wind. All the time it was all escaping—the wind and all the stars. All the time I was starving, dying of thirst in a desert. I don't understand yet why."

"She opened all your hungers and thirsts—"

"Yes, yes she did," Francis turned to him almost savagely. "That's just what she did. Hunger for work, for religion even —more than anything for the kind of love you can build on, grow with . . ."

"She opened your hunger for Ann, Francis. Admit it," Alan said almost severely. "Passion like that is a great catalyser but it isn't an answer to any hunger, not even the hunger for itself."

Francis stared Alan full in the face as if to read his heart. "If I could only believe you, Alan. If I could only believe you weren't just trying to help—I know you are. But how does one ever know the truth about oneself?"

"By taking a leap. Marriage is rather like religion, Francis, not, if you'll forgive my saying so, the vague aspirations you felt in Paris, but the real thing, the thing that changes one's life—there comes a time when you just have to take a leap in the dark. When you have to believe in the impossible, just in the impossible, and in nothing less than the impossible. You can believe me."

"Do you know, Alan, really?" Francis asked and now it was his turn to sound severe.

"Yes," Alan said, "I know." Then he smiled a mischievous smile, "After all, it's harder to take the leap when you're fifty than when you're twenty-six."

"My mother was not Ann."

"No," Alan said quietly, "your mother could only come a little way to meet me. Ann will come the whole way to meet you, if you give her the chance."

"I don't see why she should, after the way I've behaved. Ann is so straight—what will she do with a person who comes to her by such a devious path?" The more he thought about Ann, the more humble Francis felt.

"I wouldn't underrate Ann's powers of understanding, Francis."

"I'd like a drink," said Francis as if he were just waking up after a week's sleep. "As usual, I'm the world's fool. Do fools always have such wise friends?" he said with a smile so radiant that Alan was almost afraid he might have been wrong. It would be too terrible to think of.

CHAPTER SEVEN

FRANCIS WOKE to the American light, full, blazing sunlight on the walls of his room and realized that it was after nine. He stood at the window shivering, for it was suddenly autumn, and looked out at a dark blue sea. Yes, it was autumn. The Virginia creeper on the garage had turned deep crimson—overnight? He did not remember noticing it before. Now whatever it had been yesterday, every edge was sharply defined, every leaf stood out and for a moment he tried to remember what the Paris light had been beside this—that gentle envelope which turned hard stone transparent and touched everything with mystery. How different was the September morning! One might drink this air, he thought and need no other drink, and yet it was implacable as well as nourishing. It made the most mysterious object look plain and bright. And if it was time one thought of in Paris, the great river of time in which all things and people melted, here each moment was strangely isolated and brilliant, and to be lived as if it were in itself the center of eternity. Francis was thankful that he would not have to speak to a soul this morning—they had all had breakfast long ago.

He got himself a glass of orange juice from the icebox and then went out and sat for half an hour on a rock, looking at the sea. There had been wind in the night, though now the air was absolutely still but the sea remembered the wind as he remembered his long wakeful hours; the waves rolled themselves up one after another and broke in great white towers against the rocks, and the crevasses spilled over and churned with foam. Only far off all was calm, deep dark blue which seemed to absorb rather than reflect the sky. Too rough for sailing, Francis noted. He felt extremely and completely wide awake though he had only had a few hours sleep. And when he got up he thought, Now, now. Very far off there had been a night when he stood at the top of the hill and looked down at the Charles river asleep and when he had asked himself, "Do I exist?" Now, remembering it, he smiled. It was such a sure thing that he existed, all of him, from the hair on his head to the soles of his feet, climbing back up the rocks easily, in sneakers, such a sure thing that instead of answering the question he began to sing in a loud happy voice, "What shall we do with the lazy sailor? What shall we do with the lazy sailor? What shall we do with the lazy sailor, early in the morning?" He was answered by the derisive screams of the gulls. But what a plain grand day it was, this day in a life, this one day!

He found her where he wanted to find her, down in the wood, chopping again. He took the ax from her without a word and this time went at it with skill and competence. When the tree fell, he said, "There."

"Hello," she said then, "where have you come from all of a sudden?"

"Ann," she was standing just above him leaning against a

birch tree. If he had never seen her before he saw her now, every line sharp as he had seen the leaves and the sea when he woke up, and seeing her, he found no word to say except her name. So, very quietly as if every moment counted, he took a cigarette and offered her one and lighted them both, carefully.

"Did you say something?" she asked lightly.

It's now, he told himself, now. But still the leap was there to be made and he could not quite make it. She was not going to help him. Perhaps even she didn't know what he had come to ask.

"Oh Ann," he sat down on the leaves and the moss, "Ann."

But she didn't sit down beside him. She stayed where she was.

"It's a grand day," she said, looking off through the trees to a tiny glimpse of the sea.

"Ann," he said again, and then as she didn't answer, he went on to say anything, "I've hardly seen you all week."

"I've been busy sailing—what have you been doing?"

"Thinking—about you," he said with a funny cracked voice. "Sit down. I can't talk to you like that. You're too far away."

Obediently she sat down, her arms curled round her knees. But now Francis was perfectly silent. All around him the little sounds went on, a leaf falling, a chipmunk flashing past, a jay calling loudly to another jay. But inside Francis there was only an immense stillness. She was about three feet away from him and he could see the smoke curling up in the still air from her cigarette. This silence was at first very tense, but as he still did not speak he became used to not speaking and after a while, he felt himself relax, enter into the moment, the one moment which was to be for him the center of time forever afterwards. He waited until all his fear and embarrassment had ebbed away into the wood, until everything true and peaceful, everything that can grow and breathe had come slowly to the surface, and then he reached over and pulled her arm away from her knees and took her hand. When it was firmly clasped in his, he sighed as if he had been holding his breath.

"There," he said again.

"That's what you said when the tree fell," she said in a matter of fact voice, but now he had made the leap it didn't matter what she said. The bridge was thrown over the abyss. They had met and her hand was clasped in his, so hard there was no hunger between them, only arrival.

"Oh, Ann . . ."

"Yes, Francis, dear." The words, so simple, so clear touched him like sunlight. And he waited for them to go down to his heart before he spoke.

"I never thought it could be like this. I never thought there would be any peace, any time, any place where I could stay still and not be pursued. Oh, Ann"—the kiss which had stood between them, an insurmountable problem, now joined them and solved itself quite simply, like a leaf falling. It was a grave, not a passionate kiss, in which they both forgave each other for all the years of separation. Ann leaned against Francis' shoulder and as he put an arm around her he felt all at once like a brother and a father and a very good husband all rolled up into one. He knew how it would be always, how their two strengths would rest on each other.

"I really gave you up, you know—last winter, after that horrible walk." She laughed a little shyly, for Ann was not used to talking about her feelings, especially this. "I guess I had to. Just as you had to come alive away from me, I had to die away from you, had really to give you up. It made me free for the first time in my life. That sounds strange," she ended, laying her hand very gently in his.

"I think it takes a long time to get to the simplest things—they're the hardest to learn." And then Francis sat up and turned to her eagerly to tell her everything. "I had all the wrong ideas always. You see," he said, frowning the frown she knew so well. Indeed so familiar was his face to her, so much a part of her, that she hardly saw Francis. She just felt with him. "You see," he went on, hunting down the words, "I thought because of my father and mother, I guess, that I had to be exceptional, live a special life of my own, unlike anyone else's. All that tosh about never falling in love—"

"Yes," Ann grinned, "you were pretty awful, I must say."

"Then when I did fall in love it had to be Solange, someone impossible—really, Ann, because I was so scared of it, and I could go on insisting on suffering as if agony were a kind of brilliance. It was all false," he said harshly.

"No," Ann said quietly, "you mustn't say that. No love is false. It wouldn't be fair to say that—fair to her," she said because she couldn't quite bring herself to say the name, just now. He looked up quickly to meet her clear gaze and blurted out, "Do you know why I love your face?"

"Don't interrupt. I want to hear the rest."

"It's not an interruption. Listen, I love your face because it's such an American face, so clear. The truth just sits there on your face as if it felt at home."

"Darling," she blushed, "you're lyrical. It embarrasses me."

"Well, not all American faces are like that, God knows.

Most of us look like cows, bland and empty. Or worn thin by the arid emptiness inside, wooden faces, cow faces. But there is also yours to make me remember if I ever forget, that at best there is this human simple clarity and from that almost any thing can be built—first of all, a family," he said, looking shyly at her now himself, as if perhaps he had gone too far.

"We'll have to be awfully good, Francis, we're so happy." She didn't answer him directly.

"I feel practically a saint already," Francis laughed, "don't you?"

"Moderately human anyway," she teased.

"Listen, Ann," Francis was serious again, "there's just one more thing and then I won't have to talk about it ever again. When I came back, almost at once, I knew about us, you and me, I mean. But you see I felt like a criminal. It didn't seem right, or possible to come back from all that in Paris and be so faithless, so soon . . ."

Ann sat up quite straight and looked off through the trees.

"It must be quite clear between us, Ann, mustn't it?"

"You don't have to explain, Francis. I think I understand. You won't perhaps ever be in love with me as you were with her, but you mustn't worry. I don't think I would want just that from you. It's something deeper than romantic between you and me—that's why it took us so long."

"Yes, we're going to want our lives together, not only our love, our whole lives and our children—" he smiled and took her hand again and kissed it very gently.

"And I wouldn't worry about being faithless," Ann said. Seeing the tense look back in his eyes, she wanted above all to comfort him, to bring him back to peace. "I think maybe

Solange"—now she said the name, she caught her breath just a little—"will be like poetry to you always, and must be like that, but I'll be—what shall I be?"—she turned to him with a shadow of a smile—"bread and bed and house and home."

"And dear love, dear love, not terrible love," he murmured. "I can't get used to it, Ann, that it's ours, that it's going to be always here. It's very silly but I've grown to expect blows."

"I expect there'll be some, but we'll meet them together," she said quietly.

Francis was lying back again in the leaves looking up at the pattern against the blue sky. "I wonder what kind of shadow a man casts," he said dreamily.

"A plain human shadow, I guess," she said, wondering what he meant.

"Yes, that's it," Francis sat up in great excitement. "You see in Paris I talked to an awfully wise friend of father's and he said it was dangerous to be so free, that it was like being a god and gods cast long shadows. But now at last I can have my own shadow, the shadow of a man. It means all kinds of things, Ann. It means responsible love; it means what I can do in teaching, and as a father and as a human being, and it means maybe what I can be as an American, an everyday kind of person really"—he smiled as if it made him immensely and quietly happy to be just that—"for that's what we believe in, isn't it? In the unlimited power of being human." He stopped and glanced over at her, half-ashamed of all this talk. "I'm talking too much."

"Hey, kids, where are you?" It was Alan's voice, high up the hill among the trees.

"It's Alan, how lovely! We can tell him first," Ann scrambled up and gave a long call, "Hoo—ooo—come down, Alan!"

Then she turned back to Francis and gave him a long look before anyone, even Alan, broke this magic circle they had drawn around themselves. "I love you, even when you talk nonsense," she grinned, "and that wasn't nonsense. I'm glad you have a real shadow at last."

Now they could hear Alan crashing down through the leaves, and groaning. "Where are you? I'm getting fearfully scratched."

"Make a last effort, Alan; we have a secret to tell you."

There he was, panting a little, his face scratched by the branches, the picture of disgruntlement.

"It had better be a good secret," he said crossly.

"It is. We're going to be married," Francis stood beside Ann, one arm flung over her shoulder. They stood there, suddenly self-conscious, smiling foolishly as Alan surveyed them.

"You look ridiculously young," he granted, and then came over to kiss them both.

"Don't say you always knew it," Ann commanded, "or we'll bite you. It was a very close thing, wasn't it, Francis, and we feel rather triumphant. For it might not have happened at all," she said mischievously. "I might have married someone else."

Alan stood back now as if he were about to decorate them and took a little box out of his pocket. "I won't say I always knew it, but I just thought I'd bring you something, Ann." He looked mysterious and pleased. "Here it is."

"What is it?" Francis asked, filled with curiosity, longing to snatch it out of her hands.

"Oh," Ann said. The box contained a diamond brooch. "How lovely!"

"Yes, Persis told me to give this to Ann when she married

—and she didn't say when you married Francis," he told Ann with a grin.

"Let me see it," Francis took it from her. "It's beautiful," he said, looking up to catch her smile. "Darling, don't cry."

Ann tossed her head. "I'm not crying," she said, "but Oh I wish your mother were here!"

"She's here," Alan said matter-of-factly.

"She would be pleased, I think." Francis held Ann's hand in his with that firm handclasp which told her everything she needed to know. "At last I can really believe she would be pleased," and he gave a long sigh of contentment.

All around them the sunlight splashed through the leaves. It was warm on their backs.